I0583150

Moonshadows

Lela E. Buis

Moonshadows:
A Collection of Short Stories

That Ridge ~ Knoxville

This is a work of fiction. All characters and events are products of the author's imagination, or are used fictitiously.

Moonshadows

Hurricane Season
© 2013 by Lela E. Buis. All rights reserved under the Pan-American and International Copyright Conventions. No part of this book may be reproduced except for brief quotes for the purpose of reviews and critical articles without the express written consent of Lela E. Buis.

Storm and Shadow
© 2013 by Lela E. Buis. All rights reserved under the Pan-American and International Copyright Conventions. No part of this book may be reproduced except for brief quotes for the purpose of reviews and critical articles without the express written consent of Lela E. Buis.

Desperate Lives
© 2013 by Lela E. Buis. All rights reserved under the Pan-American and International Copyright Conventions. No part of this book may be reproduced except for brief quotes for the purpose of reviews and critical articles without the express written consent of Lela E. Buis.

ISBN 978-0-9850190-3-7 (print)
ISBN 978-0-9850190-2-0 (e-book)

Published by That Ridge Publishing, Knoxville TN

First Edition 2019
Printed in the United States of America

Cover photo by Stefan Keller

ACKNOWLEDGMENTS

Some of the stories in this book have been previously published in magazines and anthologies in a slightly different form. Grateful acknowledgement is made to the editors.

"Dragon Rain," *The Thirteenth Moon*, ed. Jacob Weisman, Tachyon Publications, Jan. 1996 and *Floating Worlds*, ed. Gary Bowen, Obelesk Books/Triangle 1996.

"Ground Zero," *Worthy Foes*, ed. Gary Bowen, Obelisk Books, 1996.

"Hurricane Season," *The Magic Within*, ed. Emily Alward, Diane Holmes & Alicia Rasley, WorldEdge Press, 1994, and *The Thirteenth Moon*, ed. Jacob Weisman, Tachyon Publications, Sep, 1995.

"Mixed Heritage," *Alternate Hilarities*, ed. Alexandra Zale, 1993, and *Hunkazine*, ed. Marcia Patterson, 1995.

"Winter People," *Infinity Ltd SF&F Magazine*, ed. Michele P. Mauro, Books & Bytes Inc.,1991.

"Ascension," *Icarus and Angels*, ed. Gary Bowen, Obelesk Books/ Triangle, 1996

"Carnival," *Fresh Blood*, ed. Riyn Gray and Liza Campbell, *Fresh Blood*, magazine, 1994.

"Haunted," *Dark Tome*, ed. Michelle Marr, publ. *Dark Tome*, magazine, 1993.

"Shadows," *Erotica Vampirica: Sensual Vampire Stories*, ed. Cecilia Tan, Circlet Press, 1996. *Erotica Vampirica*, ed. Cecilia Tan, Blue Moon Books, 2005.

"Entwined," *Ladies of Winter,* Aug 1994, J. Canning, ed. Published by the Nocturnal Ghoul's Society.

"Moonshadow," *Pirate Writings*, Summer 1993, Edward J. McFadden, ed. Published by Pirate Writings Publishing.

CONTENTS

Hurricane Season

Dedication

For Roger Zelazny, who inspired all of this.

"Life isn't about waiting for the storm to pass...It's about learning to dance in the rain."

—Vivian Greene

GROUND ZERO

Chary's in trouble. I knew this was a bad scene, right from the start--too hot. I told him, "You jerk, let me do it." But he's into macho shit lately. Got to do all the crap work himself, and spare the little woman. So, of course, I'm the one who has to go in after it hits the fan, and haul his ass out.

I put the equipment in gear and head for the lights and the sirens. There's no problem finding him, at least. He must have set off hell of an alarm.

We're a team for hire, any job, any time, as long as the price is right. Anti-terrorist stuff, industrial espionage, agents provocateur, you name it. The money's good, but the wear and tear is kind of heavy. We'd meant to retire next year, but the accident in Osaka put a gaping hole in our finances, so now we'll have to work another five years, maybe, to have enough in our investments to support ourselves in--what do they say?--the manner to which we're accustomed?

Tonight we're working a probe at Oak Ridge. Big anti-nuke coalition wants to verify rumors of fusion bomb research, and they're willing to cough up a bundle for hard evidence to embarrass the government. The current administration has loudly denied anything of the sort's going on, daily, at command press conferences. That, in itself, is enough to make you suspicious.

The politics don't mean shit to us, though--at least up to a point. Just pay our price, and we'll do the job.

Time was when Oak Ridge was out in the boonies, but once it was a thriving research center, somehow Knoxville grew that way. It's almost downtown now, tidy and respectable as a jewel set in a decaying web work of freeways, strip malls and fast food greasy spoons. There's still a buffer, though, because the government wants it that way.

An eight-foot chain link barrier looms, with razor wire furled like lace along the top. Anti-terrorist embedments stud the entries, ready to spike any vehicle trying to crash the gates, and the guard shacks are swarming. The compound's lit up like Christmas, so I don't bother with the gates--I'll have to make a direct approach. The fabric is lots more fragile, electrified as it is, and unprotected except for that. I cut through with a slash of insulated limbs, and find that nobody's even noticed.

My equipment's not that spectacular, actually, and common in unmodified form. If anybody really looks, they'll see I'm unauthorized and unbadged, but otherwise, once away from the hole in the fence, I could pass as a disoriented, slightly panicked employee, dressed in street clothes, heavy prosthesis, and my usual exotic face. I make good speed toward the research lab, moving along the sidewalks like a good girl, watching out for the traffic. I stop at the intersection, politely, for a convoy of armed troops on the way to surround the place.

I step on the gas then, and the amps whine. I whisper into the mike, "Chary?" and he answers.

"Llewei? Where are you?"

"Coming in. Where the hell are you, dumb ass? All we need is for you to get hurt."

"Sorry, babe." He sounds contrite. "Listen, I got the stuff. I'm back of the building, at the HVAC unit. Can you get me out?"

"Will do," I say, "or die trying."

It's unkind.

"Don't," he says.

It's a piece of cake. I set up a distraction in the shrubbery across the street--place is landscaped like the White House--and hightail it for the rear. I have to detour to evade the lights; the trucks have brought up halogen spots.

The smoke bomb detonates and a sound track starts up, automatic fire and shouting. The assembled guard shifts in a sluggish entropy, a live gigantic protozoa, a chimera of men and trucks, prickly with guns. I wait for a transit point, slip through the lines of forsythia.

Chary's waiting, and he catches onto the flex steel of my exoskeleton. At top speed I can move a hundred kph, and in within a minute we're outside the danger zone. I slow down then, and we make a leisurely exit, through another hole in the wire.

"Thanks, babe," says Chary, sitting in the hotel room. "I owe you another one. Listen," he goes on, still contrite, "I don't mean to be a hard ass. It's just that after the accident I…"

"I don't want to hear it," I say, and hand him a beer.

He shoves back a mat of reddish-brown curls, pulls an exhausted grin. I know how he feels, but I don't want to inspect it too minutely. It was me that had the accident, you see.

We're staying at a posh, neo-Aztec pyramid near UT and the Coliseum. Early morning, and the room is dim, opening out onto a well of lobby, twenty tiered stories below. It's in perpetual night, as far a real daylight goes.

Chary's warm in the bed beside me, and now he's stirring too, reaches for me. When I concentrate, I have a little sensation left, and I imagine I can feel him. Maybe it's only the memory of his hands that I have now, but still I like it.

When he's finished, he sighs, whispers in my ear, "Morning, babe."

And I say, "Mmmm."

We don't have to meet our contact until late tonight. We'll still have to work, but this is a great beginning, regardless.

Chary lifts me out of bed and into the structure of my protasis, and I can do the rest. This is a light duty rig, suitable for limited moving around in the room. It's less obvious than the heavy exoskeleton, but still I hardly ever go outside in it. I prefer the big system, and to hell with vanity. You never know when you'll bump into problems.

Showered and dressed, I tuck into the heavy rig and we head down to breakfast. The circular galleries are festooned with orchids, nearly empty, but still we're watchful. The job last night had our fingerprints all over it—harder for us to remain anonymous since the accident. We could hole up somewhere cheap, but I see no reason to change our lifestyle. I like the swank hotels.

Our table's waiting, linen fanned on the plates. I flex my joints and sit. Track lighting transmutes Chary to a glowing angel, highlights the smooth, hard bones of his face.

He's all business now, regardless of the aurora. "Pancakes?" he wants to know. "Or Eggs Benedict?"

Back in the room, we dig our processor out of the luggage. This research project has a stand-alone system—no virtual break-ins for them. So no big deal—we did it the hard way. Chary's copied their CAD onto a flash drive, and now we'll see what he's got.

I load the disk, check through our stock for compatible 'ware, and bring up the files on screen.

"Hell," I say, after a while. Chary whistles through his teeth.

We've got the whole damn bomb right here. The hotel feels like ground zero.

"Chary, what are we going to do?" I ask.

"Wipe it," he says.

I'm not so sure we ought to. "It's big bucks," I say. "Retirement right here."

"Wipe it," he insists.

"Damn moralist."

He's right. But I'll have to think about it. Maybe there's a way to turn this to money without getting our tails singed. Or maybe our tails are singed already, and we just don't know it. Whatever, we'll have to make up something to give our contact tonight.

It takes a while, picking and choosing, enough stuff to show what it is, but not enough to mean we got the whole thing. At dusk fall we have dinner, ride back up in the elevator. My reflection stares back from the glass, pale hair with a kink like crimping, mocha skin, almond eyes. It's not a Caucasian face, and now it looks edgy and tense.

Then it's wiped away. Night flares around us—we've soared through the roof in a heart-stopping rise. Below, the river gleams like a mirror, aflame with stars. A tracery of bridge arcs west, dark against a sunset sky, streaming with sharp high-beams. The lit high-rises of UT make up our skyline, fire and onyx-tinged; and traffic growls like the voice of a god.

"Figure it yet?" asks Chary.

I lean on the railing. "No," I sigh. "But somebody else will.

"Tonight?" he asks.

I think about it. "How many people know it's a stand-alone?"

"Everybody," he says, "that's ever tried to break in."

"I think we'd better high-tail it."

"You and me both."

But we have to meet our connection. It's hard cash we've got coming, and the rest is only speculation. It's a risk, but that's our business.

Midnight, and we're just off Henley Street, shrouded by industrial slums. The empty Sun Sphere towers above us, casting an umbrous shade. The World's Fair was near here years ago, and the governor went to jail over the contracts (moral: never trust your brother-in-law). The relics are old and decaying now, and never used--a fitting shrine for the man.

So far everything's gone smoothly for us, but I can't help feeling cold, like death's breathing on us out of the ruins. The shadows loom, threatening, and something rustles. I start and shift, but it's only newspapers blowing. Green animal eyes glow faintly in the weeds, then disappear.

"What time is it?" I whisper, and then something's behind us.

Chary turns, hand darting beneath his jacket, but it's only Ketchum, our buddy that's going to pay.

"Hey," says Ketchum. "Sorry I'm late." He jumps at the scrape of the papers, sucks in a breath. "Damn," he says. The man looks like a weasel. He sets down his attaché, rubs his hands together. "You guys got the stuff?"

"Yeah," says Chary. "Enough."

We've brought hardcopy with a back-up disk. Ketchum whips out a penlight, peers at the drawings. "Ha," he says. "You really did it."

He stoops then to the latches of the attaché, cracks the lid. It's rigged. It spits aerosol that burns our lungs and sears our eyes. I lunge through the cloud, but I'm years too late. Something whacks me. It *was* death breathing on us, out of the ruins.

Silence. Eternity.

I rise up slowly through blackness and pain. To a certainty of disaster. It's not comforting. Besides that, it's raining.

My eyes still burn and I want to cough, so maybe I haven't been out too long. Still, I'm out of the exoskeleton, and the protasis is dead. I lie there a while, heaving for breath, rain spitting in my face, drowning in self-pity and ready to die.

This is a battle I constantly fight. Weakness laces my dreams, nightmares of waking a quadriplegic last year. I try to hide it, even from myself. I try to convince myself it's real. But this is too close to the nightmare.

If Chary can't get to me, I'll die right here. If some pervert happens along, or some gang of kids, I'm theirs. And not only that, I'm stupid. Totally and peerlessly stupid. This was a set-up all along. The coalition is a front. Foreign agents? Terrorists? No matter, now.

They want the bomb, and they've got Chary. I'll give it to them in a minute.

Will I? I have to think about it, shuddering as thunder grumbles above.

Not only no, but hell, no.

Morals? Economic instincts? Whatever, it's immaterial if I lie here crying. If I'm not going to hand it over, I've got to get to the skeleton. Bio-feedback, the doc said last year. You've got a few nerve fibers left, and you might as well do it while you've got muscle tone. So I did, and now I'll try it again.

Concentrate, stupid, or lie here and die.

I work and strain; finally I remember how it goes, or else the pro's working, after all. I flop over on my face, shove up and drag along. It's agonizing, hell on the joints. I pant, leave blood on the pavement.

Too long. Too far. I drop flat, soaked and spent. I can't tell my tears from the rain. Lightning strikes the Sphere then, showers me in blazing plasma, and I galvanize to a new kind of fear. This is the one that produces adrenalin.

The skeleton's embrace is better than any lover's. In it I'm whole again, and alive. In it I can beat them to the hotel.

Wet, dripping, from behind a ficus I check out the room. No sign of disturbance. No sound from within. I'm faster, after all; I don't have to wait for the traffic. My teeth are chattering. Inside, I throw a towel over my shoulders. Then some feverish cyberwork--no time for finesse. I'll have to hope Chary's not macho tonight.

Footsteps in the hallway; I lunge for the closet, fall and tuck up, small as my equipment will fold. The doors are louvered. I've got my gun with me now. Tight-strung, I watch them break in.

It's hard to sit through. But I do it, anyway.

Chary looks bruised and sullen—not promising. He spits at them when they demand the full disk, takes a beating for it. They start to go through our stuff, watch for him to wince. He does it on cue, curses and struggles. One of them knocks him down, sits on him.

They boot up our processor, read the disks, find what I've left for them. Three men—I'll memorize their faces. I like to remember who I've killed, if it comes to that. If not, maybe I'll meet them again some time.

I slide my fingers around the trigger guard, articulate joints. It's hard to hold the damn thing in line. I'm still shuddering—from cold, reaction. I lock in the equipment, line up the sights.

Chary's flat on the shag. I pray he'll stay there, not make a fuss. Beyond all hope, he lies still—maybe he's unconscious.

Seeing he's limp, they leave him alone, wreck the processor out of pure meanness, trash the room. One last second of suspense—tension. My hand quivers, caressing the trigger.

They're gone.

Chary heaves up, wipes a split lip on his sleeve. He doesn't look surprised when I shove back the doors.

"So," he says. "Did I play it right?"

I'm irritated. "How in hell did you know?"

"Babe, your blood's on the carpet," he says.

He's right. The manager's going to be pissed. The place is a mess, and my arms are still oozing. I sit on the rumpled bed, dab at the clots with my towel.

"Let's get the hell out," I say. "Before they figure it."

"What about the money?" He's up, slightly battered, throwing stuff in a case. One of his eyes is swelled shut, and his lip is bleeding.

"We'll have to take a loss," I say. Then I assess the damage to his face, pull a grimace. "But just for now."

Hell if they'll outdo me. We're whole, in one piece—if limping. I've got our retirement stuck in my pocket, and it feels damn sweet. All I've got to do now is think how to pull it out.

POSSESSION

I answered an ad in the Ashland's weekly *Journal* to get the job. "Housekeeper and companion," it said, with "room and board included, competitive salary."

It was just the type of position I was looking for. I'd come to the area with other prospects which had turned out disastrous, and now I needed some time to decide what other options I had to pursue—in other words, what else to do with my life. I hadn't any references as a professional housekeeper, but the "companion" part didn't seem to require any. Plus, the estate was somewhere out in the countryside--which idea appealed. It only vaguely occurred to me that the situation I was reading into the ad might be too good to be true.

Until I saw the house, that is. Then I had second thoughts right away.

It lay deep in the old Virginia woods. Looming on a hill, craggy and windswept, surrounded by a high rock wall, it was silhouetted that night against wild, racing clouds. Twilight cast an eerie, verdigris cloak over the grounds and the twined, black ivy that muffled the house in a clattering gloom. Skeletal trees twisted against the sky, girding the knoll like sentinel wraiths, and in the dusk the shrubbery grew wild and unkempt. A dim shade of waxing moon smoldered on the horizon, useless to dispel the sere, dark wildness of the scene.

There was a signal at the gate, apparently contacting a security system in the house. Wrought iron bars groaned back for the taxi.

A buffet of wind caught me as I tried to alight, billowed my skirt and lashed at my braided hair. I paid off the driver on the cracked pavement of the drive, lifted my suitcase in a suddenly more doubtful hand. Then I raised my eyes to study the house, slightly uphill from where I stood on the walk.

A faint, reassuring glow had appeared in the far windows as the dusk fell more completely. It gave me courage to mount the steps and work the heavy bronze ring set into the timbers of the door. The knell seemed to echo forever, down through the depths of the house.

I waited for long moments, finally heard footsteps approaching. I shuddered and pulled my coat more tightly about my shoulders, glanced around at the shadows, seeming now to crowd in with the sun's final disappearance. I started as the door swung suddenly inward, silent on oiled hinges.

A figure loomed. Before I could jerk backward, the entry light clicked on. Trapped like a moth in its yellow flare, I waited, immobile, and the dark figure spoke to me first.

"Ah," he said. "You must be Ms. Mazurek.

"Um. Yes," I agreed. I was almost reassured by the man's voice, ordinary but somber, and very much in keeping with the atmosphere of the house.

"I'm Stephen Robillard," he said. "We negotiated by telephone."

"Yes," I said. "Yes, of course." Assailed by the isolation and appearance of the house, my conversation wasn't at its best.

"Do come in, Ms. Mazurek."

I was glad to get out of the wind. I reached for the handle of my suitcase, but he was quicker, his hand cold against mine. The house was a relief from the wind, but not the chill, as if winter was reluctant to give up its hold on the interior. Elsewhere spring had begun, but not in here.

The hall was paneled in dark mahogany, furnished in faded Victorian glitz. The man had something of the same character. He was tall, pallid and very straight, dressed in trousers and a jacket that seemed too formal for at-home wear in this day and age--as if he were lost in the past somehow. His hair was quite dark and very smooth, falling in wings about his cheekbones, and his eyes were very dark and riveting. His shoulders and his jaw were heavy.

"I've only come from town, myself," he said, turning, leading the way down the shadowy hall. "Pardon me that I haven't made any preparations for your arrival."

I resisted an impulse to say that I hadn't expected him to make any. After all, the man knew I was coming this evening, and it would have been nice at least if the outside light had been on. I could well be irritated.

"Please make yourself at home right away," he said, oblivious to my silence. "I'll show you the whole house tomorrow and... introduce you to my daughter. Also to Emmett, the handy-man. I would tonight, but I believe they've both...retired for the evening. This is to be your room."

He opened a paneled door for me and turned on the light, followed me in and set down the suitcase. It was a room like the rest of the house, cloistered and cold. The wall-paper was a bit ornate for my taste, but bearable, and the old woodwork offered a bit of charm. There was an iron bedstead and a marble-topped dresser. A wingback chair sat near the windows, and a writing table near the door.

I turned and we stared at one another, a moment of appraisal. Robillard frowned and shoved his hands in his pockets.

"Ms. Mazurek," he began. "I want to thank you for accepting this position. My daughter is...unwell...but she's...becoming a young woman and I hope your presence will be..." He seemed to be speaking with difficulty. He stopped abruptly, glanced around the room. "Well," he sighed, "if there is anything you need..."

"It's freezing in here," I said.

He lifted a nervous hand to brush back his hair. "I'm afraid the furnace is...somewhat dated," he said. "But all the rooms have fireplaces." He gestured at the intricate, cast iron grate in the wall. "I'll send Emmett in with wood," he appended quickly, hesitated again. "In the meantime, let me show you the kitchen." He turned, almost staccato, and strode away.

The kitchen was somewhat warmer, and he left me there to my own devices. I looked around, located the kettle. Investigating the cabinets, I found the essentials for a cup of tea, continued a brief inventory as I waited for it to brew. I'd been afraid the kitchen would match the rest of the house. In some ways it did, but the appliances were contemporary and quite adequate. I was pleasantly surprised that the plumbing seemed to work. There was a large pantry and the well-organized cabinets. The tea was herbal.

When I found my way back to my room, the fire was well caught, and I settled into the chair to finish the tea and review my misgivings. I was somewhat taken aback at the dark and forbidding aspect of the house, but I still needed the position. Finally I decided that daylight would brighten the prospect, so left the cup on the side table, unpacked my suitcase and put away my meager belongings. Then I brushed out my hair and retired to bed.

Morning dawned with the wan, cold light of early spring. The windows of my room were shuttered beneath the draperies, so that I nearly overslept. I hurried my toilet then, having meant to rise early. There was no attached bath, but I found one up the hallway. Dressed for a blizzard and on my way to the kitchen, I found the rest of the house still quiet, apparently locked up like my room. The place felt stale and secretive, buried in a deep, twilit gloom. In keeping back the daylight, it seemed to deny the existence of both the woods outside and the world.

I arrived in the frigid kitchen, cold from the night, and put on coffee this time instead of tea. Without much instruction from my employer, I wondered what I should do next. Shortly I heard stirring from other parts of the house, and Robillard appeared.

"Would you care for breakfast?" I asked.

He had transmuted to someone more casual and real this morning, dressed in a flannel shirt and insulated vest. He gave me another calculating stare, as if attempting to read my own character in the bulky sweater and heavy jeans I had chosen to wear.

"No, thank you," he said. "Just coffee will be fine."

"Here in the alcove?"

He had a paper under his arm, and I wondered at the unlucky paper boy who must have delivered it so far from town.

"In the library. If you please," he said.

Emmett appeared shortly thereafter, without any requirement for introduction. He looked to be a frail man, on the edge of elderly,

"Good morning," I said to him. "I'm Erna Mazurek."

"New housekeeper, are ye?"

"Yes," I said. "Would you like breakfast?"

He had a better appetite than his employer, asked for eggs and bacon. He ate in the breakfast alcove, lingered over coffee.

"Have you worked here long?" I asked.

"Yep," he said. "I worked for the old missus before she passed away. Been here most of my life."

"You've found it a good situation, then?"

He looked at me straight, his eyes sharp within their framing wreath of crows-feet. "Housekeepers come and go," he said. "But I look after the place."

It seemed a fierce loyalty that was encouraging. He finished his coffee and departed for unnamed chores. There was another inhabitant of the house I hadn't heard from yet.

"Should I take your daughter something for breakfast, Mr. Robillard?"

I shouldn't have interrupted. The library was as darkly shuttered as the rest of the house; he was reading by lamplight--or not. Maybe he was only staring at the page. Shadows played about him, a dark aura that lent harshness to the lines of his face and a tense, haunted shade to the expression of his eyes. I took an uncertain breath...

But he started at my voice, and the saturnine image fled. "I'm sorry?" he said.

"Breakfast for your daughter, Mr. Robillard." I stepped into the room, meaning to open the shutters.

"No," he said sharply, jerking his head up. "No. Leave them as they are."

I stopped short, dropped my hands, watched him fold the paper carefully and place it on the ottoman. Was it true that he had dreaded this moment? Somehow I thought that was so. The impression left me at a loss, that the man might fear his own daughter.

I shuddered unaccountably at the notion, clutched at my elbows through the sweater. But if it was fear I'd seen in his eyes, the lines of his face, the man faced it bravely. He stood straight and calm before me.

"Clara's room is upstairs," he said.

I went for the tray, followed him up the dark, carpeted risers. In the hallway Robillard stopped before a heavy panel, took a key from pocket, but then he stopped. He turned, and leaned his back against the door. His eyes seemed very dark and intense now in the pale frame of his face.

"Ms. Mazurek," he said. "I mentioned that my daughter is ill."

"Yes," I said, suddenly wary.

"She…sometimes suffers from mental disturbances. If she isn't quite herself today…"

"Of course," I said.

He opened the door and we stepped inside. I had meant to be understanding, but the warning did little to prepare me.

The girl was about eighteen—and breathtakingly sensual. Fair as her father was dark, like perfection itself, she sat on the floor in a glare of full light. Holding out her hands, she was transfixed by the shower of sun that turned her to milk-glass and filigreed gold. Her skin was translucent, glowing, flushed with the searing light and the warm flare of life's blood within. As we entered, she turned her head.

Her eyes held the blank innocence of an animal.

She crouched tensely in her rent nightgown, her small breasts quivering and taut, smeared with the remains of last night's dinner. Her hair was tangled and stiff. She had bloodied her nails in ripping down the draperies and tearing the sheers from the panes. The shutters hung open, the hinges broken and sprung. The curtains lay shredded and gnawed on the floor. Feathers from a punctured pillow spattered the room like snow.

The girl snarled, baring her teeth, and launched herself at the man. She had the strength of an animal, too, the blind determination to maim or kill. He fended her off, slammed her back against the shutters.

I was aghast, frozen with horror. I dropped the tray as he lunged against me, shoved me through the door. Then I turned, shrieking myself, and clawed at him. He pushed me hard against the wall.

"Do you keep her locked up?" I screamed. "Why?"

He towered over me, his face contorted, his eyes flaming. He gripped my wrists, shook me roughly. Then he realized what he was doing—his face changed, smoothed out. He let go of me suddenly, backed away, breathing hard.

"No," he said. "Believe me, Ms. Mazurek, please..."

I was panting, too, stricken by horror.

Behind me Clara Robillard struck the door, bodily, screaming in fury. Her father grabbed my arm hard enough to bruise, stalked off for the stair. If I hadn't followed, he would have dragged me.

By the time we reached the hall, I had control of myself, at least.

"Let go of me, please."

He took his hand away, turned to face me. I retreated a couple of feet.

"Pardon me," he said, took a breath. His face had twisted, but at my wary expression he regained some composure himself. "You must excuse us, Ms. Mazurek," he labored. "My daughter can be quite violent, but her...illness...is certifiable. By keeping her here, I only mean to keep her out of an institution."

"Of course," I said, rubbing my arm. I still watched him carefully.

"I'd hoped she would react better to your presence," he said. He took another breath. "After she's rested..."

It wouldn't be any different then, I thought, unless the man drugged her. But I didn't say it. I only turned sharply and went back to the kitchen.

He apparently went somewhere to rest himself, or maybe back up to deal with his daughter. I didn't know. Before lunch he appeared in the kitchen doorway to watch my back, his harsh lines softened again to something like concern.

"Ms. Mazurek. Are you all right?" he asked finally.

"Yes," I said. "Of course."

My voice was even enough. I had considered my reasons for coming here yet again, and decided I could cope. Apparently it was clear that I wasn't immediately going to bolt. When he saw it, he sat down on one of the benches of the breakfast niche, dropped his head and rubbed his face with both hands.

"My brother Charles is coming for lunch, Ms. Mazurek."

"Please call me Erna," I said. It was a move to disarm the man. It wouldn't do to become his adversary, not in a situation like this.

"A guest isn't a problem?" he asked.

"No," I said. "Of course not. There seem to be plenty of supplies in the pantry for now. Shall I make a weekly shopping trip, or do you have things delivered?"

"I have them delivered," he said. "Just make a list of what you need."

Our guest resembled his younger brother, but taller, grayer, less preoccupied. He looked me over thoroughly from my rope of jet black, thick-coiled hair to my invisible wool-swathed heels.

"Aren't you too attractive to be a housekeeper?" he asked, half-seriously.

At another time his observation might have been flattering, but not in the dark, blazing tension that hung over this house like a tactile shroud.

"No," I said flatly, and left it at that.

Charles frowned, and his back went rigid.

Stephen Robillard didn't notice either my curtness, or his brother's offense. He requested Heinekens, and the two of them retreated to the den. A few minutes later I set out that way to announce lunch, but when I heard the subject of their conversation, I stopped short.

"You're out of your mind," Charles was saying, "to bring another housekeeper here. And this woman's a bitch. She won't put up with much."

"Charlie, I have to do something," said Stephen Robillard. He sounded very fierce.

"Why do you hold on to Clara this way?" demanded his brother. His voice fluctuated as he paced back and forth. "You can't go on telling yourself she's just autistic, or just schizophrenic. You knew what her mother was when you took her into this house."

"Lupina was..."

"Dammit. She's dead, Steve," insisted Charles. "And you can't bring her back, however much you want to. You were damned crazy to fall in love with such a woman. You were insane to bring her here. And to have that feral whelp..."

My feet had been too light. I went back to the kitchen, stamped audibly on my second trip down the hall. Lunch got cold regardless. Charles Robillard left without eating, and his brother only moved on to gin.

Finally it was evident he wouldn't eat. I started to clear the food away, found myself suddenly distressed—like an attack of panic, or perhaps claustrophobia. Breathing hard, I stood in the dark dining room that adjoined the kitchen. At mid-day the house was still frigid with a cold beyond temperature, so obviously a prison for all who lived in it. My hands were shaking uncontrollably. I strode to the windows, and as the girl had, perhaps, I jerked open the draperies, slammed back the shutters to let in the light.

It was such an improvement; I went on to the library. Stephen Robillard caught me there, working at the shutters.

"Stop it!" he cried, attempting to capture me. But this time I slipped out of his grasp.

"Eventually you'll have to let her go," I panted.

"No," he said. "No. I won't."

I couldn't breathe. I couldn't stand the house, the shadows. As Stephen Robillard worked to refasten the shutters, to re-establish darkness at the heart of the house, I ran to my room for a jacket. Then I bolted out the back door for the bright freedom of the outdoors.

The dark wraiths of last night turned out to be apple trees. I turned at the edge of the hill and nearly laughed, seeing the twisted branches so different by day, clothed by sunlight in the soft pale mists of apple bloom. The wild spill of the grounds below me suggested the real woods beyond, and I breathed easier as I strode toward it down the overgrown hill. It was nearly warm in the sun. Birds flitted and sang above the hill where spring had touched last year's stubble of weeds with green. The sun called to me, and the woods. I could stay lost here forever.

But there was still the wall. I struck it suddenly, found myself trembling with renewed horror. Darkness fell before my eyes, as if it were I who was imprisoned, locked in that dank, cold room at the head of the stairs. I swung around in near terror, stared back up at the face of the house, trying to locate the girl's room in the grim facade. But all of the glass was empty, and reflecting only sky.

The child drew me with a silent calling. I spoke to her that night. At midnight I crouched by the door in my robe, leaned against the varnished wood of the jamb. "What do you want from him?" I whispered.

She only snarled and clawed at the door.

"Clara," I insisted. "Growing up means you have to make something of your life. Hate, for whatever reason, demeans you."

She growled at me, a mindless, animal snarl. Then I remembered what Charles Robillard had said about me.

"Little bitch," I said. "You're beautiful. But you have to deal with the whole world, not just your father."

Silence then. And scratching.

"Leave me alone," she said. It was a faint, small voice—but cold and determined as her father's was.

I sighed, and left her alone.

Night fell again; then three had passed. The moon continued to wax. All the girl's state didn't come from her mother, I saw. The man paced at night in the faint knife-shafts of moonlight that cut through the den, in a torment that was obvious. He doused it in drink, or furies of activity with Emmett, hacking at the shrubbery as if he could single-handedly keep back the encroaching woods. Other times he only sat, brooding and silent in the library's umbral eclipse.

It couldn't go on. I could feel the contest coming. Every whimper and scream from the girl's room pained me. Nothing I could think of would solve this conundrum. She was certifiably ill, he'd said. If he had a doctor's support, any standard response, any attempt to get her away from him, would only make matters worse. But whatever went on between them, the man had my sympathy, too. His torment was real. Somehow obsessed, I watched him from the shadows, read it in the tight lines of his shoulders, the quiet agonies of his face. There was no way to bring them together, I thought, the man and the girl, and events could only run their natural course.

The moon rose full at the end of the week, a fat, bloated disk that tore at the soul. The day had worn painfully on, as the girl moaned and clattered above. Dusk lingered in barely perceptible shades, crashed suddenly into a dank, cold darkness, pierced by the diamond white of palpable stars, so bright they struck through the shrouding cloak of shutter and drape and into the house like spears. At midnight, finally, the great eye of night had extinguished them all, eating them up with her rise to zenith. Ghostly moonshadows fluttered on the wind, tapped at the windows—night's children calling, seeking entrance through the barricades with their pale, cold fingers. Pacing in my room with my robe wrapped tight, I heard them all, felt their fiery touch myself, while I cringed at the girl's every scream. How could the others lie abed and listen to her?

Above me, she threw herself over and over at the door, building to a climax of fury. To shut out the sound I fell on my own bed, buried my head beneath a pillow. Finally, with straining, battered ears, I heard the wood above splinter and fly.

I leaped up from my cold burrow then, raced into the hallway—shied back at a barefoot phantom. It was only myself in the hanging glass—hair loose and wild, face as pale as a ghost, clad in a smudge of gray bathrobe.

I wasn't the only one to have heard the door break. Robillard lunged into the hallway, jerking on a shirt.

"Wake Emmett!" he cried at me. "He's deaf!"

I turned and ran, swung back at a crash and tumble behind me. It was the girl coming down. He had caught her on the stair, and they fell, rolled and uncoiled.

He leaped up and grabbed for her, caught only her nightgown. It tore, came away. She made the door, ripped at the lock. A crevice opened like a wound, the moonlight knifing in. He grasped at her again—too late. She'd slipped through the aperture, naked and wild, and into the night.

When I reached the door, they seemed gone, disappeared into the moonlight and the threatening, unkempt grounds.

I made a quick decision. I ran first to the security box to work the latch of the main gate, then followed them out toward the woods. I caught sight of the two of them immediately on the lip of the hill. The naked girl ran easily through the new grass, bathed in the sharp moonlight and the cold, whipping wind. She wove between the gnarled specters of trees, then stopped, beautiful, argent, her smooth arms upraised in the snowy billow of apple blow. It swirled around her like mist as she reached for the moon, caressing her body with petals of silk. When she heard the man coming, she spun, her bare, pale skin flashing in the glow, and let her arms fall. She stood there luminous, wild as the goddess herself.

"You killed her," she said.

Robillard had stopped, as well. He stood very straight, half-hidden in the shadow, a hazy figure poised ten feet away from her.

"I loved her," he said.

The girl spat, showed her teeth. "You brought her here and you killed her for your love."

"She wanted a child," he said. "And that was you. What better way to die than in childbirth?"

She screamed at him then, an inarticulate howl, and she charged. She changed in a flurry of mist and light as she ran, altering to wolf-form, and launched at his throat. She struck him and they fell, writhed, twisted to the edge of the hill, struggling wildly. She snapped and strained within his grip, still luminous, still pale, still trying for his throat as he held her away. They rolled over a ledge of rock, fell hard. He lay still then, bleeding, but she slid and came to her feet, meaning to return.

I was between them.

The blood-scent had called me. It was a spear that had struck where the moon could not change me. We crashed, fought, heaving and snapping, night's children together under the sky. The girl fell and rolled belly-up in submission. She lay panting, her tongue dripping, her sides heaving for breath. I moved to stand over the man then—ignored the lust that had seized me—the moon-driven thirst for blood. Slowly I came back to myself, took a breath.

"What I said was true," I insisted. "Hate transforms. It will turn you to an animal in truth.

"Will it?" the girl gasped. She lay in her human form again, still panting, staring up at the moon.

"Find out for yourself. The gate's open. The man is mine now. Get out."

She fled.

I closed my eyes, breathed more easily. I had only the man to deal with now—and his desires--the complement of hers. We should be a good match, the two of us. He lay at my feet, his shirt torn, his pale body half-exposed, his ribs straining over the smooth, flat curve of his belly. His hands lay slack and empty, one forearm slashed and bleeding. My own blood surged and sang with the moon, lifted with the glowing borealis of light. I wanted to howl in triumph.

The man stirred and groaned.

"She's gone," I said.

I stood above him, naked myself and cold in the moonlight. The wind whipped my loose hair around my breasts, interwove shadows with the light.

"You knew," he said.

"Yes," I said. "We recognize our own."

NIGHTSIDE

The stars lay terrible, beneath her feet, at the tips of her fingers. Her eyes saw the solar wind, tracked the radiations of infinity as they pierced the membranes of her senses. But that was really *Gaslight's* sensors, not her own.

They were closing in on a ship. It was drifting, damaged and probably unmanned. Matisse knew it before she rounded the cargo modules, before she even scanned for damage. *Gaslight* was a salvage vessel, and it was a gut feeling that came from seeing a lot of dead ships.

On her screen the cargo modules were fragile iridescent clusters against the infinity of space, like soap bubbles in a rainbow field. Tractor dipoles clasped the bubbles within the horns of a crescent moon. Forward, the alloy skin of the parabolic drive module shimmered. The company name and registration was quietly emblazoned along the side, and Matisse logged a memo without really reading it. The ship was far from new, but it was well-maintained. It made her own little ferry look like a garbage scow.

She edged in cautiously, skirting the hulk. When she came in sight of the bridge though, she braked her trajectory, quickly flicked her senses up to max. The bridge was a shell of smashed metal and twisted struts, with a melted scar that ran down the side of the ship like dark elemental blood.

The quadrant around her looked dark and empty. Still she took the time to double check through several wave-bands of sensors before she let her breath out. What gave her pause was the fused quality of the damage. That didn't come from a chance collision.

This was a strange place to find a cargo ship. It was well off the usual stellar routes—a fact that didn't increase her assurance. But the cargo modules looked undamaged, and they were worth a lot of pesos. Part of her brain was ebullient, busy estimating the value, while she still scouted the situation.

Wrecks had to be abandoned before they could be claimed as salvage. From the looks of the bridge, there'd be no problem with a live pilot on this one.

"You're not on a salvage run, kid. But opportunity knocks." She was equipped for it, after all.

On a synchronous course, Matisse set her alarms on auto, downloaded briefly from the ship's systems to herself—sometimes the computer interface gave her delusions of grandeur. The terrible cosmos was gone, and she was back in the ratty cabin, amid a clutter of cables and dangling fiber optics, patched-together panels and screens. But the situation looked the same—a pricey abandoned wreck and a clear quadrant, with no one to dispute her ownership.

"We're rich, kid," she said to the computer. She grinned, and ran into a problem right away.

She had to record a detailed scan to log with a salvage claim, and it turned up a faint life spark in the bridge. Another scan produced the same result.

"Damn," she said, as the pesos vaporized.

Docking and towing a wreck was no big deal. But cutting into the hull here in open space by herself was something else. There was a lot of room for accident.

"Dad, Paul, where are you when I need you?"

She leaned her chin on her fist, drew her straight brows together. If someone really was alive in there, they wouldn't survive while she towed the wreck, or even long enough for her to get someone to help.

"Damn," she said again.

She grappled the module and brought her robot arms around. It was six weary hours before she got him out, well into what should have been her sleep cycle—all of it fine, nightmare work with the cutting torch. Through the arm's video, he looked slight, smashed and bloody, pinned under the console. In just a flight suit, he had no sign of an air pack, and if there had trapped atmosphere, she had ruptured it with the arm. She maneuvered the body into a pressurized rescue bag and reeled it in.

He looked smashed and bloody in her cargo bay, too. He was slightly bigger than Matisse expected—through the ship's sensors everyone looked small—and somehow he was arresting. He was slender, apparently young, and his hair was vivid black, a startling contrast to skin like bone china. It was more than just the pallor of shock—she had never seen skin so fine, as if it was untouched by UV, blue-shadowed by veins beneath. Beside the alabaster fineness, her sturdy hand looked like brown ironstone. There was no sign of pulse or respiration. She got him up to the gravity quarters and into the medical unit, just in case.

"Matisse, you could have been sleeping," she muttered. She rubbed her aching head, leaned on the unit, waiting for the scanner to report him dead. It seemed to hang fire, cranky, and she thumped on it. "Bastard!" When it came down on a decision, she almost choked. It said he was still alive.

Well, there was a fine line between brain death and life. The damn thing didn't register any vital signs—but neural impulses, apparently. It was enough to prod the weary Matisse into cleaning the guy up and having a closer look.

The unit printed out the traumas: bruises, broken ribs, blood-vessel ruptures, internal damage—a few burns from weld spatter. Lucky the rescue hadn't done any more damage than that. She cut off his flight suit, let the autofunction fix him up. There was a deep wound in his side that had to be sutured, where a spline from the console had speared him. Oddly, there had been no hemorrhaging. He should have bled to death from just that. Matisse considered resuscitation and life support, but decided against it. After all, if he died, the wreck was hers.

Wearily she crashed into her bunk and slept like the dead, herself, dreaming of midnight. When she went to check on him in the morning, he was breathing.

The swelling had already receded from his bruises, the colors shading from purple to green and yellow, leaving a young face sharp with panes and angles. His breath was subtle as moonlight, but just as sure.

On the upper deck Matisse sat in her pilot's chair and studied the cargo ship, still grappled. *Silence*, it said, and the company was Transvania, out of Centauri.

When she went to check on him again, the unit was empty.

For a surreal second she stared in shock. Around her the silence, the emptiness, was suddenly eerie, the familiar ticks and creaks of the ferry become somehow ominous in a matter of seconds. She shivered, glanced around at the empty sick bay, the blank walls that told her nothing of where he had gone.

A wisp caught her eye, like smoke, drifting, a ghost of something that wasn't there when she looked. She edged backwards, feeling the sigh of the ventilation, jumped at a ping from the frustrated monitor, where the electrodes were pulled loose and hanging.

A flicker of panic stabbed her. But there had to be an explanation. What? That someone in that condition, apparently dead, could get up and walk away within twelve hours? Another flutter of ectoplasm caught her eye, nothing when she swung round to look. Her heart speeded, jumped. She quivered, suppressed an impulse to flight, and decided on a retreat to the bridge that she could seal off from the rest of the ship. She turned hurriedly—in light that was abruptly golden, liquid as champagne, that clung to her like lust, hindered her movement and dimmed her sight.

A force she didn't see swept her violently against the bulkhead, crashed her head against the steel. A curtain of darkness fell over her, sheer and blood-tainted. But not so dark that she didn't feel a weight that pinned her to the deck, cold fingers that twisted her head back, and touched her throat with ice.

She thought she died.

Consciousness lapped over Matisse slowly, like incoming tide. She decided her head hurt and her mouth tasted foul. When she tried to move, the dark curtain swept down again, brushed its hem along her eyes.

But the darkness was incomplete this time, and she struggled to her feet and felt her way to the head only a few meters away. In the mirror her face was ashen. A purple bruise was swelling her forehead, and a smear of blood tarnished her chin.

She splashed cold water over her face, decided she would live, after all. Still she felt terrible—weak and clumsy. Her mind was moving slowly, as if caught in the blurred sub-consciousness of a dream. She wondered what was wrong.

Her dullness was shattered by an alarm, and she bolted automatically, forgetting her weakness. She stumbled, rested a second against the passage bulkhead.

In the bridge, she collapsed into the pilot's chair, interfaced and snapped up the sensors, remembered to seal off the rest of the ship. The forward screen was filled with a black shadow against the blackness of space, a night-blot that cut off the flickers of stars. Still in motion, it pirouetted before the ferry, cutting off escape. As the black belly turned, it brought the white slash of a broken cross into view, bisecting the sky.

"Shit!"

The ship-to-ship activated.

"*Resurrection* to *Gaslight*," it grated. "Do you read?"

They must already have her registration. Too late to run. Matisse hesitated, opened the channel.

"*Gaslight*." She tried to make her voice stronger. "What do you want?"

"Cast off, *Gaslight*."

"It's mine," she said, without thinking—it was automatic. "I'm making a claim."

"This ship belongs to the new God. The Almighty will cleanse it."

No question now how the ship got damaged.

"*Gaslight*," said the black ship, "where is the pilot?"

She had forgotten him. But she wouldn't tell them so now.

"Dead," she lied.

"Do you have him on board?"

"*Resurrection*, this is none of your business. Space salvage law states..."

"You have three hours, *Gaslight*, to produce the pilot."

They broke contact.

Matisse slammed off the ship-to-ship and closed her eyes, but it didn't take the black ship away. Fortunately, she was too weak to panic.

Three hours. And there was still a dilemma below.

Perhaps she could negotiate. She clicked the intercom icon.

"Listen," she said to the ship, "Could we call a truce? There's a Black Church cutter parked across my bow, and they want your dead body. In three hours they'll blow us both to kingdom come. Do you want to talk about it?"

No response. But then she hadn't really expected any. Even if the attack on her had been surprisingly violent, he couldn't be in any condition to do something about this.

If the damned cutter just weren't so close. *Gaslight* was trapped between it and the mass of the cargo ship—if they were to back off a little, she could swing the little ferry around the cargo pods so they couldn't shoot at her directly. Still, it would only be a delaying tactic. She couldn't outrun a cutter even if she let go of the other ship—probably they'd open fire as soon as they saw her disengage.

Watching the ship through the sensors, she started at a faint sound behind the hatch panel.

For a span of seconds she wasn't sure what to do; then she flicked to the security screen for a view of the passage. Her passenger was behind the panel, wearing a pair of Paul's coveralls.

She studied him critically. He looked believably human, leaning against the bulkhead—insubstantial, but hardly a ghost.

She lay back against the hard cushions, touched the intercom. "Yes?" It came out a harsh whisper.

"I want to talk," he said in a voice as soft and dark as the solar wind.

She reached to get her Colt from the storage cabinet, then unsealed the hatch and lifted the pistol, swiveled to face him.

He looked at the gun, waiting for her to shoot. His eyes were as black as his hair, and even more vivid, smudged beneath with shadows.

"Is it too late to apologize?" he asked, finally.

At least he didn't look so great, either. She'd had a secret, superstitious terror that he might be completely well already.

She let the laser fall to her lap. "Come on in," she said. She watched as he crossed the short distance, eased into the co-pilot's chair. He stared at the image of the cutter still on the forward screen, charcoal and midnight, with the scar of the broken cross.

It was the look of the hunted, she thought, the animosity of a wounded animal, in a brief, marginally safety.

"What do they want?" she asked.

He shook his head. "I'm sorry I hurt you," he said. "I wasn't rational when I woke up."

"Are you some kind of evil new space mutant?" she asked, and this time he looked at her.

"No. Something old," he said, "adapted."

"Hell of an adaptation," she said, and meant it. "What's your name?

"Nicola Dumas."

"Matisse."

"Whose coveralls?" He touched the fabric.

"My brother's."

"Family salvage business?"

"Yes. Any ideas how we can get out of this fix?"

"You could let them come on board," he said.

"They'd take my ship, too."

Slack in the seat, he looked delicate as porcelain—but of course he wasn't. He must be tough as nails just to be walking around. He sighed tiredly.

"Where are we?"

"Sol system."

"I just clicked on a jump at random," he said, "to get away. Do you have a jump drive?"

"No. This is a ferry."

"What does *Silence* look like?"

Matisse shifted the screen; and he grimaced at the hole that had been the bridge--and the controls. "The engines are okay."

"Looks like it."

"We're docked," he said. "If I can use your computer to calculate, I can load a jump manually."

Matisse laughed suddenly, harshly.

"What the hell? Where to?"

He looked at her with shadow eyes, smiled tightly. "*Centauri Station*. Call in your salvage claim. You can have the ship if you'll leave me there."

She was surprised. "It's yours?"

"My grandfather's. Family shipping business. It's a total loss, looks like, so our insurance will pay."

"Oh."

"I'd rather you had it than them. Three hours?"

"Two and a half."

He had the calculation done in an hour. She wondered if it was valid; he couldn't be up to checking it. She was about to trust her life to his math, and the awkward double vessel might not withstand the stresses, but she couldn't think of anything better herself. She felt rotten, wondered how much of it was physical and how much was total, abject fear.

"Do you want me to go over with you?" she asked.

He was still slack in the co-pilot's chair. "No." He shifted his head to look at her. "Do you think you can stall?"

She grimaced.

"Does that mean you can't do it in time?"

"Close," he said.

He went out the hatch and down through the hold. She got out a suit with air-pack and locked the ramp for him to cross the short distance to the access hatch in the shimmering opposite hull, made sure he was hidden between the ships. Then she watched the time read out in empty silence.

"*Gaslight*, your time's up," the receiver cracked. "Have you got us a body?"

Her heart jumped. She had lost track of time. She slammed on the transmitter.

"No," she said. "I can't help you."

"You'd better produce one."

"What do you want from me?"

Her anger provoked contempt, a laugh. "Are you dense? We need a body."

"I never said I had one. I can't just produce one out of thin air."

They must have scanned before and found *Silence* dead. If they checked now, they'd pick him up. The seconds flicked by. She licked dry lips, tried a different tack.

"What's the matter?" she taunted. "Did you lose him?"

The voice growled. "You've got him."

"No. You just blew him the hell away and you won't admit it."

The voice was flat and deadly. "We're coming aboard."

She was out of strategy, out of time. They would kill her, take the ferry—or maybe worse. The black ship stirred, loomed, and the broken cross, like a spear, aimed at her heart. She punched up her shields, checked her Colt. Damn. How had she ever gotten involved in this? The twisted Black Church with their corrupt notions of good and evil was the scourge of the sector.

Gaslight's shields were for debris, not naval assaults. The cutter spat. Rainbows arced on the ferry's skin, and the hull shuddered. Photons clashed and spattered like sunflares, sheared off into space. Stressed, the shields weakened, colored the screens with dying bursts of scarlet flame.

"Damn. Damn."

Matisse slammed down switches, diverted power to turn the fire-storm. Screens turned a sickly yellow then, as the flares died in a final blinding jolt. Readouts bled, screaming damage from the sensors. Alarms shrilled.

"Dammit, dammit." She should have left the cargo ship alone. But no, she thought, watching them reach for her with steel-clawed arms. That wasn't right. She was the hell correct. It was just a shame she had to die for it.

The black ship was meters from grappling her. She gripped her hands into white-knuckled fists, knowing that if she moved the ferry the calculations would be off. Sorry, she thought, sorry Dumas—we've got to go. Her hands jerked out. She interfaced, brought up the controls, slammed down the icon to pulse away.

Reality spasmed, and the black ship was gone.

Quiet then, and the blank emptiness of drifting. The nothingness was interrupted by a touch on her face. It was warm fingers this time.

"Matisse, are you all right?"

She started awake. "What happened?"

"We came through fine. There's some damage to your grappling crane, I think, but it's not bad."

She blinked, groaned, struggled up to sort through the data. "Not bad for a manual-load," she decided. She heaved a breath, gave him a quick grin. "The jump's right on target."

Centauri Station, on the forward screen, offered them a slip on the sunward side.

"No, please," he said. "It has to be nightside."

She glanced at him sharply, then opened a channel to argue with the tower.

They docked with a clank, and he slid out of the seat. "They'll figure it out," he said. "I have to go."

"Wait. Don't you want to call a medic?" she asked, jerking up, ducking through the hatch behind him.

"Just a delay," he said. "It wouldn't help that much."

"What are you going to do about Silence?"

"Nothing. The paperwork's all yours."

She trailed him out. At the hatch he turned suddenly, reached to touch the spot below her chin. She flinched, but it was almost a caress, an afterthought—a skim along the line where the blood had been.

"Don't worry about this," he said. "It won't cause you any trouble." He smiled, dark and oddly sweet, and then like a wraith in the lights he was gone, leaving the Silence behind.

Well damn. Winning skin-of-the-teeth moral victories was just fine, Matisse thought. She propped her hands on her hips to glare over the cold machinery of the docks. But how the hell was she going to get home?

She fainted going through customs, woke in a clinic.

"What happened here?" the starched medic asked.

"Where?"

"On your throat."

She didn't know what he meant, and he had to show her in a glass. It looked like a bite mark, bight punctures over her carotid artery. It was nearly healed already.

MIXED HERITAGE

I always did like Jimmy's dog better than him. But Jimmy never did get it. He was big and handsome, and had the most beautiful, brown eyes.

The dog, that is. Ralph.

Maybe I should explain.

I was walking in the park. It was a gorgeous day, late spring, chilly; but with a little bite in the sun. Enough so I had on a skirt. The trees were still bare, just starting to bud out, and here and there some kind of bulbs were blooming. It was a busy day at the park, kids with candy and old folks feeding the pigeons. I stopped at a wrought iron fence to watch this team make a double play, and a Frisbee hit me right in back of the head. Well the dog was right behind it. I went down and my skirt went up. Ralph wagged his tail and whined, and then Jimmy was there to pick me up from the concrete and dust me off.

When he was done, he gazed into my eyes and said, "My, what beautiful eyes you have! What color is that?"

The big, bad wolf had better opening lines.

"Green," I said. They're really yellow, but it saves a lot of explaining. He liked my name too, but then most people do. It's unusual.

"Let me buy you a drink."

"Okay," I said, looking at Ralph.

He was some sort of retriever mix, chocolate-colored and shaggy. *So* dignified, and *so* sorry to have knocked me down. His eyes were just too soulful. It was love at first sight, and I forgave him right away, even though I'd skinned my knee and torn my best pair of leggings.

Ralph had to wait outside the place while we had a beer, but I started seeing Jimmy just to see him, too. It didn't last long. It never does. The moon was new when I was at the park, and as it phased, Jimmy and I got on less and less.

Jimmy was some sort of jock. I wasn't really interested, so I listened to all the play-by-play with just half an ear, all the time loving Ralph—this secret affair—and never did identify what Jimmy played in college. Football, maybe. He had big shoulders and reddish hair and blue eyes—God's gift to women, you could tell. He never asked me where I was from or any of that stuff. Just as well. And when I told him the first time I couldn't come over to his place, he actually sulked.

"But why not, Luna?"

"I can't explain, Jimmy. I have this sort of monthly cycle, and I don't go out when I'm not feeling sociable."

"Are you talking about your period, for Christ sake? I already got take-out."

Well, he pouted for two whole weeks. But that was okay with me. When he called up again, I was ready to see him. And I had missed Ralph, really bad. He'd missed me, too. He barked and wagged, followed me around the apartment all evening, touching his nose to me, licking my foot. I was really affected.

So when the next month rolled around, Jimmy was really pissed. He chewed me out. Made me mad, actually, so I wanted to get back at him. I'm sort of emotional at that time of the month.

About three a.m., I went over there. I scared shit out of this alley cat, and prowled around in the dumpster. I shouldn't have been so easy to side-track, but when the moon's full I'm distractible, too, and it smelled so good.

I got to Jimmy's door just as this other girl was leaving, and I scared shit out of her, too. They yelled and called the cops, but I got away with Ralph. He loved it.

I had to move, of course. But we've really lived happily ever after. The pups are cute, too. Roly-poly, half-wolf and half-whatever-Ralph-is, with big, soulful, brown eyes. And when the moon's new, they change into beautiful, yellow-eyed little girls.

THE HATCHLING

Mist curled up from the Rhine valley like early morning smoke from a cook fire. Gentle waves lapped the shore of the river, spreading out from a mercantile barge headed at full speed down river. The air was brisk and sharp, just the sort of morning to be out and about, demanding tribute from the traffic.

Unfortunately, Lord Clovis' raid had been interrupted by a surprise visitor that had arrived out of the cloudy mist like a thunderclap. It now lay up the hill, coiled around the base of his castle in gigantic golden rings, its wings folded close and its sulfurous stench rising to join with the fog above the central keep. Lord Clovis and his liege men crouched in the brush at the edge of the Rhine and stared upward through the shifting mist, aghast and horrified. A little distance away, the servants and household staff huddled in a fearful knot, protected for the moment by the trees and wondering what dragons ate.

Because it rose so naturally from the stone cliffs, Vogtsburg Castle was popular with crows and ravens, along with the usual spring flock of nesting songbirds, but this sort of visitor was a surprise development. The barge was escaping downriver without paying a penny in tribute, but at least no one was trapped inside the castle. Except Flora, that is: Lord Clovis' beautiful, golden-haired daughter.

The dragon poked his nose at the various openings of the castle until he found the main doors. He folded back his crest and slid his huge, scaled head inside the great Rittersaal like a serpent. He flicked his forked tongue and blinked one golden eye at the acrid wood smoke issuing from the great central fireplace. In a moment he located the stairs to the tower and negotiated the turning spiral, leaving his nose pressed against the heavy timbers of the door.

"Flora," he said in tones like a cathedral bell. "Art thou behind this portal? Come out, my beauty!"

"God's nightrobe!" cried Flora. "Get ye away from my door!"

Actually, she couldn't come out, because Lord Clovis kept her locked in the tower, which explains why she was trapped when the rest of the household escaped. Flora normally languished in the spire attended only by a lady's maid and a tutor. She yearned for her freedom constantly, throwing flowers from the battlements of the tower, watching as they fell gracefully three hundred and some feet to the rippling surface of the Rhine below. From thence they flowed to parts unknown, and Flora daydreamed of the wonderful places they visited when she couldn't.

From the windows of the tower, she had seen the dragon descend and stormed the door in a frenzy, beating at it with her tiny fists, but it was heavy and iron bound, and there was no way to open it without the key. She was fifteen, fair and blue-eyed, dressed this morning in a heavy blue velvet gown and beaded slippers against the chill. Now she cowered behind her chest, as far away from the door as she could get.

"I am thy lover," said the dragon, "come to claim thee. Come thee out, my sweetness!"

"What are ye talking about!?" screamed Flora. "Go away!"

It was a stalemate, of course, as Flora couldn't open the door. The dragon bumped his nose against it, testing the timbers, but the hinges hardly rattled. Possibly he could get enough leverage to breach it, but twisted as his neck was by the spiral of the tower, it was unlikely. He hissed, emitting a small flame of disappointment, and inside the tower Flora squalled in an ecstasy of terror, sure she was to be burnt alive.

Down by the Rhine the air of emergency was mitigating somewhat, as the dragon seemed intent on coiling around the castle, and not despoiling the castle staff or even the nearby village of Trechtings Hausen. Lord Clovis' men had carefully emerged from the bushes and made a run, one-by-one, for the trees that offered better cover. The household staff had vanished, but inside the tree line they met a bevy of children that had escaped from their mothers in the village.

"Get thee hence!" Clovis barked when he saw them, and his chief knight Gerhard yelled and waved his sword. The children disappeared, but it was unlikely they went back to the village. A copse of bushes up the hill waved as if disturbed.

Lord Clovis sat on a rock and removed his helmet. He wiped his brow, leaving a dark stain of moisture on his leather glove. He was sweating despite the chill that rose from the river.

"By the Rood!" he exclaimed. "Gerhard, have thee any ideas on this?"

Gerhard squatted before him, his mail shirt beaded by condensed moisture. "Nay, lord," he said. "Think ye that our force is strong enough to defeat such a foe?"

Clovis evaluated the heavily armed and mailed band of liege men now cooling their heels in the cover of the trees. They were a brave bunch, though slightly loose of morals, as might be expected when they served a robber baron. Their first terror had passed and they were now engaged in boasting of their past victories and sharing whispered tales of dragon slaying. They had always considered these tales as myth, but now they might provide a bit of courage to those in doubt of it.

"Aye," said Clovis. "They will serve. I want the beast out of my keep. How shall we accomplish this?"

"A priest?" suggested Gerhard.

Clovis glared at him. He had no liking for the clergy himself, and he wondered darkly if this was sarcasm. "We will try the armed men," he said. "Would darkness be to our advantage?"

"Yea, lord," said Gerhard. "It will offer cover for our approach, at the least."

They sent to the village for provisions and Clovis had a lunch prepared over an open fire. They tore at bread and meat under the trees and spent the afternoon planning their attack on the dragon's rear.

In the tower, Flora had grown weary of cowering behind the chest. Eventually she emerged and made an attempt to evaluate her position. There was a bowl of fruit in the room, a fresh loaf of bread, a cheese round that her maid had cut for breakfast, and a full pitcher of water. It was small provisions to last out a siege, so Flora decided she must hope for a quick rescue.

By afternoon she was bored. Normally her tutor Marnie came in the morning to teach her the womanly arts of conversation, weaving and embroidery. However, Marnie could also be prevailed upon to gossip and tell tales of the world beyond the castle walls whilst they were working. Flora paced, picked up her latest piece of embroidery and put in a stitch. She was distracted, though, and lost the thread out of her needle. She huffed in exasperation and threw the piece on the floor, paced the span of her cell again.

The dragon had been quiet since she shrieked at him, and now she began to wonder if he was still there. She turned and addressed the door.

"Dragon," she said. "Are ye there still?"

"Aye, sweetness," he murmured. His head rested comfortably on the landing, and he had no thought to move.

"Have ye a name?" asked Flora.

"Basilisk," said the dragon.

There was a slot in the door at about waist level to pass things through, and Flora bent to peer at him. Not much was visible. It was dim in the stairwell, unlighted as it was by windows. Still she caught the molten glint of his scales and a glimpse of golden eye. She leaned against the door.

"From whence come ye, Lord Basilisk?"

"From Mittelgebirge," he said, warming that she would speak with him. He had been a bit crestfallen at her aversion to flame.

"The low mountains. There are many fat sheep there which suit my palate."

"Where is Mittelgebirge?" asked Flora.

"Eastward, near the Alps," said Basilisk.

"And what are the Alps?" she asked, deciding that it might be a lovely afternoon, after all. She pulled a pillow off the nearby stool to cushion her rump and got comfortable against the stone. "Tell me about the world outside these walls."

By twilight Lord Clovis' men were making their way up the final slope near the towering fortress. The Castle Vogtsburg was pretty much impregnable, perched as it was on the stone cliffs over the river. Still, the dragon seemed to have his head buried inside, so they hoped to take him by surprise.

The climb had been arduous. Burdened as they were with armor and weapons, they were afraid to take the winding road up, and had climbed through the rough terrain in a straighter approach. Now they assembled in a hollow just below the castle to catch their breaths and whisper in a quick strategy session. The dragon's long neck seemed entirely within the castle, but his huge belly lay within reach, wrapped about by another coil of tail. All was quiet and still within the woods. The night sounds had been interrupted as the men approached, but now the frogs started up again, as unimpressed by their presence as they were by the dragon. A full moon was rising in the wake of fading sunset, shedding a soft light--a good omen, the Lord Clovis hoped.

The men worked up to a position slightly above the dragon to improve their attack and then stormed down the hill. Screaming their war cries and waving sword and shield, they fell on the dragon's belly full force, hacking and smiting on the scales like golden plates. However, the scales were more like iron than gold, it seemed, and they turned the heavy blades as if their wielders were mere boys instead of seasoned men. They fell back in frustration, and then the manly Knight Aachen strode forth with his battle axe and took a hearty swing and pierced the golden skin now lighted to silver by the moon. Blood spattered forth and he screamed as its acid fire burnt along his arms.

Basilisk flicked his tail as he felt a sting in his side, resettled his hind legs and tightened his coils a bit more securely around the base of the castle. Inside the tower Flora heard the screams. She peered out the windows but couldn't see anything on the landward side because of the dark trees and heavy brush. On the river side, all seemed peaceful, the moon lighting a magical path along the river, stars less visible than usual, but the Evening Star riding high and fiery beneath the moon. Flora sighed and looked for her nightgown in the wardrobe. Normally her maid Lucy laid it out for her, but it wasn't that hard to find, even by candle light.

"Good night, dragon," she said.

"Good night, sweetness," said the Lord Basilisk. "I will watch at thy bedside until morning gilds the sky."

The men limped down the slope in the darkness, helping their wounded as best they could. The Knight Aachen was burnt by the dragon's blood and several others were bruised and battered by the lash of the dragon's tail. They reached their camp by the river near midnight and tended their wounded by firelight.

Thus defeated, the Lord Clovis sat by the coals far into the night, contemplating his sins and coming up with another plan. By late morning his knight had returned from beyond the village with the Wizard Drefuss. Luckily the mage had been in residence in his solitary tower a distance down the river, and the knight had woken him from a sound slumber in the dimness of early dawn. The old man studied the golden coils that wrapped the castle keep above the camp.

"I'm not an exterminator," he said. "Have you tried a virgin?"

"Hah," cried Clovis. "Good one!" He smote his thigh and laughed in a grim mirth.

"Oh, I see," said the wizard. "The dragon's got the only one within reach."

He looked around the camp at the battered and groaning men. "I see thou'st already tried an armed attack."

"I have decided this is your fault," said Lord Clovis.

Drefuss raised his bushy brows in horror. "Mine!"

"Ye are the man who traffics with magic, aren't ye?"

Drefuss looked around at the camp again, but more sharply this time. "This is not the venue to talk of magics," he said. "Let us walk by the river."

They took the open path down the bank, girded with rocks on the one side and ducklings on the other. Sun glinted off the choppy water, causing Clovis to squint against the glare. Out in the river a fish jumped for a dragonfly and fell back with a splash.

"So," Clovis said, after they had put a little distance between them and the camp. "Tell me of the night Flora was conceived."

"Are ye sure ye want to know about this?" asked Drefuss.

"The time has come," said Clovis darkly.

Drefuss frowned. "Ah, well. Perhaps so," he said. He considered, searching through memory. "It was a dark and windblown night," he said. "The day had been full of storms and lightning. All the omens pointed to a portentous alignment of the stars. The fair Lady Jasmine came to me herself, disguised in a washerwoman's robes and attended only by her chambermaid. They hammered on the door to my tower and would not be turned away. Your lady had spoken to me a fortnight before on what she wanted, and now I tried in vain to dissuade her. 'There must be a balance,' I told her in my hall. 'Ye must give up something dear to you in exchange for what you want.' 'I have brought gold,' she said, and I said, "That is not likely to be enough.' 'Anything,' she said, 'I must conceive or I am nothing.'"

The Lord Clovis winced slightly at this--perhaps it had to do with one of his own sins.

"So," Drefuss went on, "I brought her a potion and she drank it, and that night she bed with you and conceived your daughter Flora."

"And the price was?" he asked.

"I gather it was her life," said Drefuss, "since she died in childbirth."

"And there was nothing ye could do about this?" asked Clovis.

"Not once the magics were in motion," said Drefuss. "The powers always come into balance. A life for a life…" He shrugged, stopped to look out over the river. A gust of wind ruffled his beard, snapped the hem of his fine tapestry robe.

"So where does the dragon come into this?" asked Clovis.

"I don't know," said Drefuss. "Did you ask him?"

"God's blood!" said Clovis. "Do you think I should march up to his snout and ask such a thing what it wants from me? Why, he would burn me to a cinder!"

"So you want me to ask him?"

"I don't care," said Clovis. "I just want rid of him."

"I'd say he's come for Flora," said Drefuss.

"My daughter?" cried Clovis. "Why! How!"

"Well, you see," said Drefuss, "the potion the Lady Jasmine drank was made from a dragon's egg."

He turned and shaded his eyes to look at the castle on the cliffs above, girded about by the golden rings. It looked like a gaggle of village children were sitting on the dragon's rump.

Flora had no flowers to throw into the Rhine this morning, so she tossed the contents of the garderobe pot out the window instead. They fell as gracefully as the flowers, but not so fragrantly. She had to throw into the wind, and down below some of the refuse spattered into the camp of armed men. They cursed and shook their fists at the castle, but the fair damsel in the tower could not hear them.

Flora considered using some of the precious pitcher of water to wash, but decided against it, finally just put on the same blue gown she had worn the day before. However, she did spend a few extra minutes checking her reflection in the looking glass and putting up her hair in a beaded net. After all, it seemed she had a suitor, however unlikely.

"Lord Basilisk?" she said, settling on her cushion by the door.

"Aye, sweetness," he answered. "What would thee have of me?"

"Are ye hungry yet?" she asked. "When will ye go to hunt?"

"Nay, Flora," he said. "I had a fine ox for my dinner three nights ago, and yet I am sluggish with the weight of it." He seemed to consider. "And art thou hungry?" he asked.

"Not yet," she said. "I have a little food in here."

"Why do thee not come forth?" asked Basilisk.

Flora decided to be honest about it. "The door's locked," she said. "And I have not the key."

Basilisk rumbled in his throat. "Why is this?" he asked.

"I suppose I am my father's greatest treasure," she said, which was something a dragon could understand.

Basilisk flicked his pointy ears and breathed on the door's outside, noticing a spot of char that was developing near its base.

"Lord Basilisk?" said Flora.

"Aye, sweetness?"

"Why is it you have come for me?" she asked.

"Thou art mine," he said.

"Yours?" she asked. "In what way?"

"We were betrothed as egglings," he said. "Thou art my soulmate forever."

"What *are* ye talking about?" she asked.

"Doest thou not feel it?" he asked. "Is there no fire for me within thee?"

The Lady Flora made no answer, and he huffed a sigh at the door again, making a slight curl of smoke rise from the spot of char.

"God's word!" swore Clovis by the river, "So ye have given me a dragon's spawn for a daughter?"

"Eh?" said Drefuss, turning from the hill and arching his bushy eyebrows in response. "'Twas not I, good sir."

Clovis flailed both arms. "Well, by the Rood, ye must fix this!"

"'Twould be much safer to just give her to the beast."

"Safer?" shouted Clovis. "She is to bring me fortune and alliance. She has attracted the attention of my greatest rival, the king's evil tax collector. What do you mean, 'twould be *safer?*"

"There's yet the problem of balance," said Drefuss. "Once ye have interfered with the natural order, then ye have these odd results for your sins. Regardless of dragons in your keep, this is a stable situation."

"But there *is* a way to be rid of this thing?"

The wind lifted, bending the reeds. Drefuss frowned. "More chancy magics, of course. Wilt ye throw the dice on this?"

"I will *not* give up my daughter to this devil's spawn," said Clovis. "Get him out of here."

Above them, the lovely Flora was explaining to Basilisk why she could not fly away with him.

"But we are such different creatures," she said, toying with the fine cloth of her embroidery. "How practical is this plan?"

"I will carry thee away to foreign lands," he said. "Thy father cannot follow us through the realms of air."

Wind surrounded their tower, flirting with the stones, fingering the roof slates and glazed casements. "And then what?" asked Flora, letting her linen fall. "Shall I live in a dragon's cave and gnaw at the gristle of sheep and oxen?"

"I will find thee a fine house," said Basilisk. "And serving women as thee have here."

Flora thought about it. "And what else? Shall we wed? Have children?" she asked. She searched for the root problem. "How can we consort in a marriage bed?"

"Hmmm," said Basilisk. "That is a problem." He shifted his snout and hissed sharply, doing more damage to the door. "Perhaps thou art right, my love."

"Thou art mightily sweet," she said. "And thy proposal is seductive, but methinks I must remain here with my father. He has made plans for my wedding day already."

The quiet stretched between them. "I will abide by thy wishes," he said at last. "But I shall not forget thee, my sweetness. Let us frame our good-byes."

His crest lay limp and lifeless in the chill of the stair, and beyond the portal, a single tear fell from her eye onto the linen cloth.

Storm clouds gathered over the Rhine. The sun fell, the wind rose, and the village children fled from the dragon's back as he twitched to life.

The day was gone. Dusk was falling. The hearth fire was long dead. Basilisk backed out of the stair and the hall as he had entered, mindful that the tapestries did not entangle in his crest or snag on his pointy ears. Safely outside, he shook his head and lifted his snout, loosening the golden coils that had held the castle bound. He raised his wings, feeling life and darkness in the storm winds. Thunder rumbled faintly in the distance. Above the crags, ragged clouds scudded across the moon, torn by the forge of an invisible smith. Below, the river lay like a silver worm, twisting with unease. Ill though the wind seemed, it lifted him, and he rode away on its back.

The storm swept in quickly. It was fueled by the magic of peridexion wood--dragon's bane--and torrents of slashing rain. Lightning played about the tower like the hellfires of the Almighty and hail beat at the shutters like a volley of arrows. A distance away, the villagers huddled within their beds, deafened by thunder and sure the devil had come to claim them. In a solitary tower downriver, the Wizard Drefuss stood frozen before his scrying glass, arms upraised, enthralled by his own darkest spells.

Basilisk had not quite escaped. The gale before the storm carried him into a microburst downriver, and he spiraled out of control, crashed into the heaving trees of the mountainside. He fell, thrashed, and left claw marks down the side of a sheer cliff. It was to no avail; the dark Rhine swallowed him in a mighty splash. An explosion of steam burst upward, hissing as it met the rain.

The storm seemed to coalesce into a solid giant of wind and cloud, a towering knight armed with spears of lightning and the crashing hammer of the rain, striding down river from the glowing wizard's tower, all lit about with Saint Elmo's fire. The earth shook under his weight. The demon knight turned its gaze to and fro, searching for dragons.

Basilisk was quenched and drowning in the Rhine, but little Flora was still defenseless in her tower, burning like a flame. At the first lightning flash, she had hurried to fasten the shutters, but rain spattered onto the stone floor before she could pull them shut. They flapped wildly in the wind until she could subdue them, finally lashing them tight. Flora was used to riding out storms in the tower, but it seemed she had never known one so fierce as this. She had tried to light a candle, but the storm winds snuffed it out. Now she crouched behind the chest in full darkness, her heart aflutter as the tower bucked and shivered beneath her.

"Dragon's spawn!" screamed the wind. "Where art thou?"

Flora stopped her ears, sure she was imagining demons and monsters in the storm. Still the screaming continued, grew closer. Lightning flashed just outside, and thunder shook the tower. The winds ripped at the stones, slashed at the shutters. The lashings gave, and the wooden panels ripped away. Rain sprayed into the room.

Now Flora could see the demon in the storm, and she shrieked and flew at the door. She bashed at it with her fists, threw her weight against it. Burnt by two days of dragon's breath, it cracked at last, and Flora wriggled through. She ran for the stairs.

But the storm demon had seen her through the window, and now it attacked the tower in earnest. Lightning blasted at its circular belly, and stones flew outward, dislodged by the storm's fury. Flora tried to run downstairs to the great hall, but the lightning struck below her again and again, forcing her upward instead. Sobbing now, she halted at the tower's flat roof, still cowering in the stairwell. Another lightning strike burnt the stones below, and the tower shifted beneath her, tilted sharply. It was falling. Flora called upon God to save her, and dashed out into the rain.

The demon of wind and fire towered above her. It took another stride closer, and its scream was deafening. "Die, hatchling!"

"What are you talking about?" screamed Flora. "What have I ever done to you?"

The demon giant struck at the tower again, and this time the stones gave way completely, the massive tower head crumbling in slow motion toward the river below.

Clearly, there was no time for talk. Flora prayed instead for dragon wings, and leaped out as far as she could over the tower's crenellations. Below her a bright glimmer was rising, suddenly visible as she fell.

"Dragon's spawn," screamed the wind, "die!"

"No!" cried Clovis, and he rushed forward to cast down Dryfuss' scrying glass. It broke, but that only cut off their view of the falling tower.

"What happened?" he asked.

"Fool," said Drefuss, looking up from the broken shards. "How am I to know?"

Outside the wind continued to howl. The demon storm lashed at them through the night, keeping even the most fool-hardy under shelter. However, Clovis was out to make the trek upriver at the first pale glimmer of light, accompanied by the Wizard Drefuss.

Morning had broken fully. The keep above them was a smoking ruin, the tower fallen into the Rhine. Not all of it, though. Clearly some of it had collapsed on the Rittersaal roof. It would be expensive to fix.

"God's blood," said Clovis.

"Don't complain to me," said Drefuss. He was still angry about the broken glass. "Ye threw the cursed dice."

A little way downriver, the first of the village children appeared on the path.

Eastward, on a farm near Mittelgebirge, it was raining rose petals along the Rhine. Bess the farmer's wife lifted a rough hand to catch them, floating down like snowflakes, turning and shifting as they fell, now pink and now velvet red in the sun.

"Husband," she said. "Look at this!"

He leaned on his hoe and shaded his eyes, peering upward. Through the pale morning clouds he spied a glint of gold and a fainter wisp of blue. "Wife, we must hide the sheep," he said. "That's the dragon returned. What's he got there with him?" He frowned and squinted again, wondering at the blue rider.

"Is he throwing down rose petals?" she asked. "What's gotten into the beast?"

DRAGON RAIN

I woke with a start from a restless dream. The hotel room was dark and quiet--only my breath in the silence—only the faintest intrusion of outside noise from the street. It was a fright like waking from a nightmare—but it wasn't the dream. I'd heard something move.

I lay there waiting, staring at the dark, and I heard it again—a faint rustling sound, a whisper of movement. My heart had already lurched, and now it settled into a fast, pounding rhythm.

The rustling grew sharper, a rattle more like cellophane crackling, and then I heard munching sounds.

God. Was it rats?

This was supposed to be a nice hotel. I jerked up. "Who's there!"

I fumbled for the light switch, quickly surveyed the room.

Nothing.

Well, there was something, too. Once I'd gotten up, I found the torn cellophane beside my back-pack, a residue of crumbs from the cookies that were supposed to be inside. The trail led from there to an antique, cast-iron kettle my grandmother had forced on me when I left her house, and then it stopped.

What the hell? The kettle's developed a taste for cookies?

Somehow the damn thing looked different in the lamplight, too. I'd thought it was decorated with ginkgo leaves, but now it was obviously pine cones.

It was four a.m. I decided I couldn't cope with the Twilight Zone this early, so I groaned, fell back into bed and slept until daylight—rats or no.

I was stuck in Tokyo for an extra couple of days. This pilgrimage was a college graduation gift from my parents, a visit to the old country to spend the summer with relatives in rural Hokkaido—and to get me away from what my mom gingerly called an "unhealthy romance."

Well, I'd gotten away all right. I'd met at least a hundred cousins. *Sobo,* my grandmother, was so pleased, she arranged treks all around Japan for me, visits to Fuji-san, to various shrines. I'd never been exactly bilingual, but I'd made remarkable progress in the language, gotten into the customs and daily life. Over the summer, I'd spent very little time thinking of what I was going to do about Kevin—which was the thing I'd really meant to accomplish on the trip. Much as I'd wanted to, I hadn't even talked to him on the phone—likely what Mom had planned. Kevin was going to be furious, and we hadn't settled anything.

Yesterday I'd gotten into town burdened by gifts, made a panicked dash through Ginza for more, and then thrown everything in a suitcase to catch my plane back to Los Angeles. Well, it didn't take off. I was trapped by a typhoon that turned up churning and muttering off the coast, dangerously close to Narita Airport. All but emergency flights were canceled until the thing made up its mind what to do. All my underwear was dirty. Most of my clothes were at the airport. It was hell of an anticlimax to the trip.

By midnight Mom had already called twice from California to make sure I was all right. I'd only been stuck one day, but still, maybe she had a point. The hotel room was a cheap Western style thing, bland and close, and I couldn't make any plans. I was already hearing noises at night—early symptoms of cabin fever, at a minimum.

Now here was another day to kill, when I wanted with all my raging hormones to be flying home. Yesterday I'd sworn not to call Kevin. I'd meant to wait until I got home to talk with him—to postpone the upset, I had to concede. But this morning I was pacing like a junkie. I was thinking of sex with him, the heat and the sweat, the feel of his body. I wouldn't admit it, I couldn't stand it—I broke. Holding my breath, I jabbed in the number. The call crackled through—and his voicemail answered.

Dammit. All that build-up, and he wasn't even home. I collapsed on the bed.

Lying there with my arms blotting out the room, the best I could come up with was to go out to breakfast. It was brunch actually, by the time I had shoved up, dug out enough clothes and struggled through the shower. Standing at the window naked and still damp, I thought maybe the restless dreams had carried over, or maybe it was the typhoon that made things still seem like an avatar of unreality. The air was gray and oppressive, thick with moisture that almost took shape. Out there over the Pacific hung a big low-pressure swirl, a powerful, elemental force I could almost feel. Traffic groaned from the street below like a monster's voice, echoing off the clouds. It made my head ache just thinking about it. I dried the last moisture off my breasts with the hotel's towel, and went irritably to put on my clothes.

When I got all the way down to the street level, I realized I'd forgotten my umbrella. That looked like a bad idea—the moisture was definitely thicker now, and the shape fairly obvious.

It was rain. I cursed in aggravation, took the elevator back up, turned the corner of the hallway and collided with a guy that had his hand on my doorknob.

"*Ah! Sumimasen!*" I squeaked automatically, and he reached out to steady me.

He was a boy, I thought at first, dressed archaically in clothes I hardly recognized: a *hakama*—a traditional dark, split skirt—elevated wooden *geta* clogs and a coat with the shoulders extended. Pale golden skin, chiseled bones, a turned down nose. He had long hair tied up in a samurai's *chonmage* style.

"*Kore wa watashi no heya desu,*" I explained, thinking maybe he'd mistaken the room.

He blinked and stared, probably at my gawdawful accent, and took his hand off my arm. Then I thought he was older than my first impression. His eyes were odd, long and flat with the Japanese formal *tatemai.* He turned without speaking to me, walked away up the hall to the elevator, where he glanced at me again with those curious eyes.

Well. I frowned and shrugged, turned to open my door. It was only one more strangeness in an already too-weird day.

The boy was standing in the lobby when I went down, staring inscrutably out at the rain. Probably he'd forgotten his umbrella, too. With mine open, I hiked down the avenue to the cafe where I'd had breakfast yesterday. Chrome and laminate with wide glass windows—it was visibly Western, too, but with a difference—notably the menu. I gotten to like the Japanese-style breakfasts, salad and fish with rice, but today I'd meant to be home, and as a defiant gesture I ordered sausage and eggs.

The grease gave me indigestion—likely a signal of adjustments to come. I dawdled at the restaurant over coffee until it started to rain heavily, and then decided I wanted to go back to the hotel room.

The kettle was gone off the chest.

The thing was such an aggravation. It was heavy and bulky to pack, hard to keep up with—but there hadn't been any way for me to refuse it. The pot had been handed down through my dad's family for generations, *Sobo* said, and had insisted I take it.

So now I'd have to carry it home, problem or no. Unless someone had stolen it.

Well, not likely. Not something that damn heavy.

The room had been cleaned, and I thought the maid must have moved it. I found the wayward thing under the bed. Now the ginkgo leaves were back. I'd swear they'd been pine cones at four a.m.

A spatter of rain and a gust of wind rattled the window, hissed across the panes like a *kami's* spit. I shuddered and closed the curtains on the sickly, roiling sky, read a magazine for a while. I was trying to keep my mind off being stuck—and off Kevin, too. Against all my resolve I tried to call him again, but he still wasn't there. Only the voicemail. Dammit.

Finally I fell asleep. It was dark when I woke, to another call from Mom.

"Yes, Mom," I assured her, "everything's fine. No, Mom, I haven't heard anything about the weather. No, the typhoon's not here, just some rain."

No mention of Kevin, though I knew she wanted to nag. I washed my face and tried to plan the evening. Sparkling alternatives: More reading. A movie on TV. Maybe dinner first.

That settled, I tidied up a bit. It didn't help to have slept in my jeans. I put on a denim skirt, not to be outdone by the Japanese girls, and then covered it up with a bulky raincoat so no one could see it. Hat. Umbrella. I started off for the same cafe.

It was pouring now, rain slanted sideways, gusting in squalls along the street. Maybe I should have considered a taxi, close as the restaurant was. Dinner was damp and unsettling, as thunder crackled outside. I nearly had the place to myself, chose a spot near the window to watch the flailing deluge. Mom had known more about the typhoon than I did—the waitress said it was headed inland now. I shuddered at a flash of violence, the crack and rumble of thunder. The electric lights seemed frail and dim, barely keeping back the dragon.

Well, hell.

I had delayed my return to the hotel as long as I could, but nine o'clock was long enough at the table. The waitress was inattentive, staring worriedly out at the downpour. I managed to catch her attention, paid the check, collected my things: Raincoat. Hat. Umbrella. Outside, the rain was sharp as needles—sharp as dragon's teeth, snapping at my face.

I had to cross one street, barely an alleyway, and the dragon almost got me. It was a flash of headlights, a squeal of brakes, a coiling hiss of spray as the car slid at me, unable to stop.

Then something hit me from behind. It was over before I knew it. I'd lost the umbrella, skidded on the pavement myself. Someone was lying on me. I tasted blood. My knee hurt.

Car doors flew open. Voices erupted into the darkness. It took me seconds to realize it was the driver shouting apologies.

Three men helped me up, ghostly figures in the rain, backlit by shimmering lights. The damn bulky raincoat had protected me from most of the damage.

"I'm all right," I managed to say. "I'm all right."

I wasn't sure I really was. My tights were torn, and I was soaking wet. I refused offers of a hospital, offers of a ride. Mortally embarrassed and starting to shake, all I wanted was to get to my room. I looked around for my umbrella, saw it a distance away, blowing in front of the gale.

One of the men chased it down, splashed back through the puddles, the eerie, spectral gusts.

"*Dozo*," he said, offering it.

"Thank you."

I held it immediately in the proper place. Too late to keep any of me dry, but at least it kept the fucking rain out of my eyes. The men sorted. One of them took me by the arm.

"I'll walk back with you," he said.

I decided he must be the one who had shoved me out of the way.

"Okay, thanks," I said. I was unsteady on my feet, I decided, and shaking from more than the wet. The other men bobbed, phantoms in the shimmering rain, and disappeared into the car.

Accompanied, I splashed on to the hotel, buffeted by the wind, slashed by the rain. In the lobby my companion took the umbrella and closed it up. We got into the elevator, waited, got out, walked down the hall to my room. I looked at him and saw he was the boy I'd bumped into this morning.

"Are you staying in this hotel?" I asked vacantly.

"Yes," he said. "In this room."

He took the key away from me and opened the door, shoved me inside.

"What the shit?" I swung around to face him. "Who the hell do you think you are?"

"My name's Wakashi," he said. "And I'm a *tengu*."

I'm definitely in the Twilight Zone. I can hear the theme notes loud and clear, accompanied by driving rain against the windows.

"Your knee's bleeding," he said.

I escaped to the bathroom and locked the door. Sitting on the toilet seat, I shivered blankly for a while, but finally I got up and shed the wet clothes, took a blazing shower. By the time I had my hair dry, I'd figured it out.

Wakashi. It's that damn wayward kettle that *Sobo* gave me, the one with a taste for cookies. Very old, she'd said, with the faintest of knowing smiles, and very valuable.

So the damn thing's possessed, and Grandmother knew it all the time. I brushed out my hair, wrapped in my robe, took a breath and resolutely opened the bathroom door.

By then he'd gotten completely comfortable, sitting on the bed in the hotel's complementary *yukata*, watching TV and eating the last of my cookies.

"You can't stay here," I said. "You'll have to go back to Hokkaido."

"Oh?" he said. "How am I supposed to get there?"

"If you're a *tengu*, you can fly."

"The dragon will get me," he said.

An age-old rivaltry. Well, I wasn't going anywhere in the damn typhoon either.

"What do you want from me?" I asked.

"Tell me about Kevin," he said.

I sat down hard on the other bed. He'd been going through my things, had Kevin's gift out, the wrappings torn away—it was standing on the night table. By no small coincidence, it was a dragon cast in bronze, a symbol of lust and other violent powers, as old and expensive as I could buy.

"It's none of your damn business," I said.

"Tell me anyway."

I didn't want to talk about Kevin, or even think about him--the relationship was too primal. But maybe the time had come when I'd have to, or else give up thinking at all. It was that kind of relationship—pure lust—or at least Mom insisted it was.

I'd hated her for that at first, but maybe this trip had done what she'd wanted after all—given me some perspective—so I could think rationally about what staying with Kevin could mean.

As long as I was close to him, I couldn't think. Mom insisted he used that fact to abuse me. Well, maybe she was right. He'd never actually hit me, but we had that kind of fight-and-make-up relationship that kept me on a wild roller coaster, always off balance and falling his way. He was completely dominant, and deadly jealous, too.

"Give him up," Wakashi said.

The very idea left a gaping hole in my life.

"The hell," I said. "What am I supposed to do instead?"

His eyes flickered with amusement. "I'm available."

"No way," I said.

"Why not?"

His smile was out in the open then. His eyes were lively, the *tatemai* gone. They were sharp like *Sobo*'s—like he saw right through me. His hair was damp and loose now, and it fell well below his shoulders. He looked perfectly solid, very wry and hardly magical at all.

"Damn you," I said.

"Japan's a nice place," he insisted, fishing another cookie out of the cellophane, watching the TV. "You could stay here. Your grandmother said she'd find you a job."

"I am going home," I said firmly.

"Well, that's fine," he said, "but still there are other aspects to life."

"How can I get rid of you?" I asked.

"You can't," he said, holding the cookie in his teeth to punch up another channel on the remote. "*Sobo's* cursed you forever."

"I am going to bed," I decided. Then I did, and left him propped on the pillows, watching TV by himself.

He didn't stay there. Sometime in the night I felt him slide up against me. I tried out the feeling, the warmth of his belly, the silk of his skin—decided it wasn't half bad. He was welcome in the cold darkness, while the storm's violence howled and raged, clawing at the windows. I turned toward him, and he slid his hands inside my robe. We stroked one another, shrugging the robes off, exploring. In a few minutes we'd found a way to fit together, and mated fiercely in the darkness.

Morning, and the storm had come to a pause. Wakashi's hair was scented somehow of wide, serene outdoors, open pine forests, high, snow-capped mountains. I propped on one elbow to study him. He stirred, slid one lazy hand along my thigh.

"We're in the storm's eye," he murmured. "Maybe your plane will take off in the foreseeable future."

"What am I going to do with the bronze?" I asked.

"Give it to a priest."

"A temple?"

"No," he said. "A shrine. Shinto will deal with it better. You can ask for a blessing."

"Can I get you exorcised?"

He pulled me closer, buried his nose against my throat.

"No," he said.

I gave the bronze away, felt immediately better. To hell with Kevin. Life sparkled, its facets catching the light. Packing my bags to make the plane that night, I looked around for Wakashi.

Damn him. By then he was only a kettle again.

THE WINTER PEOPLE

Atta whined and lagged, dragging her basket. "Kajia," she said, "carry me. I'm tired."

"No," said Kajia, panting from the climb. "Atta, I'm carrying Juji already."

"Juji can walk," complained Atta. "I'm tired."

"Sorry. Just keep going."

Kajia, struggling ahead of the little girl, had left off a breathless humming to answer. The world spread below them, bluish and indistinct, mist-softened by a cloud come down to touch it from the sky, so the trees appeared to wade in a hazy river.

The air was cold, and a pale blossom lay on the earth. It was the first green spring Kajia had seen in her few years, a wonder of magic, and thus she sang, honoring the spirits of bloom and fertility. She was hoping to gather some of the vitality to herself this way, for her people believed that the world was place of power. Atta and Juji hadn't seen such a spring before either, but of course it didn't matter so much to them.

They had been climbing for a while, but still the spider webs held dew enough to snare the sun. A rocky slope stretched down the hill, and beyond that, rolling hills breasted the ground fog, afloat on nothingness. Above them, wispy cirrus painted the sky with snow. Kajia boosted Juji a little higher on her hip, where he clutched at her bare breast. She took his hand away absently and gazed up the hill, looking for the sweet froth of acacia to fill their basket before the sun got hot.

"Why can't you carry me, too?" asked Atta, with the single-mindedness of a toddler.

"Because I said so," Kajia insisted. "You can rest when we find something to eat. Don't tear up the basket, Atta."

"Can't I rest here?" asked Atta.

"No," she said. "Stay close to me so you don't get lost."

"I won't get lost," Atta, insisted. "I want to rest here."

"Go," said Juji, black-eyed, with dirty fingers in his mouth.

The limestone was sharp, and unexpected pebbles cut through her hide shoes, but rockiness kept the brush from growing so dense. Kajia labored up, pulling herself from bush to sapling, burdened by Juji, while Atta trailed, complaining, dragging the basket still.

"Don't tear up the basket, Atta," Kajia called down to her. "It's the only one we've got."

At the top she settled Juji in a patch of knee-high grass and shoved back her ragged hair. She was sweating a little now under her wrap, and was grateful herself to sprawl on a stone that was still cold with winter. Grassy and nearly bald, the hilltop was fringed in trees, with deep hollows below filled by a white blow haze--it must be plum. Kajia had caught her breath by the time Atta struggled up the hill.

"Can we rest now, Kajia?"

"Yes," she said. "Sit here and give me the basket. I see acacias over there. But watch Juji, while I pick. Okay?"

The children wandered about while Kajia worked, and she stayed quietly alert, tracking them by their faint rustlings in the grass behind her. The green shoots snapped easily in her strong fingers, tender and pungent, while the sun climbed marginally higher, casting a sweet warmth over her shoulders. The acacia growth was thick, and the basket filled up quickly, so Kajia had to find a better way to carry the bounty. She took off her wrap to fill that, too.

Then running feet snapped her straight from the task, trembling, alert as an animal. But it was only Atta flying through the grass.

"Kajia! Come quick!"

"Where's Juji?" she hissed.

"All right," Atta said. "But come quick."

She was already running back the other way. Kajia followed.

Blood stained the grass, and Juji stood staring at it, sucking his thumb.

Kajia swept him up.

"You shouldn't have left him here."

"Kajia, what is it?" asked Atta. "Should we run away?"

Kajia glanced quickly around, but the clearing was as open and innocent as before. There was a lot of blood; the sharp tang of it widened her nostrils, quickened her pulse. It shattered the sweet peace of the morning.

"You know the way back to camp, Atta?"

"Um-hum." Atta was sucking her thumb now, too, big-eyed.

"Don't be a baby," Kajia said. "Hide behind this rock with Juji. I'm going to see what it is."

"Kaji..."

"It's clotted," she said, "and not that fresh, Atta. From last night maybe. I'll see what it is."

Something heavy had dragged itself along the grass, bleeding, likely dying—but it had left no clear track that she could identify, even in the soft ground. If it was an animal, they could use the skin, or the meat; but alive and hurt, it would be dangerous. Kajia followed the trail cautiously, sidling, glancing over her shoulder, to where the track ended in a thorny growth of brush. She knelt to peer into the thicket, poised, ready to sprint.

"Atta!" she called.

Running feet pounded up behind her.

"What?" Atta panted.

"Go get somebody to help me," she said, "Makia or Jen. It's a man, a boy. And he's hurt."

Atta bent to peer through the brush.

"Go on!" insisted Kajia.

Atta ran.

Insects hummed through the air, flies circling the lure of blood, and a horde of gnats danced in her eyes. Kajia crept into the brush, tightening her lips as she got close—thinking he would be dead, after all. But when she touched the boy, he opened his eyes, and when he lifted his bloody hand she took it.

Atta did well for such a little girl. The sun was still only three-quarters high before she was back with the clan's matriarch, Makia, who was Kajia's grandmother, and Jen, her oldest son. They had brought Laj with them. Dark and sensitive, married in from another clan, he was closest they had to a shaman.

They dragged the boy out of the thicket where they could look at him. His eyes were closed now, his hand limp and still.

Jen leaned on his spear. "Best end his suffering," he said. "He's not going to live."

But Laj was kinder-hearted. "He's lasted over-night," he said.

"His belly's ripped open," Jen said. "And look at his leg. The bones are splintered. Even if he lived he'd be a burden."

Makia unbent from the boy's side painfully, arthritic, old at thirty. She was a pragmatic woman, as a leader must be in a harsh and uncertain world.

"His people must be here somewhere," she said in her matriarch's voice. "Follow his back trail, Jen, and see if you can find out what happened to them. No, Atta. Stay here with us, child."

It didn't take long for Jen to come back, wading through the grass with his spear balanced on one shoulder.

"One of the bear-folk," he reported. "It looks like a hunting party killed a deer, then ran away when the bear attacked. There's another one torn to pieces." He jerked his head back the way he had come. "Over there."

Makia looked at him. "They didn't come back for their dead?" she asked.

"Not that I could see. Ran straight away." Jen shrugged in his slow way and pounded his spear haft on the ground. "Maybe they're afraid," he said. "Maybe they've angered the bear spirits."

Makia frowned, fingered the coarse ends of her graying hair, thinking about going away and leaving the dead without rituals to placate their souls.

"The bear-folk have nothing against us," she said. "We'll take care of them, I guess. Laj, what do you think about the boy?"

"I don't know," said Laj. "Maybe."

"He'll be a burden," repeated Jen.

The decision lay on Makia, and she took the responsibility to follow her vision, however it might affect them. She weighed the boy's fate, and perhaps his spirit.

"This is kinder country than we knew," she said. "Jen, we don't understand it's ways. And his people may come looking for him. I think we can afford to keep him a while."

Sitting in the grass then, holding the boy's still hand in hers, Kajia curved her lips into a quiet and fleeting smile.

Their camp was temporary, a circle of brush set against a rocky outcrop. There was no cave as Makia would have liked, but at least there was an overhang that kept the dew off and offered some shelter when it rained. They carried all they owned, a few tools and skins and storage baskets, traveling south away from stomach-pinching cold and rivers of ice that had taken the clan, one by one, until now only twelve were left.

Laj and the dour Attani built a litter and brought the boy to the camp, while Muki and Bu, Kajia's younger brothers, were sent to build a cairn for the dead man, and to bring his weapons.

Laj sewed the boy's wounds together with bone needle and gut thread, and bound the leg up between sticks. He had no herbs nor medicine, nothing that he could recognize in this strange land, so they only washed the boy and covered him and left him by the fire. That night he breathed the shallow breath of dying, but in the morning, somehow he was still alive.

Kajia went to look at him, and her mother's sister Koha, suckling a new baby at her breast, came to sit beside her.

"Maybe he'll live, after all," said Koha, studying the boy, shifting the heavy Kata in her lap. She was Juji's mother, too, serene and thoughtful. Not much older than Kajia, she was Makia's youngest. It was she that had brought Laj to the clan, willing to give up his home and travel with them to have her.

"He's so pale, and his eyes are sky-colored, Koha."

They looked at one another, and Koha smiled. "Yes. It is a wonderful magic," she said.

"How old do you think he is?" asked Kajia, her eyes falling back to the boy's angular form.

"Fifteen?" guessed Koha. "Laj says he's one of the southern people the traders talk of. They're built lighter than us, but taller. See how long he is?"

"Are we that far south? You think he's a man then?"

"Yes," Koha said. "His beard's not heavy, but see?" She nodded her head at him. "It's growing there on his face."

Their conversation was cut short. "Where's that lazy Atta?" called Tiza, headed toward them past the fire. "Are you two going out to dig roots or not?" she growled. She was Kajia's mother. An old break in the arm-bone, healed crooked, troubled her when it was cold, and she was always cranky in the mornings. She threw a frayed basket down at their feet.

"We're going. We're going, Tiza," Koha said, secure in her place as a young and fertile woman. "Just give us a little time." She sighed and slung Kata on her back. They found Atta and went out to dig in soil that was amazingly loose and warm, thawed from the permafrost that lay behind them. That was a wonderful magic, too, like the spring.

The boy took fever from the wounds, and they thought again he would die. He tossed and whispered in a tongue they didn't understand, but somehow he clung to life. Laj and Jen met another hunting party in the hills and tried to ask about him in the bastard trader's tongue, but the strangers didn't know anything helpful.

He woke to sense quite suddenly. The men had brought back a deer in the morning, and Kajia was cutting meat into strips to hang over the fire and smoke, while Tiza and Koha scraped at the hide a little further away.

"This is fine country," Makia had said about the deer. "Look how fat the meat is at the end of winter."

"There were plenty of tracks," answered Jen.

"So," she said. "It won't be so hard to get another one."

It was confirmation of Makia's wisdom, which Jen had sometimes doubted openly—still he had followed her on this long and dangerous journey, on which so many of their kin had died. Kajia remembered it less than her elders, but the hardships had left their mark on her, too, so that nothing seemed sure in her life. It was a new concept that the world could be kind.

Kajia flint knife wasn't the best in the world. Her work on the carcass was laborious, but at least she had set Atta to work collecting sticks and didn't have to bother with her. She hacked and tore, and after a while she became aware that the boy was watching her. She wiped her hands in the dirt and went to sit next to him.

"May the spirits give you strength," she said.

He answered something in his foreign speech; and Kajia shook her head. He closed his strange eyes and licked his lips, and when he tried again it was in the pidgin trader's tongue.

"I thought you were a dream," he said.

"No," she said. "I'm real. What's your name?"

"Chantel."

"Do you want some water?"

"No," he said, "something to eat."

He ate broth and after a while went to sleep; but now he needed more of someone's time, and Makia said he was Kajia's responsibility, since she had found him. So she stayed in camp with him, watching the meat smoke, while the others went out to forage.

"You're the Winter People," he said, propped up a little, weak, but surprisingly alive for all his wanness. "You've come from the north and the snows, haven't you?"

"From the north," she echoed. "Yes. That's us."

She sat with a stick to tend the meat, glancing over at him now and then as they talked. His hair was as dark and shaggy as her own, and the ugly wounds marred his chest and belly, but his eyes were sunny, like the spring, and he smiled a lot.

"Are these all your people?" he asked.

"There were more," she said. "Makia's children and her mother's. But they've all died of the cold."

"Oh," he said. "It's always winter there?"

"Yes," she said. "Colder. Harder. The ice moves south, a little more each year. Makia always said it would be easier here, with more to eat, and it seems to be that way. But we've been traveling a long time. I don't remember the north country very well."

He hesitated.

"How old are you?" he asked then. His eyes had swept over her, stopped at her breasts.

She flushed and dropped her eyes, dug at the dirt with her stick.

"Thirteen winters," she said. "I'm a woman."

"But you don't have a man?" He had already noticed her disgrace.

"No," she said.

"Why not?"

She dug with the stick. "I just haven't chosen anybody."

"Chosen anybody?" His blue eyes clouded.

"Everybody expects me to take Attani," she said. "He doesn't have a woman since Mota, Atta's mother, died in childbirth, but I just haven't." Kajia shrugged, got up to feed the fire, came back to sit down. She glanced at him, but found no censure—only confusion.

"Our women choose outside the clan," she explained, "but I haven't had a chance since we move around so much. Koha found someone, but I'm not as pretty as she is."

"Oh," he said. "Your customs are different. Here the men choose and pay a brideprice for the girl."

"A what?"

After a while he said, "I want to get up."

Kajia didn't think he could, but he did. He leaned on her heavily, but he relieved himself and lay back down white with pain. He was a head taller than she was, even though he didn't stand up straight.

The next day he told Jen where to find his clan, but the men put off going to find them. It was further than they'd thought, and thaw had made the bottomlands mucky. They waited for dryer weather, and so it was nearly a moon before Jen and Attani set off on the journey, taking the dead man's things as a sign of good faith.

They came back several days later, late in the afternoon, but without any strangers. Jen and Makia went off to talk. When Kajia tried to ask Attani what was going on, he just shook his head and went on gnawing a strip of deer meat. So she had to wait for Makia and Jen.

It wasn't long. The two of them came back and went to speak to Chantel. Lying by the fire, he watched them come with eyes that seemed flat and pale.

The trader's tongue was blunt.

"Your people aren't coming for you," said Jen. "They say you belong to the bear-folk now."

Chantel didn't answer, only turned his face to the cold rock wall, away from the warm blaze of the fire.

It was hard to see the life go out of him. He didn't stir the next morning, or ask for anything to eat.

The others glanced at him and went away to their various chores, left Kajia as usual to tend the fire and the children. She sat on a woven mat, working the dried deer hide with her hands and teeth to make it soft, watching the children sometimes, but mostly the boy where he lay by the fire.

At mid-morning she went to touch his shoulder.

"Chantel?" she said.

"Don't, Kajia."

"What are you doing?"

"Just leave me alone," he said.

She could feel his shame. She left him alone, but still she watched him.

Rain flooded the rocks the next day and a cold wind sprang up after it, swept a breath of snow over the camp. They moved closer in the darkness to sleep huddled together between the cliff and fire. In the morning Tiza found Kajia sleeping against the blue-eyed boy.

She grumbled all morning after that, as they tried to find wood that would burn. They'd had enough stored under the cliff for the night, but today they had to gather wet sticks, and the fire sputtered and smoked all day, burning fitfully and without much warmth.

"Sleep with the children," Tiza said at dusk. "They need you more than he does."

But Kajia moved again in the darkness, to lie against Chantel.

"Does she think I want him?" she thought to herself. With her arms tight around him, she felt his ribs rise and fall as he slept, the warm pulse of his heart against her. It was a strange thought that she'd had, and it was a long time before she went to sleep.

Tiza was angry the next morning and tried to talk to Jen about it, but he only shrugged and went about his business. She sent Kajia out to gather wood for the day, invented obvious errands to keep her away from camp.

"Look Kaji," she said, as night closed in, "you're a woman, and you can choose your own man, but not him."

Kajia was respectful of her elders and she held her tongue, but once Tiza was asleep, she moved again.

The next day was already warmer, the thin mat of snow retreated before the sun. It was hardly daylight when Tiza sent Kajia to dig tubers with Koha and the babies.

"Are you going to take Chantel for your man?" asked Atta, as soon as they were away from the camp.

They had descended from the ridge into a wooded dale where pale flowers shoots thrust up beneath last year's rotted leaves. Hogs had rooted in these woods, but the tumbled track was old, and likely tubers had grown in again beneath the soil.

"Atta, go dig somewhere else," answered Kajia, testing the ground with her fire-hardened stick.

"Well, are you going to?" asked Koha. She was bent under Kata's weight on Kajia's other side.

Kajia frowned, began to dig as her stick found a root under the dark humus.

"You'd better hurry, if you are," said Koha. "You see he's not eaten. He'll die for sure this time, because he's got nothing to live for. No kin. No woman."

Kajia kept digging.

"Kaji?"

Koha's brown hand stopped the stick from moving.

"I can see what you see in him," she said. "Do you want him or not?"

Silence, stillness lay on the earth. A faint breeze stirred the branches of an evergreen, cast a monstrous shadow.

"I want him," Kajia whispered.

"Well, go back and talk to him then. Tiza's gone for water by now."

"But..."

"If you want him, does it matter, Kajia?"

"You know it does, Koha."

"Ask him," Koha said.

"How can I?"

"Will you let him go without trying, then? You're a woman, Kajia, but you're unproven. How strong is your magic?"

Kajia pulled the tuber from the earth, straightened and dropped it in the basket, feeling how the dirt, like time and life, slipped through her fingers. It was a terrifying thing to feel.

"Chantel?"

He still lay with his face to the wall.

"Chantel," she said. "Sit up and talk to me."

Perhaps her tone reached him this time, because he rolled over and pushed himself up on his elbows.

Now that he was waiting, staring at her, patient and hollow-eyed, Kajia was afflicted with shyness. She sank down in front of him, her eyes downcast, and tried to think of something to say.

"I'm sorry you...can't go back to your people," she began.

Nothing, and she glanced up at his face. It was sober, waiting. She chewed her lower lip.

"I mean...I don't think...Did you expect them to come for you?"

The trader speech was so awkward. She was afraid to offend him, but it only seemed to hurt. He closed his eyes.

"Yes," he said, quietly.

She picked at the bindings to her wrap. "Why didn't they..." she asked. "I mean..."

"I'm tainted by the bear's claws," he said, "in more ways than one, I guess."

She hesitated, not knowing how to respond to the irony, but then she found a way to the subject she wanted, after all.

"Did you...have a woman?" she asked.

"Betrothed," he said. "I'm...I was saving for the brideprice."

"Oh." She took a deep breath. "Chantel, you could...I mean..."

"No, Kajia," he said.

"Why not?" she asked.

"I don't want your pity."

"I didn't think it was pity."

Taken unawares, he stared. "Kajia, I'm not a man any more. I'm dead."

"You don't look dead to me."

He closed his eyes and covered them with his hands, as if he could shut out his life.

"I am," he said.

"Why are you here, then?"

"I can't walk," he said. "I'd go if I could."

"You'll get better."

"No."

"Yes."

"Kajia," he said, "I wouldn't be able to give you anything, or take care of you. I'm a cripple. My leg's not healing well, and I'm... torn up inside. I can't even stand up straight. Your mother knows. Listen to her. Your people can't afford to keep me, like this."

"We're keeping you well enough now," she said. "I can keep us both."

"Have you talked to the others?"

"It's my choice."

He stared at her then, but she wouldn't look at him.

"No," he said.

The quiet was so intense that even the fire sounded loud. Then she looked straight at him, pushed up. "I thought you were stronger than the bear," she said. "But I was wrong. It's killed you after all."

The next day the clan moved on, packed up the camp at the cliff's base, and left him there alone.

The midnight before, Chantel had lain awake, waiting. Night sounds whispered around him, uneasy; an owl cried down slope. Sleepers huddled quiet by the fire.

The dark was peopled by ghosts. They spoke in the owl's voice, sighed in the trees, beckoned with spectral hands. He shivered, knowing he was one of them now, by his own choice.

"Die," they whispered. "We are your kin."

He tried to close his ears so he couldn't hear their chill voices, so he could draw them to himself bravely. But then a rustle crept up behind him, and a hand brushed his shoulder, light and uncertain. He didn't respond, but still the girl's warm body slid against his back and her strong arms tucked around him. A goddess, he thought, older than his own people, come down from the cold and forgotten north.

He found his own peace then, finally. And when her breathing evened in sleep, he touched her hand gently, where it lay against his scarred belly, holding him tight.

Mist rolled off the reedy lake, pooling along the shore. A change sharpened the morning air, and it wasn't the lowland weather. It was something different in the climate of this new camp.

Everyone rose and went about their business as usual. But Kajia became aware there was a private exchange of glances, and subdued giggling from the round-eyed children. Then beside the fire, Attani came and sat next to her, and she knew what it was that waited.

She avoided it all day, but evening was the time of choices, when fortune could be set beneath the stars and the full, fertile moon.

"It's time you made a choice, granddaughter," said Makia, when they were done with eating. "The clan continues," she said, "though we are small. That which we receive from our ancestors, we must pass along to our children. You must choose, child, and we must begin the rituals. You're too old to be unmarried, almost fourteen winters, and you had rites of passage near two years past."

She waited then. Kajia looked around the circle of eyes. They fastened her with the responsibilities of womanhood, the customs of life and death. Distorted by distance and circumstance, they trapped her into a choice that was no choice at all.

She took a deep breath and lifted her chin. When she answered, it was to all of them.

"I want Chantel," she said.

There was silence for a moment, and then something burst within the fire; a log slid in a shower of sparks.

"Enough!" cried Tiza, jerking to her feet. Her voice cut like a knife, and baby Kata began to cry. "Daughter, you can't..."

"No," said Attani, harsh and bitter. "It's my turn now. The man was nothing, cast out by his clan, given to the bear-folk..."

"If you..." Koha started up, the flames reflected in her eyes.

"Stop," interrupted Makia. Silence fell at her gesture.

She took a breath and gathered her authority about her, but when she spoke, still she seemed more kindly than the others. "Child, she said, "I weighed the boy's spirit myself, but I wrong. The bear people offer us no terror. We are a strong people, and we might have taken him back from them. But Kajia, he chose to die in spite of you, and we honor his decision. He's not here for you to choose."

It was the truth, and it hurt. Tears burned her eyes, and Kajia fled the circle. She didn't go far though, not beyond where she could see the fireglow--it was her safety in the dark. She was bound to her kin, to their needs and their protection, but still she had wanted something better. She huddled against a rock to cry at the riverbank, where water lapped the rising moon.

But she wasn't alone. A touch grazed her shoulder, and she started up. A shape wavered before her, a pale apparition haloed in moonlight. She caught her breath, and dark fear gripped her hard. She poised to run--but the creature was between her and the fire.

"Goddess protect me!" she cried. "Are you a ghost?"

"No." The answer was full of pain and cynicism. "Not yet anyway."

"Chantel!"

She grasped at him, and he sagged against the rock, put down his stick.

"Wait," he said, fending her off. "I brought you something."

It was a crude shell, seemingly made of dirt; but when she took it, it was stone in her hand.

"What this?" she asked.

"A pot," he said.

"What?"

"A gift," he said. "It's clay, baked in the fire. You cook in it, keep water. I know you don't have anything like it."

Oh," she said. "I know. The traders talk of it. You made this?"

He took an unsteady breath.

"Yes," he said. "It's not much. A little thing, and crude. But a brideprice, if you'll have it—to save my pride."

She looked up from the clay shell, her eyes still wet with tears. As the moon broke free of the lake, she touched the fine bones of his face and laughed.

Forty-five thousand years ago, fleeing the advancing glaciers of northern Europe, a sturdy and rugged people, called today Neanderthal, migrated south. In southern Europe they met Cro-Magnon the advancing front of evolution's new wave.

HURRICANE SEASON

I kept the glove. It was iridescent, like an exotic shell. The fingers curled slightly, titanium composite claws; and its colors ran in subtle, prismatic rainbows, like oil slick on the water.

It was way too big for my hand of course, but I would play with it; put it on and lurch after Ulys and Johnny, clawing the air and growling like some automaton of a bear, not knowing any better.

They would play along, running and screaming. Sometimes we played hunter, and they would try to track me through the kudzu tangle, or along the rocky beach. But I was quick at hiding my trail, and often as not I got away.

"When I grow up, I'll be big and strong like the enforcer," I would say.

"Aw, Ada Lee. You're just a gurl!" Ulys would say.

Younger than me, he was freckled and dishwater blond. His hands and feet always were too big for him. Like Papa had looked.

"So? What does that matter?"

My hands were grubby, little-girl hands. But later, when they were longer, I could feel the faint tingle of the electro-senses still alive in the fingertip contacts, and I didn't play with it any more.

Mama never knew I had it.

We lived south on the Appalachian Islands; our steep shanty town hidden in a cove where the ridge sloped right into the ocean. The rocks were so close under the water you had to be careful where you swam, and only a couple of places were safe to dive.

Mornings, we were shaded by steep bluffs, and the sun set in front of us. The shacks were built on rough pilings that leveled the floors and kept us above the winter storm surge, though we were mostly protected by the cove and the rocky crags hidden in the sea. The settlement had gardens hacked out of the kudzu, fenced with rusty chicken wire, laced with barbs to keep out the pigs and deer, and everyone had a pirogue tied under their shack; but mostly we lived on salvage. The same rocky ridges that broke the surf brought us storm wrack, wood planks, electronics, delicacies of strange food and fine clothes from the shipping lanes to the west; the spice of distant places, with enough left over to trade. And we thought nobody could blame us if we helped nature a little. We were wild as the pigs and 'coons, barefoot and indolent, but there was no need for anything else. The living was good.

He came from the north, following the chain of islands, armed exoskin fashioned into the sleek, aerodynamic shadow of a hawk, ominous, silent then; though we had heard the sonic shock as he dropped below mach speed and thought it was thunder.

On the beach the iridescent composite broke up into man-shape, too fast for us to hide. We had been clamming.

Frozen tableau: I thought he was a robot, and we were all dead. I hung on to Uncle Lon.

"I want to speak to your chief," he said through quartz synthesizers—dispassionate, arctic.

Silence at first. Then Uncle Lon, shifted, ready to tell him to git, I reckon; but Mama was first.

I had always known Mama was tough, but I had never known she was beautiful. I saw it then, somehow, reflected in the stranger's rainbow skin.

She straightened from where the tide foamed, let her skirt fall.

"He's been dead 'bout three years," she said, matter-of-fact, cool as the stranger in his anonymity.

He hesitated, facing her.

"What can we do for you?" One hand on her hip, the other shading her eyes from sunglint off his armor, while the skirt washed on the swell, clung wet about her legs.

"I'm here to investigate a report of pirate attacks in the shipping lanes. Under maritime law, it is piracy to damage or forcibly remove cargo from a privately owned vessel. Do you know anything of individuals in violation of this law?" It was a clipped, un-modulated query.

Aunt Jean and Uncle Lon just looked blank and stupid, like they didn't understand what he said, but Mama took her chance.

"Where've you come from, man? North? West?" Her face was ardent. "Where?"

Hesitation.

"North."

The voice had not changed, but the word was a concession.

"Ah! From the city? Can you stay with us awhile? Talk?"

He didn't. Not then. But we saw him—the fine con trails of his jets where he guarded the ships, watching the sea, tracing the surf. Under the faint trails we played at city for a while, as best we could from imagination. To the west was Denver, Mama said, and to the north N'York, though most of it floated nowdays since the land had sunk. It was so big, sometimes at night we could see the lights, borealis on the clouds. We tried to pump Uncle Lon for information—he had been to see N'York. But he wouldn't say much about it we could understand, except it was big, and different.

"What's the enforcer's name?" Johnny asked him.

"Hush!" said Uncle Lon. "To us he don't have a name."

We gave up the play, finally, for want of details; but the enforcer didn't go away. It was early summer, and we should have been fat, already storing away for the next winter. But we were scared shitless of him, wouldn't go out in the pirogues for fear he'd see us as pirates, so we starved on the sparse gardens and ever sparser clams.

Glow of fire below. Wavering shadows on rough planks. Whispers, overheard from the loft of our shanty.

"...can't have him here..."

"...ruin us all..."

"...get rid of him somehow..."

"...kill him..."

"Hush!" That was Mama. "...oughta know better!"

"...Anna Mae..."

"...with that skin on?" She almost hissed.

"...just a man, Anna Mae, with the skin off..."

Stillness.

In a minute the quiet had deepened to something you could feel. Taut. Straining to hear, the three of us in the loft almost held our breaths.

Finally Mama said, "Okay. We can give it a try."

The bite was gone out of her voice. And I could almost see her shrug, casual. That was all. But it was awhile after they left before we went to sleep, wondering what they'd meant.

Later I saw him walking with Mama on the gritty sand where we had first seen him, north of our cove. I was surprised when I saw the helmet off. I couldn't see through it to the man beneath like the grown-ups could.

I scooted through scrub, mosquitoes whining around my head, trying to get close enough to hear what they were saying. But even without the parabolic mikes, he had quick ears. And sharp eyes. He had me in a minute, and Mama scolded. His eyes were altered, yellow-metallic gold, with an iris you could see dilate when he looked at you.

There were some enforcers that were just a machine with a person's brain, and then some that were just machines, too. The alterations enhanced him to interface with electro-senses, the application specific integrated circuitry, so he was really part man and part machine; but mostly man, in this case, I guess.

Not long after that, a sow got Ulys. We had caught her shoat. We knew it was dangerous, and Johnny was too little, so we had left her in a tree. The little pig wriggled and squealed, hard to keep a hold of, and the big sow came out of the kudzu right on top of us, grunting, ears flapping. We let go of the shoat and ran. I got away all right, but Ulys tripped on a big root.

She would have ripped his belly open, but he jerked his knees up and she laid open his thigh to the bone instead with her big yellow tusks. When I heard him screaming, I turned around and quick hit her right in the eye with a rock so she left him be. Then for a breathless minute she couldn't see to find me, and he laid quiet, so she ran off after the squealing shoats.

He was bleeding bad, crying; and he kept rocking and saying, over and over, "Ow, ow..."

Johnny came running, white-faced, and I told her, "Tie his leg up tight in your shirt, honey; and watch for the sow. I'll go for Mama."

It would take too long through the kudzu, so I cut across to the beach. I was already out of breath when I got there, with nearly a mile to run, still. But I didn't have to go all the way. I nearly ran into him, I was so upset; gasping and starting to shake with reaction. I skidded and fell in the sand, tried to scramble back the other way, to get clear of him.

He was so close I could hear the servodrive amps hum as he moved. The rainbow glove caught me by the ankle. Completely out of control, I kicked and screamed, sobbing for breath.

"Stop, Ada Lee," he said.

I hadn't thought he knew my name. Or maybe it was the authority in his voice. I quit screaming.

"Let go! I have to get Mama."

"What's wrong?"

He went back to find Ulys and Johnny, skimming over the tangle like a bird. I could never have found them from the air, but he uncovered them on the first pass. Infrared. He could read their body heat.

Johnny shirt was soaked with blood, but he put something else on instead, a milky autofilm that molded to fit Ulys' leg. It sealed the ragged slash, and must have been anesthetic, because Ulys quit moaning.

Mama's face was ash when she saw it. She glanced quick at the bloody slash and then up at the enforcer holding Ulys gently as a baby. I never saw her look so strange.

By rights Ulys should have lost his leg. A hog's bite is so nasty, it always gets infected. But he was okay in a month, because of antibiotics we could never have gotten for him.

And the next time the enforcer came, he brought Mama something. It was late already, and I had started to go out and pee. But when I heard them on the porch, I waited.

It seemed like they talked for a long time. After he left, I went out and sat by Mama on the edge of the porch. The moon was in front of us, laying out a white channel on the water so clear it looked like you could walk on it. Off to the right, the land circled around dark, to make the mouth of the cove. All the shacks were dim, and the water lapped restless against the pilings under our feet. Mama didn't say anything, just kept looking out at the water.

"What did he bring you?" I asked.

For a minute she just sat there like she didn't hear me. But finally she looked down and opened her hand. It was a little bottle of perfume. And when I took it to see, her hand felt moist and warm.

It was always dry in the spring, but late summer was storm season. Hurricanes bloomed like flowers in the warm water, scouring the island with wind and rain so it was fresh and green, then twirling off to the west or north to die in the Arctic cold. Usually they missed hitting us square. There was a fast current off the east coast; a Stream, Uncle Lon said; and high pressures that held them off us. If they came in it was from the east, and we were protected by the ridge behind us. But the barges that carried goods between the big cities didn't have any protection. Like as not there was at least one that got lost and ran afoul of the submerged peaks, spreading a slow slick on the ocean and storm wrack on our beach.

It happened early that summer, just after it got really hot. It was a freak season all around. The Stream current had shifted out some and the storm formed up inside it. In the evening it was hot and still, and by morning the sky was steel gray and eerie, wind whistling like banshee in the kudzu.

When the wind started we could tell it was coming straight in because it blew dead south. By noon the rain was horizontal, trees were laying over and the surge was rising. We moved out of the swamped shanties and up towards the ridge top with whatever waterproof scraps we had to take shelter under the kudzu tangle. The three of us huddled with Mama under an oiled tarp, wet and cold, to wait it out. Uncle Lon and Aunt Jean had a plastic slicker. Johnny whimpered in Mama's arms as the wind tore the flapping tarp, but we were really safe enough.

It was a big storm, and disorganized so the eye was narrow and unstable. In the calm we came shivering out from under the tarp to see a ship stuck about a quarter mile off the point. Any other time we would have gone out in the pirogues to strip it before it broke up, but now we just stood watching from a little clearing, some of the men folk complaining quiet-like. Mama didn't say anything.

In a while the four-man crew was out on deck, lowering a life boat. It was some sort of white, unsinkable composite and rode high, though it wallowed in the heavy swell. They made for the cove, but the breakers out beyond the mouth were perilous, crashing brown with silt clawed from the bottom, and they hadn't the skill to ride them in. They tried to cut across and the boat swamped before they got clear. It shot back up, capsized, engine sputtering. We thought they'd drown in the undertow, but then we saw Mama was right. The enforcer came plunging down out of the steel sky to pick them out of the whitecaps just as they were sinking.

He circled once, a little sluggish with the weight, and picked us up on the hill. Banking, he jetted a little burn to stall and settled in our clearing. In a second everything had gone to shit, because the flush-faced Captain recognized Mama as the pirate chief. He coughed and gagged, got it out.

"Pirate bitch…"

The enforcer's helmet snapped around. Poised, we had all seen it coming, scattered into the brush like deer. All but Mama. She stood a frozen second facing him, until he moved to take her. He was so fast, I don't know how she got away, but Johnny screamed, so shrill it hurt, and then Mama was gone in the kudzu. He pulled up, took to the air, tracking. I guess she tried to get down to the cove, but he dived, pulled up as she changed direction.

I don't know what I meant to do, except help Mama somehow. I set Johnny down by a rotted log and told her to stay, ran up the hill after them, gasping, the brush dripping rain water in my eyes. I came out above the bluff in time to see what happened. Nobody else did, it was so quick.

Mama must have been in the brush at the bluff, and he burnt it with flame laser, the fiery track driving her towards the open. I thought she was dead, heart in my throat, thinking I would smother; but Mama was smart as well as tough. When she flushed, it was sudden, and she didn't hesitate. She ran straight out and leaped off the bluff as if she could fly away. It was a long second before gravity took her, and then she closed her arms and snapped her head down in a dive, cutting the treacherous cove clean as a razor. He followed her, of course; but she knew the water and he didn't.

In the rising wind, blowing north this time, the kids and old folks watched as Mama took everybody out to strip the barge and ride the stained breakers in before the gale.

It was while they were out I found the glove floating up from the sharp rocks beneath the waves. Mama never said anything, but I heard her crying that night. I didn't understand it then. But now that I'm in her place, sometimes in the dark summer evenings I wonder what his name was.

Storm and Shadow

Dedication

For Andy, gone too soon.

"Lord, grant me chastity and continence, but not yet."

--St. Augustine

HAUNTED

It's February again, and the mist roils thick as memory. It rises from the unseen ground like a ghost from the grave. Winter's breath, cold, impalpable, it caresses my car's hood, the fenders, and eddies in the low beams, obscuring the road as if I'm driving into unreality.

It's not really necessary that I see the road, though--I've come this way so many times. It's like the face of a lover even in darkness, as I remember the familiar turns, the spectral shadows of trees that crowd out the sky, making the lane dark and eerie even in the day. It seems almost brighter now with the mist, and my lights fall down over the air as if it's a solid chasm waiting to engulf me, and something I could touch.

The house is there on the hill finally, like a cliff, overhanging and precarious. It's a two story, Victorian style. There's a village below, but it's obscured by the fog as if it doesn't exist tonight, and can't intrude on my purpose. I sit in the car a moment before I get out in the rocky drive. The house looks abandoned from the outside, sagging slightly with the gravity of age. It has missing boards and a cracked window pane. The yard is scraggly, overgrown with forsythia so tall it must block the front windows with color in the spring, but it's bleached and insipid now in the winter of my soul. I remember how it looked before, with the shrubbery blooming and honeysuckle running along the fence, and I can almost smell the attar, the memory that chases the image.

My trepidation in the car is only fleeting, quickly gone. Once I'm through the door, it all becomes the same. The carved furniture sits properly against the walls, undisturbed, and the carpet seems as free of dust as it did when it was new. I walk through the dim parlor as if in a ritual, touching the lace curtains, the tapestry-upholstered chairs, and here and there a photo, gilt-framed. It has no business changing, after all, of departing from what it was, from what I remember. Beyond is the hall with the mauve-striped wallpaper, and the kitchen.

I hold my breath, in fear that he's somehow forgotten. But of course there's no need. It's here.

It's a valentine as Victorian as the house, for tonight, the night for lovers. A lace-trimmed heart, red as blood and pierced with Cupid's arrow; it's propped on the counter beside the sink, with a bouquet of long-stemmed roses, where it's always been, so I'll see it when I come through the door. I laugh when I see it, in a sharp pleasure; and I think, oh, Sal, it's been so long!

I go back to the entry, still smiling, and hang my jacket and scarf on the coat rack that stands there. I'm early. It'll be a while yet before he comes.

I try to sit in one of the stuffed armchairs, but I can't. I find myself up and pacing for the third time, tugging at a loose strand of my hair, checking my watch. The hands creep towards midnight. The stillness remains unbroken, the emptiness of the house, and I begin to worry that something will go wrong, that something will keep him away. It seems too quiet, the mist through the lace curtains too heavy. Am I wrong that it's different tonight?

The two hands are almost one on the dial, and still there's no sign. I can't sit here anymore. Anxious, I get up to wander through the house again. In the kitchen I lift the roses, pick up the bloody heart. I take the stairs in the back of the house, climbing towards the bedrooms. Now there's no sound, as there should be, of my shoes on the treads. It's as if time and place have warped suddenly, as if the mist has come in, invaded the house with a malevolent presence that rises behind me, cold tendrils reaching for my back. I turn swiftly, but there's nothing there.

"Sal?"

I hear my voice quiver, and the sound dies quickly in the unnatural stillness. A whisper seems to come from above me, and I swivel again, looking up. Nothing.

"Sal?"

The stair rail is cold beneath my hand. I take another step up, another higher. The hall is semi-dark, lit to shadows by windows at the ends of the house with deep window seats. Perhaps the sound was only branches tapping the glass. But still I'm afraid. The rooms are murky and black. The doors seem suddenly gaping like mouths to devour the unwary.

I slink down the passage, hoping to find a vantage point at the window, where I'm not looking into the light. Something is wrong. I can feel it. The certainty makes my skin crawl like gooseflesh, chills me to the bone. My breath falls into smothering, cloying stillness and disappears, except in my own ears, where it sounds loud as a bellows.

Another creak from somewhere, and I start, remembering how isolated this house really is, how far from any neighbors. Sure there's someone else here, I move cautiously backwards, holding my breath now, hoping he can't hear the pounding of my heart, hoping to make the safety of the stairs again. But the ancient floor betrays me. It squeals like a traitor beneath my first step; and he leaps out at me!

He's big, a dark shadow, too heavy for anyone I know. I scream and run, but I know he's too close. He carries something uplifted in his hands. It catches the light, glitters. An axe. He's a crazed burglar. He bellows like a maddened animal, drowning my screams. I slip at the stairs, try to stagger up, knowing I'm going to die.

The axe swings upwards, falls towards my back; and I lurch forward. But I fall into waiting arms. There is no death, no pain. The phantom is gone. Sal's here now, holding me. And he's warm and solid as I am, at least for a while.

"Oh, Sal," I say, lying slack against him, with relief, as my breath shudders out. "I had forgotten. I thought something had happened, and you weren't going to come."

"Cassie, I'll always come," he says, and his voice is as sweet as all of life.

He's tall, and smells comfortingly familiar, dressed as he always was in jeans and a flannel shirt. His shoulders are as wide and solid as the earth. In the daylight he's blue-eyed. I turn my face up to be kissed; and he's there now to kiss me, as I want, as I remember.

We go back up to the bedroom, and we make love on what was once our bed, among the roses, scattered, and whisper about the last year, while we've been apart. Finally we sleep, and I hold him in my arms.

Feeling the loneliness already, I wake before dawn, knowing it will be the end of our time together. I want to watch him for a while, his face as he lies there sleeping, the strong lines of his forehead and jaw, the curve of his throat. This is all I have left of him, this brief touch in darkness, cloaked in mist and winter, with the roses, and my heart pierced with pain as surely as the valentine he's brought me.

The years seem hardly to have changed us. Perhaps it's only the magic of the night, but he is as beautiful as when I first saw him. He seems to shine with the radiance of my longing, so intense on this one night that has to make up for the distance that death has put between us.

How long has it been? How can I count the years of his life? I reach out to smooth his dark hair, to feel his warmth, the rise of his breath one last time--for I am the ghost, haunted by a living man.

The mist thins, the light grows, and my hand on his chest fades slowly away, leaving only the roses, and him, behind.

NIGHT AT SLOAN POND

"Joy," said Isaac Bain. "This place is pure bad luck."

Joy was making bread, folding and kneading the sourdough on the kitchen table so it would rise and she could get it baked before dinner time.

"Bad luck happens to everybody," she said. "You can't say we've got any worse troubles than anybody else."

"I've been thinking it ever since your Ma died of the cholera," he said. "Then I got crippled…There's just too much that goes wrong around here. That trouble last year, and the drought is killin' us. We're fightin' an uphill battle trying to keep this place."

"So what do you think we should do about it?" she asked.

"If I was younger, I'd go back East," he said. "Can't you find a good boy to marry and get away from here?"

"Pa," she said. "You know I've not got any prospects."

"There's a barn dance coming up at the Elmer place this month. You oughta go."

"There won't be anybody there I want," she said, pushing escaped brown curls out of her eyes with one floured wrist.

"None of them boys is good enough?"

"Everybody's got troubles. There's not much kindness in folks." She glanced at him, laughed suddenly. "Why don't you pester Nick to get married?" she asked.

"I do," said Isaac. "I'm not making any headway with your brother, either."

"You'd better let things be," she said, squeezing the dough in portions and shaping it quickly into loaves. "What would you do if both of us got married and moved off somewhere?"

"I'd get along," he said.

"I've lived here all my life," she said. "And I'm not giving up." She wiped her hands on a dish towel. "I got work to do. I'll be back in later to cook us some dinner."

Joy was shelling corn when she heard the dog. She was sitting on the porch of the cabin, shoving at the dried kernels with her thumb so they broke off the cob and fell into a dishpan between her feet. Her back ached and the pad of her thumb was already blistered, but it was last year's corn, and they couldn't afford to waste it. It was moldering a little and she meant to shell it all this morning for chicken feed. The season was late spring and already plenty hot, so she had her skirts hiked above her knees, her legs bare and brown above her worn leather shoes. When the dog growled, she straightened in her straight-backed chair and looked to see what was wrong. Buck was old, but he didn't make any mistakes.

There was nobody coming from the direction of town, but off to the east a rider was making his way down from the hills. Joy let the corn ear drop into the pan, stood up and shaded her eyes against the sun's glare. After a moment, her mouth tightened and she reached for the double-barreled shotgun leaned against the planks behind her. She stepped out into the dusty yard, holding the shotgun ready. The rider was Raidy Hart.

He rode on past the bunkhouse and the barn big as life and stopped his horse in front of the house, took off his dusty Stetson and rested it on the saddle horn.

"Mornin,' Joy," he said.

Hart was about twenty-one or twenty-two. He was slim and dark, and his hair was black, long enough to curl across his shoulders. He wore black chaps and a vest with silver Concho trim, and something about his cheekbones said he might be a breed. Joy knew his eyes had a dash of yellow, like a wolf, maybe.

"Mornin', Hart," she said.

He was an outlaw, but it looked like he meant to be polite this morning—maybe because of the shotgun.

"Is Nick around?" he asked.

"He's out on the range, working on the fence," she said. "What do you want with him, Hart?"

He looked at the gun. It hadn't wavered.

"I thought maybe we were friends," he said.

"Maybe," she said. "That depends on what you're doing out here."

He swung his leg over the horse's neck and slid out of the saddle, and Joy backed up. He was quick and intimidating and she didn't want him too close to her.

'I was hopin' to stay a while," he said, perfectly smooth and not a little bit brash.

"What?" she said. "Stay here?"

"Yes'm, that's what I said."

"Alright, Raidy Hart. What kind of trouble have you got trailing in your wake?" she asked.

"Nothin,'" he said, innocent as you please. "I just thought you folks could use some help." He glanced around at the ramshackle barn and the bunkhouse. "The place is pretty run down, and I know Nick can use some help with the fencing."

"We've not got the money to hire any hands," she said.

He looked down, fiddled a little with the horse's reins. "I know that," he said. "I can work for room and board."

"What about that trouble in Klamath Falls last year?" she asked.

"Lou Burke had a gun," he said. "Folks will have forgot about it by now, don't you think?"

Maybe so. She gave it up, lowered the gun.

"You'll have to talk to Nick," she said. "He's out on the north range."

"Up near the ravine?" he asked.

"I guess," she said.

"I can find him then. How's your dad?" he asked.

"Alright," she said. "He's in the house."

He turned toward his horse, and Joy looked past him then, saw a gray coyote sitting under the trees by the barn. She had the shotgun in her hand, raised it automatically and pulled the trigger.

Quick as she was, though, Hart was quicker. He shoved into her and knocked the gun up so the blast went harmlessly into the air.

"Don't…," he said.

"What's wrong with you?" Her voice was sharp. She had been braced for the blast, but his weight had knocked her off balance, and now he held her in a too-tight embrace. "Let go of me! It'll be eating our calves…"

"Joy?" came Isaac Bain's voice from the house.

Hart looked distressed, but then he laughed suddenly, let go of her.

"It might be one of my kinfolks," he said, like it was a joke. "Please don't shoot him."

He looked toward the trees, but the coyote was gone—so he mounted, tugged on the reins.

"It's okay, Pa," shouted Joy. "I just shot at a coyote."

As Hart started off for the north range, she turned and went into the house to see to Isaac.

That night Raidy Hart moved his bedroll into the bunkhouse. Joy sort of expected that Nick would take him on, so she had enough supper for all of them ready when the two men came in from the fencing. Hart seemed a little awkward, like he didn't quite know how to behave around polite folks, and when he finished up, he borrowed Joy's broom and disappeared.

"Joy," said Nick. "I hope you don't mind if he stays here a while."

Joy didn't turn around. She was busy washing the blue-willow dishes, lathering them up with lye soap and rinsing them in the dishpan.

"I just don't want any trouble," she said.

"He got us out of trouble last time he was here," said Nick.

She glanced at him, saw the stubborn set to his jaw.

"Alright," she said. "If you want him, it's fine with me."

When she went to shut up the chickens, she saw the coyote sitting under the trees again. It seemed to have come to stay a while, along with Raidy Hart.

Oddly, the animal didn't seem that interested in the chickens or the calves, only lurked at the outskirts of the yard. She caught glimpses of it during the day when Nick and Raidy were out mending the fences, sometimes caught its quick shadow closer to the house in the dusk of early morning when she went out to get wood for the cook fire.

For someone who probably got his money from holding up stagecoaches, Raidy Hart did well as a ranch hand. He and Nick fixed up the barn and the bunkhouse, and did some work on the house, too. It wasn't long before the place started to look a little more prosperous. Still, the fencing was what needed the most work, so the men stayed gone on the range most of the time. It didn't really matter, though, because Joy was used to working by herself.

The drought that had plagued the range for the last six years broke suddenly about two weeks after Hart came to stay. They were all sleeping and woke suddenly to thunder and a heavy downpour. In the morning when Joy opened the door, the yard was wet and the water still puddled on the porch and steps. It was cause for celebration.

Her garden soaked up the moisture and turned green. Joy got her hoe out of the shed and went to work making sure a sudden growth of weeds didn't take the corn and beans that would keep them through the winter. This morning the squash vines were blooming, and the bees hummed back and forth over the blossoms. She bent to see if any of the squash were mature enough to eat, and when she straightened, the coyote was sitting clear as day right at the end of the row. He was big for a coyote, sleek and dark, with black tips to his ears. He looked straight back at her with his yellow eyes, and then turned and trotted off toward the brush.

She watched him go, thinking what a strange animal he was—and getting bolder, too. She was still concerned about the calves, but Hart was basically doing a lot of work for just room and board, so she meant to respect his wishes about the coyote.

In the afternoon, she went to pick blackberries up at Sloan Pond. She fed Isaac his dinner at noontime and made sure he was comfortable on the porch. Then she saddled her spotted mare and led the horse up to the house, tied on her basket for the berries.

"Joy, you be careful," said Isaac from the porch. "Them boys of Eisner's are still around, and I thought I saw an Injun the other day."

"Dad, we've not had any problem for a while," she said. "I'll be fine."

"Can't you take the dog?" he asked.

"No," she said. "Buck's too old for it this year. He'll never make it there and back."

"You take my gun," he fretted. "I'll feel a lot better about you going off alone like this."

"Alright," she said.

He was still believing in the bad luck, she thought, but Isaac had a good head on his shoulders, even if he did have his faults. Nick had the Colt, so Joy went into the house and got the old man's Winchester and its scabbard to fasten onto the saddle.

She didn't have a fancy sidesaddle, so she mounted astride from the front step, draping her skirts over the horse's rump. "I'll be back pretty quick," she said.

It wasn't far to the pond, only about a half hour of riding. They had almost fought a range war over it last year during the drought. It was fed by a spring that didn't go dry, even in the worst of the summer heat. Today the water was clear and clean from the recent gift of rain, and it was surrounded by dark fir and thick brambles of blackberry canes, hanging with ripe berries.

Joy dismounted and let the horse drink from the pond. As the mare went to grazing, she untied her basket and set to work picking, working deeper into the thicket. She hummed a little tune as she worked, celebrating this little bit of bounty. The basket got full pretty quick, and Joy turned around, started to work her way out of the brambles.

The mare screamed suddenly.

Joy stood shock still, then fought through the canes in a frenzy. She had left her rifle on the saddle. Oh, God, she thought. Oh, God. The thorns caught her skirts, tore at her skin. She broke through the last of the vines, saw the mare in a lather, rearing and jerking at her tether. The horse was facing a grizzly bear that roared and snarled, while a gray coyote circled and snapped at its heels.

Joy jerked backward when she saw the bear. She slipped on a bare rock and fell, felt a sharp pain in her ankle, dropped the basket. She rolled and cursed, trying to get up. The mare broke her tether and sprang away, disappeared into the firs. The bear broke away, too, lumbered into the woods. The coyote looked sharply at Joy, then disappeared as quickly into the brush. Dammit, dammit, she thought. Isaac's bad luck had caught up with her, and she was lucky to be alive.

On the good side, she hadn't lost the berries. She had prudently fastened the cover on the basket before starting back. However, she had serious trouble now. Her ankle was swelling and hurt like the dickens. There was no way she could walk home on it—or even far enough to catch the horse.

She hobbled to the pond and took off her shoe, put her foot into the cold water, thinking that would slow the swelling. The ankle looked bad, felt worse, and she hoped it wasn't broken. She tried to think what to do.

Nothing was the best plan, she decided. The mare would likely go home. Raidy was gone to town for supplies, but Nick would be home by supper time, and by then they would know she was overdue. He would probably be here before dark.

In case the bear came back, she would need some kind of shelter. There was a rocky bluff on the west side of the pond, and she found an overhang there about half way up, with a deep crevice underneath—almost a cave. She stowed the berries there in the cool shade, hoping they'd keep better. She could see the pond well enough from the bluff, so she sat down on the rock and propped her foot up, hoping that would ease the ache.

It was a long afternoon, and she had plenty of time to think about what she'd seen when she came out of the brambles. That had to be the coyote that hung around the house. It had the same sleek flanks and black-tipped ears. So what had it done? Followed her all the way here? Attacked a grizzly bear to save her horse? To save her? It didn't make sense in coyote terms. Wild animals just didn't do that kind of thing.

She worried the question as the afternoon wore on, and after a while she noticed the weather was starting to turn. It had been sunny in the morning, but now dark clouds were forming up, and Joy kept a watchful eye on them. Sometimes the spring storms could be violent, and she didn't have much shelter here. The wind was already colder, and she had neither a slicker nor a coat. She looked around for dry leaves and fir boughs to pack into the crevice for warmth. She gathered some wood, too, thinking she might need a fire.

By the time her stomach said it was supper time, the rain had started. Big droplets spattered the rocks, and Joy retreated under the overhang. Still, there was no way to stay dry. The wind picked up and drove the rain under the rock, wetting her through to the skin. Darkness fell quickly within the storm, and thunder crackled in a constant roar. It began to hail, but the rocks did protect her from most of that. Later, the rain settled into a steady downpour. Once it was full dark, Joy knew Nick wasn't coming. The storm would have cut him off, and she needed to make it by herself until morning.

When the rain started, the temperature had dropped like a stone. Joy's teeth chattered, and she worked her way as far as she could into the nest she had built under the overhang. She felt for the firewood and found it was dry, but now it wouldn't do her any good. The box of matches in her skirt pocket had gotten as wet as her clothes.

There was nothing to do but try and sleep. Joy managed to doze, but she slept restlessly, and things went from bad to worse. After a while, she became aware it was snowing. She thought she was freezing to death, and then she dreamed she had a fur coat. It was warm and sensual, and breathed softly against her. She started out of sleep then, and realized it was the coyote lying against her.

She lay there for a moment, making sure she was really awake. Everything seemed real enough. The rock was solid against her back; her clothes were still damp from the storm. Beyond the animal's fur, the snow drifted down softly. Still, something was seriously wrong.

"Alright," she said to the coyote. "What are you?"

The animal stirred slightly, didn't answer, of course.

Isaac had seen an Indian.

"A skinwalker," Joy guessed. "What are you doing hanging around with Raidy Hart?"

"He's my cousin," the boy said.

He had shifted in an instant that was hardly perceptible. One second she was lying by a coyote, and the next second there was bare human skin against her side.

"Ah," said Joy. "He said that, didn't he? Kinfolk? What brings you to this range?"

"The Modoc wars," he said. "I was with Captain Jack at the lava beds, and the U.S. army would really like to find me."

"What's your name?" she asked.

"People call me Johnny Blackhand," he said.

"And you're a witch?"

"Yes, if you want to call it that."

He moved, sat up. The snow provided a faint contrast, and his shadow was dark against it. Cold moved into the spot where he had been.

"Is this firewood?" he asked.

"Yes," she said. "But my matches got wet."

His shadow began arranging tinder. "Give me one of them," he said.

She moved further out of the crevice, shivered as the cold air flowed around her. The matches in her pocket seemed a little dryer now, and she got one out of the box, held it out. His warm hand closed over hers as he took the match.

When it lit suddenly, she could see he had started it by twirling a stick between his palms. The phosphorus in the match had caught from the heat, and he blew on the spark, got the tinder to burning well, and then added sticks of the dry firewood.

Joy moved closer, held out her hands to catch the warmth.

"You did well," he said, flashing her a quick smile. "There might be enough wood here to last until daybreak."

In the golden firelight, he looked to be about her own age. His body was long and muscular, and he was naked except for a g-string. His hair was straight and black, heavy around his shoulders, but maybe he wasn't a full-blooded Indian. He had the high cheekbones, but like the coyote, his eyes were light-colored.

"Isaac is right," he said. "There is a curse here."

"What?" she said.

"A darkness," he said. "Something old that hangs over your ranch—over most of the range, actually."

"How do you know?" she asked.

"I can see it," he said, "with a sort of second sight."

"Well, damn," she said. "That's not good news."

She rubbed her face.

"What do you do about a curse?" she asked.

"I'm not sure," he said. "I can counter it some, but I can't remove it. My uncle is a shaman. I'll have to ask him about it."

"God," she said, hugging herself. "I'm still freezing, fire or no."

"We can go back to sleep," he said. "The fire's pretty well started. If you're not too worried about propriety, you can lie next to me."

It seemed to be a legitimate offer. It was either that or brave the freezing temperatures on her own.

"Alright," she said, and worked back into the nest of leaves and fir needles she had built in the afternoon. Johnny Blackhand lay down against her, and after a while she was warm enough to fall into a real sleep.

She rose back toward consciousness when he got up to put wood on the fire sometime in the night. It was only the cold that woke her, and she drifted again as soon as his warmth was back in place against her.

However, he didn't go back to sleep. Instead, he slid one hand through the curls of her hair.

"Joy," he whispered against her ear.

"Um?" she answered.

"You don't have a man, do you?"

She was suddenly very aware of his nakedness. She ought to have known this would be trouble, but now that it had arrived, she found she really didn't care a whole lot. She thought she had been dreaming about it, the way his body fit against her back. She stretched a little against him, coming further awake.

"No," she murmured. "Not in a while."

His hand slid down her waist, over her hip. Because the day had been warm, she was wearing only a light dress with a simple chemise beneath. There was no corset or thick layers of petticoats to insulate her from his touch. His hand drifted back up, lightly touched her breast. She heated suddenly--maybe already half aroused by the dream—and her hand closed over his, keeping it in place as her nipple rose into his palm.

"Ah," he said, and curled around her. She felt his lips against the nape of her neck, against her ear. He stroked her through the thin fabric of her dress and rubbed against her back. She felt him harden against her thigh. He slid his hand inside her bodice, fondled her breasts. In a moment he was lifting her skirt and chemise, tugging at her drawers. And then he filled her emptiness.

He held her tightly against his belly, moved smoothly against her, and quickly she was panting from the sweet pleasure of it. She groaned, arched against him. It lasted a long time, and when they were done, she lay still in his arms.

"Johnny?" she said.

"Hmm?"

"How long are you going to stay around here?"

"We'll have to see how it goes," he murmured. "Some rancher might shoot me tomorrow."

Joy woke in the half cave to full daylight, with the embers of the fire still faintly glowing. It was late for snow, and already melt was dripping from the trees and rocks above her. The ice-coated firs sparkled in the sun, and below she could hear wild geese honking on the pond. The tableau was wild and natural, but there was no sign of coyotes or witchy lovers, either one.

She wondered if the whole thing had been a dream, but she had the warm feel of satiation, regardless. She washed quickly in the snow melt, ran her fingers through her hair and twined it up where it had escaped from her hairpins so she looked less like a ragamuffin. The berries were safe in her basket, and she ate a handful of them for breakfast, sitting on the rock by the fire and shivering slightly. Even though the sun was warm, the air was still sharp.

She heard Nick's hail before the sun ever rose clear of the firs.

"Here!" she answered, and slid off the rock to start the slow hobble down to the pond. She didn't have to go all the way, though, because he met her at the bottom of the bluff.

"Joy," he said. "Are you alright?"

"Fine, I think," she said. "But there was a bear, and I am *sooo* glad to see you. I have really messed up my ankle."

He pronounced it just a sprain, wrapped her in a blanket and boosted her onto the back of the big sorrel he was riding

"Wait, the berries!" she said, and he handed them up.

They rode down the trail. Looking back, she thought she glimpsed a gray shadow following through the brush.

CARNIVAL

Come, dance your lust on Bourbon Street. The crowd surges bright and hot; the sax ripples, turning, bobbing, notes sparkling in the air, champagne to my ears. I turn, dancing to it, humming with the tune, as if I'm alone.

Fog rises from the cities of the dead, the tombs, masking the eternal flame of the refinery down-river, while boats mourn on the muddy turning current, hot, restless, piercing the mist with their bronze horns, bass to the brassier jazz.

Dark hair, dark eyes, Creole on the tongue. The feathered masques ripple. Crumbling, the city sinks eternally, and only the frail levee where I stand dams the sea away.

Carriages still ride over the French Quarter streets, and the horses' nostrils flare red at the ardor and sweat, foaming at their bits, their eyes rolling white. It's the eve of Carnival, Mardi Gras, and life strains at the bonds of mortality, swirling in the streets, the hotels, the cemeteries of the dead.

Still point in the returning dance, the dark eyes. Blanched skin beneath a masque, a satin cloak. A tux-costumed vampire with dark hair, a flash of fangs. It's my companion, a friend I've met somewhere.

I'm giddy. My girlfriend Julia was here a moment ago, with a friend she'd found. We promised to stay together. But she was swept away in the swirl of champagne and sax. In my drunkenness, I regret losing her.

"Where did Julia go?" I ask.

"It doesn't matter," he says, as he lifts me down from the wall. We've been on the riverboat. "She'll come back to your room, won't she?"

His accent is beguiling. So far from New York. I laugh, loving it.

I'm dressed in a low cut frock that brushes my ankles with petticoat lace, and a blond wig. Historically authentic, the tag said, French--but I doubt it. I remember vaguely that Julia and I giggled over it in the costume shop. I tug at the bodice, trying to make it higher; and my companion kisses me, wine-flavored. The fangs click against my teeth, and we dissolve in drunken giggles. He is cologne and sweat, and the musty smell of antique satin, with his arms around me, hard and real, when nothing else seems that way.

"What's your name?" I ask.

He laughs. A secret. "What's yours?" he asks.

"Rosalie."

"So nice..." And he kisses my lips, my throat, my breast, cool and sweet. I wonder if he can hear Brooklyn on my tongue.

We catch a glimpse of Canal Street, the wild orgy of the Rex parade. Then the crowd surges and we're on Bayou Street, somehow. "Home of Marie Laveau," the sign says, "Voodoo Queen." There seems to be magic everywhere, in the old Quarter, intersticed between the haute couture and cheap souvenirs. But here is a fortune teller advertised.

"Stop," I say, with another giggle, and drag him inside with me.

"Beware the *loup garou*," the woman whispers over my hand; and she looks at my companion. The brown eyes lock, and he laughs at her. I don't understand. She's golden-skinned, in a kerchief tignon and old-style dress. The shop must not have changed in a hundred years--like we've stepped back in time.

"A quadroon," he says, outside.

"What?"

"The fortune teller. One-quarter black. How much did you pay her?" he asks, amused.

The party escalates. Another ball, another bottle of champagne, a room somewhere, with wrought iron view. I remember the dress sliding down my shoulders, the ruffles gone from my calves. He sheds his masque like a skin, and under it he's red-haired, dusky-skinned. He kisses my toes, my breasts, and I'm inflamed. Our heavy breathing marks the quiet, against a distant party. There's nothing but lust, warmth, and him.

"Who are you?" I whisper, near to climax.

And he says, "The *loup garou*."

I woke with the worst hangover of my life, in an alley off Bourbon Street. Dizzy as hell, I staggered up, in a dirty dress and smashed blond curls, caught a taxi back to the hotel.

Julia was showered and fresh-faced. She'd done better than me. She had her guy's name and a phone number to take back to New York with her.

"Damn," she said. "What happened to your throat?"

SOULS

I come in the door just in time to catch the phone. "Detroyer," I say, expecting it'll be Craig Noe.

It's Joel Angstrom instead.

"Wait," he says. "Don't hang up, Anna. It's business."

"I'm expecting a call."

"I'm in trouble," he says.

"Call your dad."

"I can't," he says. "He's out of town."

Shit. So what am I now? A surrogate mom?

"Listen, Joel," I say, clearly and distinctly. "I don't want to get involved with either one of you right now. You'll have to find somebody else to help you out."

"Anna..." he insists.

There's a desperate note in his voice. I hold the phone above the cradle for a minute, trying to analyze it. Then I heave out a sigh, shift one hip onto the desk and the phone back to my ear. Shit, again. Why me?

"What's wrong, Joel?"

"I..." he says, and breaks it off. "Anna, could we meet somewhere for lunch?"

"Tell me first what's going on."

He thinks about it.

"Some guy's following me," he says. It's hardly loud enough for me to hear over the phone.

"Do you know who?"

"Yeah," he says. "He's a black guy. His name's Macoute."

"What's he following you for?" I ask.

"That's what I need to know. It's like..."

"Like what?" I prompt. "Like he's in love with you or something?"

"Anna," he says, "don't laugh. That happens sometimes. Usually I just say 'no thanks' and that's it. But this time...I mean...it's like he's...well...stalking me, or something."

Well, I'm not surprised that guys hit on him, too. Joel's a sharp-looking kid. But I don't like the sound of this stalking. Maybe he's got reason to be upset.

"There's no reason for him to follow you?"

"None I know of."

"Okay," I say. "Vinnie's, one o'clock."

There's a message from Craig on the voicemail. "Anna," he says. "I can't help you out this week end. I've got this dive job down in the Bahamas. Next week, okay? I'm gone."

Shit. There goes a good job down the tubes. The clients are offering a big pay-off, but they need the work done right now. As in pronto--this week end. I tap my nails on the desk, sit there listening to the growl of traffic past the office windows. It's already Friday. I ought to be calling dive shops to see if I can get another back-up for the week end, but instead I'm thinking about Joel Angstrom.

I've not seen the kid for a while. He transferred to college at Florida International in the fall, and I met some of his friends before his dad and I had our falling-out. I'm not a P.I. for nothing, and I've got plenty of time before one o'clock.

I take a chance and riffle through the book, luck out on the second call.

"Teresa?" I say. "Have you seen Joel Angstrom lately?"

"Who is this?" she says.

"Anna Detroyer," I say. "I'm a friend of his dad's."

She thinks about it. "I've not seen him," she says. "Try Audrie Benoit."

"Is she in the book?"

"No," she says. "Got a pencil?"

I try the number and a damn voicemail answers. But I've got one myself; I can't complain. Maybe she'll call back before noon.

"This is..." I start, and then the phone clicks.

"'Alo," it says. The woman's got hell of an accent.

"...Anna Detroyer," I finish up. "Can I talk to you about Joel Angstrom?"

She has to think about it, too. "Wha' for?" she says.

"I'm a friend of the family."

"Okay," she says finally. "Wha' you want to know?"

"I'd rather talk in person. Have you got time for coffee?" I ask.

The north campus of Florida International is up Biscayne Boulevard in the same general direction as Vinnie's. It's late winter in Miami and shirt-sleeve weather today. Sun glints off the water in brief, bright flares, then I make a turn into the developments and it's gone.

I know when I see the girl she's Haitian. We're in a hole-in-the wall coffee shop near the campus. I order mine heavy and black, sit down opposite her in a booth. She's gorgeous, creamy pale, pouting lips, svelte in designer jeans and a flame silk shirt. There's a slight kink to her shoulder-length hair and a slight spread to her nose--the only indications of black ancestry--and you have to look hard to see that. The accent's the tip-off: high class French. Her family's not off some refugee raft.

"Teresa said I should call you," I say. "What's Joel up to these days?"

"You begin to wonder?" she asks.

"Yeah."

"That boy, he run with a bad crowd these days. Maybe soon he drop out of school."

I have to set my teeth. "What's the problem, Ms. Benoit?"

"I don' know him that well," she says. "We go out, maybe one time, maybe two. Then I think maybe he's not so good for me, after all."

I have to wince at that, and the girl catches it. Her cool eyes flick up at my face, slide away. She's not drinking her coffee, just stirring it, watching the swirls with frowning concentration. Maybe she thinks I'm not so good for her either.

"I talk to you because I like Joel," she says. "I think he is..." She doesn't finish.

"In bad trouble?"

"*Oui,*" she says, and frowns harder. "If not already, then soon."

Shit.

"Do you know the people he's hanging around with?" I ask.

"Some of them," she says.

"He says a guy's following him. Somebody named Macoute."

I jump as her spoon clatters down. "I have to go," she says, and reaches for her bag.

"Wait a minute." I grab after her, catch a handful of flame-red silk. "Who is this guy?"

"Let go of me," she says.

Her face has lightened enough for me to see freckles across her nose. Her eyes are suddenly as green and vivid as a cat's. I realize what she's said, look down, let go of her. She throws two dollars on the table and jerks out of the seat. Bells clatter as the door slams behind her.

I've lost my taste for coffee. Maybe I should go down the street to the Club Bar instead.

Headed back south again, I roll down the windows to let the heat out of the car and click on the radio. Planning on that dive job, I've been watching a cold front roll down through Georgia, hoping it'll get past us in time to leave good weather for the week end. The radio tells me it's stalled now over North Florida, promises it'll stay there. Shit, again. I don't need any more complications to my life.

By the time I get to Vinnie's, I'm totally pissed off. Joel's already there, sitting in one of the booths that line the back wall. I have to look twice to realize it's him. His hair's shaggy and unkempt. It looks like he's lost weight, and he's dressed in rags of faded jeans and an old flannel shirt.

He's still got grace to spare, stands up when he notices I'm there. I slide into the seat across from him, drop my elbows on the Formica shine.

He doesn't look good close up, either. There are years more in his eyes.

"Are you on drugs?" I ask.

He gives me a look that's almost venomous, glances away.

"No," he says.

I reach out and catch his chin, pull his head around so I can see his eyes. The pupils aren't dilated. He flushes when he realizes what I'm doing, reaches up and knocks my hand away.

"Anna..."

"Sorry, kid." I look at the menu. "What do you want for lunch?"

He orders spaghetti and I get ravioli. The waitress brings us salads.

"You look different," he says. "Younger."

"You look different, too. It's been a long six months."

"I didn't have anything to do with it," he says.

"Yes, you did." Then I catch his expression. I have to look away myself, study the plastic grapes on an overworked trellis nearby. "Maybe you just didn't know it, kid."

He sighs, rubs both hands over his face, digs the heels into his eyes. "All right," he says. "We can leave it at that."

"Are you okay, kid?"

"Yeah," he says. He drops his hands, but he still won't look at me. He starts to pick at his salad.

"So what can I do for you?" I ask.

"I told this guy I had a steady girlfriend, but he didn't believe me. Let me hang around with you for a while, sleep on your couch for a couple of nights."

"You really think I'm going to do that?'

He won't look at me.

"Why not talk to your dad about it?" I ask.

"I've not seen him in a while."

He catches me staring, glances away again.

"Where are you staying?" I ask.

"An apartment."

He starts visibly as the waitress shows with our orders. Joel's not eaten his salad, so she leaves it, takes my plate away. He doesn't seem to notice the spaghetti.

"Eat your lunch," I say.

He looks at the plate. "I'm not hungry," he says. He shoves the dish suddenly, jerks sideways out of the booth.

"Joel." I know better than to grab at him.

He stops, shifts his feet. "Yeah," he says.

I'm looking at his back, but at least he's not running away from me.

"Sit down."

His shoulders twitch, but he does it.

It's the innocence that's gone out of his eyes. He's not the same sweet kid I met last year. His face is leaner and harder, the bones standing out clear and sharp, heavily shadowed by dark smudges beneath his eyes. All of the sudden he looks less like Paul and more like somebody I don't know very well at all. I want to ask him how it is between him and Paul, but I can't find the words. It's clear he's always idolized his dad, and now…Well, I've had that same feeling.

"Can you drive a boat?" I ask.

He blinks. "Huh?"

"You know. Those things that run along the water. People use them to…"

"Dammit, Anna," he says. "I'm serious."

"So am I," I say and reach across the table for his plate. "If you're not going to eat your spaghetti, can I have it?"

He gets possessive. "I'll eat it." He finds his fork, pokes at meatball.

"So, can you drive a boat?" I ask.

His eyes flash up at me. "Yeah," he says. "What about it?"

"I need some help for the week end. Heirs looking for missing papers. They're supposed to be off the Keys in a sunken yacht."

"You do salvage work?" he asks.

"Not usually." I shrug. "I've got a friend that passed the job along to me. She's going to rent me her boat, but I can't go out by myself--it's too dangerous. I'll need at least one other person to back me up."

"I'm not a diver," he says.

"I can do that part," I say. "Just run the boat."

"All week end?" he says.

"No," I say. "Back Sunday noon at the latest. We'll have to get an early start, so you can sleep at my place tonight. All right?"

"Okay," he says, and frowns. He pokes at another meatball.

The kid just knocks me over with his enthusiasm. I sigh, search around in my wallet for money to pay the check.

"I've got arrangements to make," I say. "I'll see you tonight. Nine o'clock at my apartment."

Back at my office, I call Geraldine about the boat. Also, I need to know who this guy is that's after Joel. I tap my nails on the desk again and decide to call Gloria, my best buddy down at the police station. Maybe she can get me the goods on him.

Her voicemail answers. Damn machine.

"Hi, Gloria," I say to it. "It's Anna. You got anything on a guy named Macoute? Black. Maybe Haitian. Ugly type. I'll be gone for the week end, but leave me a message for when I get back. Thanks."

I drop the phone back on the hook. I need to get my air tanks filled now, and all my gear down to the boat by tomorrow.

By nine thirty I've decided Joel's not going to show. Damn the kid. This could be some kind of joke--or worse. In a contest between Paul and me, there's no real doubt in my mind which way the kid would swing. Hell. Maybe they're up to something again. Maybe I've rented the boat and gone to all this work just to be stood up at the docks out of pure vindictiveness.

But then, I don't like the way Joel looks right now--the hard, haunted quality around his eyes, the set to his jaw. The kid's at risk somehow. Maybe I should worry about him instead.

Welcome to mom-hood, Anna.

The doorbell rings at ten thirty.

He leans over the rail in a graceful curve to check out the parking lot below. Then he turns back to me, drops one shoulder against the stucco wall. With me standing on the step, we're eye to eye now.

"I forgot to ask," he says. "Did you have something planned for tonight?"

"I rented a movie," I say.

For the first time I see the ghost of last year's grin on his face. He glances out over the clattering fronds of palm trees that circle the pool. "Was I supposed to bring popcorn?"

"You missed the whole damn thing." I'm not going to point out it's not a date. Damn kid. I move back so he can get in the door.

I sleep restlessly, thrash when the alarm goes off. I feel around for it, and then remember I left it across the room. Joel's still face down on the couch, starts violently when I rumple his hair.

"God," he says. "It's still dark."

"It will be until seven o'clock. Want some espresso?" I ask.

I check the weather report one last time and it sounds fine. The cold front is dissipating in front of a warm air mass pushing up from the Caribbean.

"Let's go," I say, and drop the cups into the sink.

Joel wrinkles his nose when he sees the boat.

"What is this thing?" he asks.

"Workboat," I say. "It works better than it looks." I start handing him gear to load onboard. "Belongs to some friends of mine in the salvage business, but the guy had a heart attack last month and they're up in New York. They may have to sell it now."

Geraldine and Flynn started out with just a hull and modified it themselves. It's thirty-five feet. Big engines under the deck, extra gas tanks, a water-tight cabin--the thing could capsize and still float just fine. A dive platform opens out right to the waterline in back. Inside the cabin there's a cramped head and a tiny galley. A couple of bunks are packed into the empty space up under the bow.

I nod at the pilot's seat. "Go ahead."

It takes Joel a couple of tries to start it. He flips on the instruments like he knows what he's doing, backs it out of the slip.

"Okay?" I ask.

"Yeah." He's frowning. "It's just bigger than I'm used to."

The diesels provide a solid, dependable pulse as we head on out through the port. The docks are eerie and deserted this time of morning. Reflections shimmer on the water. The big cruise ships are outlined with lights like Christmas, and the air has a faint stink of oil.

We follow the channel markers and the jetties out through the glimmering, chilly darkness, turn south. The sun comes up red through a drifting, bloody haze.

"God," I say, watching it. "I don't like that."

"What?" asks Joel.

"The sky."

I try the weather service again, but it just gives me the same report: Front breaking up. Warm and sunny today and tomorrow. It's the usual optimism, mandated by the tourist trade. Florida never has foul weather unless evacuation's imminent.

Watching Joel run the controls makes me feel better about what I've done. I've taken a serious chance in asking him along as a single tender, little as I know about his skills. But he does fine with the boat. He understands what I'm talking about when I show him where we're going, sets the heading, turns on the autopilot. Then he takes a look around the boat for himself.

"Did they build this themselves?" he asks.

"Yeah," I say. "What do you think?"

He shrugs, "So far, so good," and gives me a grin.

Joel's come alive in the sun, and his eyes flash like rays off the water. He takes off his shoes and shirt and beads of spray catch on his brown skin, scatter the light in bright flares. The wind whips his hair around his face. He sits on the deck to stare at the wake, and I watch the long curve of his back, the flex of his shoulders as he adjusts to the swell. I have to look away--damn the kid. He turns his head to follow a dolphin's splash, and I notice his nose is already red. I dig in my gear for the sun block.

"What have we got to eat?" he asks.

By afternoon I'm watching the weather again, but south of us this time. I give up on listening to the radio and check the barometer instead. In another hour we'll have the Keys off to starboard, and Joel starts monitoring our position on the GPS. The wind drops and the air feels close and muggy. When I check the barometer again, it's falling.

"Shit," I say.

We're there now. We've found the Coast Guard marker. But the damn barometer's dropping like a rock. A squall line dances along the horizon. The weather service doesn't know jack shit about predicting the weather. I'd bet my ass there's a tropical depression forming in that warm air mass--and here we are right beneath it.

It's too early in the season, but then, shit happens.

We've come a long way, and it's all wasted if we head back now. If I put off the dive until this blows over, it'll be too late--Murphy's laws set the odds. The wreck's not that far down, and the dive shouldn't take me that long. I need the money bad. I'm going to gamble I can beat it.

"What are you doing?" asks Joel.

"Going down," I say.

"Is that safe?" he asks.

"No," I say, "but then, neither is running home through a tropical depression. One hour shouldn't make that much difference."

The air may feel heavy and close, but the ocean's at its coldest this time of the year, the currents carrying northern arctic waters barely heated by a quick churn through the tropics. I've brought a wet-suit for insulation and get suited up in a hurry--all the time keeping one eye on the sky.

The squalls seem to be keeping their distance. The swell is running six or eight feet, but that's not bad. We drop the buoy and the dive flag. I shrug on the tanks, check my regulator and mask.

"Stay close," I tell Joel, and roll backward into the water.

Green depths close over my head, a hiss of fine bubbles rising. Sun flows down from above like a watercolor wash. Flickers of silver glance away from me, fish startled by my sudden arrival. I turn and orient downward, start the descent with a resolute kick.

The yacht's in about a hundred feet of water. I can get down to it quick, but coming back up will be slow because of the time I'll need for decompression. Make it fifteen minutes on the bottom, max--about an hour for the total dive.

If this was a bigger wreck, I'd worry about making the dive by myself. But this is only a luxury yacht lying below me--twenty-five feet, with a minimal cabin to get trapped inside of. In a few seconds more, I locate a pale smudge on the bottom with the beam of my light. It shimmers like the ghost of a yacht. The water's indigo around me, shading to black. The silence is deafening, punctuated by the periodic rise of CO_2.

The pale smudge differentiates into a solid boat shape. The *Seduction* is lying over on her port side, the sharp point of her keel extended like a stiff phallus--an incongruous appendage for a female boat. Closer, I can see the tangle of lines and deck chairs still bound to her rails, the sail lying snugged along the boom. The stern end looks dark, vaguely charred from an engine fire. The damage doesn't look to have reached the cabin though, where I can expect to find the papers I want.

They're not in the safe. Geraldine's given me the combination along with the job, and it works like it's supposed to. There's a few thousand dollars in packs of hundreds, but no water-tight package of documents. I stick the money into the net bag fastened to my waist. Maybe it'll help if I can't find the papers, but somehow I doubt it. Anybody who would own a yacht like this won't miss a few thousand bucks.

I'm starting to feel the cold. The mixture of helium and air that I'm breathing is safe, but it can increase the effects of hypothermia. I shudder and flash my beam around the cabin again. If the damn things aren't in the safe, then where else could they be? There aren't that many options, but it'll take a while to sort through them. My time estimate for the dive is way too short. I start a systematic ransack, and find--nothing at all. Hell.

Maybe granny hid them under a loose deck board, but I can't take the whole damn yacht apart on this one trip. If the family wants to pursue this, they'll have to get the hulk raised and towed into Miami. I slide out of the cabin and start my ascent.

Thirty feet and wait, then twenty, then ten. I can already tell at twenty feet that something's wrong up above. The blue glow I left is deadened to an ominous gray. At ten feet I can feel the turbulence. I've been down a lot longer than I expected. The decompression's interminable; the wait for daylight and clear air is a worrisome, fretful need.

I rise into a raging storm. My head breaks the surface a few feet from the marker, and lightning splits the sky, a slash that leaves me half blind. Thunder crashes down, and rain hammers across the water. I gasp for air around the regulator, search the thrashing waves.

Dammit. There's no boat.

I push down a surge of panic, ride the swell up. It's rising twenty-five feet by now, if it's a damn inch. Visibility near zero. It's dark from the storm, getting late--near the winter dusk. Rain shrouds the sky, fractures the waves. Dammit. Dammit. If the boat was anywhere close I'd see the running lights. I slide down the swell to forever, fumble for my light in the trough. As the swell rises again I signal, search the sea for something, anything. Rain slashes across the light beam so it refracts and scatters. Lightning blasts it to nothingness.

The little shit. The bastard. What the hell's happened to Joel? He's supposed to be here. I'm gasping, floundering. I can't stay afloat in seas like this. I've tried to signal and that's all I can do for now. I grip the regulator in my teeth and duck back under the waves.

That cuts off the immediate fury. It's quieter here, calmer. I'll use up less energy. At first I can hear the hiss of rain along the surface, the crack of muffled thunder. Further down there's only the tug of turbulence again. Panicked and breathing hard, I try to relax--I'm still using air too fast. This is hard work. It's too dark, too close--I can't stay here forever. Dammit, I haven't enough air.

The gage falls too fast. Fifteen minutes and I have to go back up. The rain's still there waiting for me, the flailing storm, the bucking, heaving whitecaps. I'm an insignificant speck in the iron-gray sea, lost and forgotten--hanging above an infinite pit of empty darkness and numbing cold.

Hypothermia's creeping up on me. I'm out of air, and the tanks are dead weight now--I'll have to let them go. I've swallowed way too much water. I can't fight this any longer--can't kick--can't breathe.

Still there's nothing out there. And then there is something: A shadow looming through the wind and rain.

Thank God. It's the boat.

I fumble at my belt with numb fingers, flash my light at it. The shadow seems to slow, turns slightly to port. The dive platform swings past the buoy and I reach for it. I've got no energy left, and I miss. A wave closes over my head and I swallow water as I go down. God, this is so hard. I want to relax and drift, fall down slowly through the indigo depths, and never worry about anything again.

Hell, I'm going to drown with the boat right there within reach. I rouse and manage a feeble kick, break the surface again, and then he's got me. I have a vague notion of being dragged up over the platform edge, then a shift through the air and the deck comes up hard under my back. The rain's slashing right into my face now.

"Anna?" he yells at me. "Anna!"

There's a white haze in front of my eyes that's more than the rain, and for a second it's all I can see. Joel shakes me. When I don't respond, I feel his fingers on my jaw. He's forcing my teeth apart. He holds my nose, and then his mouth closes down over mine.

I have just enough presence of mind left to know what he's doing. I turn my head to the side, pull away from his hand.

"No," I cough. "'M okay."

I don't know if he's heard me above the wind, but he's felt the movement. His arms slide under me again, and then the rain's gone out of my face.

There's deck plate against my back again. The noise level has gone down, and there's wan, greenish light from the instruments above me. I can feel the boat roll like crazy. Joel's got a towel, wiping off my face. Then he's tugging at the zipper to my wetsuit, jerking the rubber down over my shoulders. I'm not wearing anything underneath, but I'm so far gone I don't care.

Once he's got me stripped and rubbed down, he throws a blanket over me, wraps me up in it and drops me on one of the bunks. I'm starting to shiver by then, big shudders that rack my body from head to toe. My teeth sound like castanets. Joel's gone somewhere, and then he's back.

"Anna?" he says, and he's got something in his hand: a hot cup that smells like coffee. "Here," he says.

It's laced with bourbon, and I choke, get it down. I'm still shaking like I'll never stop. What I can feel of me is like ice. My hands are still numb, and I slide down into the bedclothes, fold them inside the blanket against my ribs.

"God. 'M ff...freezing," I say.

It must be hardly coherent through the clattering of my teeth, but then there's movement above me in the glow of the lights-- Joel stripping out of his shirt. He slides into the bunk behind me, tugs another blanket over us. I can feel the pressure of his body where he hugs me against him, but not a degree of warmth. It's like I'm made of ice.

"Joel. The boat..." I say, and I feel his hand slide over my wet hair. He whispers into my ear.

"Shh," he says. "It's okay. I closed the hatch. The autopilot's doing the work."

He's right. The ship's rolling like hell, but it's not wallowing in every trough. We're making headway. For a long time I can't relax for the shuddering, but then suddenly I do.

I've been asleep. I don't know for how long. Joel's asleep behind me, still wrapped around me under the blankets. I can tell he's used to sleeping with a woman by the way his arm curls over me and up between my breasts. His breathing is deep and regular and I can feel him clear and sharp through a thin layer of fabric between us.

The storm seems to have died down outside the cabin. The rain has nearly stopped, and the boat's not rolling so bad now, but still I'm sick. Likely it's the salt water I swallowed.

When I move Joel tightens around me.

"Let go," I say. "I've got to throw up."

He moves his arm and rolls backward. I make it to the head and unload my stomach, splash some fresh water over my face to clean it up. I look like hell in the mirror, pale as death. I wrap the blanket tighter around me and snap the light off before I step back out into the cabin.

I go sit back on the bunk and run one hand through my hair, notice Joel's heating up the coffee again.

"Never mind," I say, and heave up to get the bourbon and the cup.

"Do you think you ought to drink that straight?" he asks as I splash out a hefty dose.

I down it and cough, wipe my mouth and splash out another one, carry it back to my spot on the bunk. Joel's leaning against the pilot's seat now with his arms folded. He's a vague, pale shape in the lights, dressed only in brief dark underwear.

"Thanks for coming back for me," I say. The bourbon feels like fire in my stomach. My tone isn't quite friendly.

I can see it go over his face. "Anna..." He uncrosses his arms, ducks to sit on the end of the bunk opposite me. "Let's talk."

"What about?" I ask.

"Did you really think I'd leave you?"

I have to look away from his eyes.

"We lost the anchor," he says, "and I didn't realize it until I'd drifted way the hell off. I had to make half a dozen passes to find you."

"I didn't get the papers," I say.

"Why not?"

I take a breath. "They weren't in the safe. Weren't in the cabin anywhere that I could see. Maybe that was the real reason for that fire in the engines." I shrug, hug the blanket around me. "Whatever, it's up to the family."

"Bad luck," he says.

"Well, shit happens." I shrug. "At least they'll know there's a problem. Maybe they'll hire me to follow up."

I unscrew the bottle cap, spill out more bourbon into my cup. The stuff tastes like crap.

"You shouldn't drink all that," he says.

"I feel like getting crocked."

"What for?" he asks. "The wasted trip?"

"Yeah," I say. "And partly it's a general comment on my life to this point."

I catch the anger in his eyes before he can look away to hide it.

"I didn't know Dad meant to rip you off," he says.

"I know. You said that."

"Then why can't you let it go, Anna?" He looks down at his hands. "If it makes any difference," he says. "Dad and I had a fight about it."

That snags at my attention.

"We've been out of touch," he says. "Last night I tried to call him. When he wasn't there I left a message I was going out on a job with you."

Not getting along? Hell of an insight into what's going on here. And how he might be using me. I inspect the idea, and don't much like the way it feels. "Your dad's going to be pissed."

"I don't give a damn what Dad thinks," he insists. "I make my own decisions."

"Don't lie to me," I say. "I don't believe that."

There's another flash of anger in his eyes. "You've had enough," he says. He shifts position, reaches for the bottle. I splash another shot into the cup, let him have it.

"So what do you really want from me, Joel?"

In answer he leans over and kisses me hard on the mouth. It's a complete surprise.

For a long moment I stare at him from a two inch distance, and then I manage to get my breath. "I am not even going to ask about your motivations for doing that," I say.

I've realized my own lust, of course, partly the cause of my troubles last year--and I still have plenty of bitterness wound up inside me. The kid reminds me so much of Paul, and he's got that long, taut, muscular body that's so alive that I can't keep my eyes off of him. The psychology of this is just too complicated.

He inclines away from me, stows the bottle. "Why not?" He sounds stubborn, and he's not talking about the motivations.

"I'm a lot older than you are."

"So what?" he asks.

"Who's seducing who here?"

"Who cares?"

I close my eyes and notice I've got no resistance. Damn, it's too late. He's so close to me I can feel the heat off him. I've slept against him already, felt the hard lines of his belly and thighs against my back, the tightening of his hand between my breasts when I tried to move.

"I'm not exactly sober, you know."

"I said you shouldn't drink so much," he says.

"God, Joel," I say, and I draw a long, shuddering breath. "You are over eighteen, aren't you?"

"Twenty," he says. "You're safe."

His mouth clings this time, works across my cheekbone. He breathes into my ear, a breath as quick and unsteady as my own. Then he slides a tentative hand inside the blanket still wrapped around my shoulders. He traces the lower curve of my breast, drifts the hand downward over my waist and thigh, tightens it on the flesh above my knee.

That's enough. The blanket falls away. I roll him backward and come up sitting astride him. Only the thin silk of his underwear is between us now. He takes a sharp breath, and I can feel him twitch and harden beneath me.

He lies there for a brief pause. "Does this mean 'yes'?" he asks.

In answer, I rub back and forth across him, then reach down and snag back his underwear.

My breasts aren't that big, but they fit perfectly into his hands. The dark nipples swell and harden, thrusting into his palms, into the warm embrace of his mouth. As he kisses them, his hair brushes like fine silk against my nose, my cheek, my lips.

He works inside me slowly, flexing the long, smooth muscles of hip and flank into ripples that work gradually deeper. His every move sends a dart of pleasure upward. He kneads my waist, my hips, reaches up for my breasts. His pale shoulders tense and curl beneath me, outlined by the soft glow of the instrument lights.

When he bottoms out, I start to move back and forth, rubbing slowly against him, stroking both of us. I run my hands down over him, feeling the smooth, sweet lines of his chest, the hard-pointed tips of his nipples, the flat, warm arc of his ribs.

He rises beneath me and I gasp at the hot pressure, the swell of him against me. As he begins to thrust, I fall forward to search for his mouth. We cling together, heating up too fast, our hands searching, stroking, demanding. His sweat oils my straining belly and thighs, trickles across my ribs. Joel gasps suddenly, and his arms tighten around me. He picks up the pace, bucks and groans at the first hard pulse of climax, rides it down.

It's a good match. He's quick, but so am I.

He's young, and after a few minutes he's ready to do it again, but slower this time. God, it's so sweet. Later, lying there beside him and easing down into sleep, I like the way he holds on to me. I'd like to think this wasn't all just a line of BS.

I wake up the next time to clearer light and a dull headache. It's morning, a gray daylight outside. The cabin is gloomy as hell and boat's still pitching, but the rain seems to have stopped. A warm body stirs behind me. I roll over and verify who I'm sleeping with, and then I bury my face in the pillow and groan.

"God," I say, "this trip has been a complete disaster."

"That bad?" Joel asks. He tries to sound hurt, but he can't. He looks smug.

"You son-of-a-bitch."

He laughs, then slides over to wrap around me.

"Just a minute," I say.

I get up and go to the head, check our position, alter the speed and heading so we might get home sometime today. And then I sit in the pilot's chair to think about things in the cold light of morning. What the hell was I thinking, to get myself drunk like that?

But considering it doesn't do any good. My mind just drifts, and thinking about Joel lying back there in the bunk starts that lance of pleasure up again.

I think I'd better not inquire too much into my own motivations here. People have just so much capacity for truth.

Hell. Maybe life's what you make of it after all.

It's four o'clock Sunday by the time we get back to Miami, a rough trip all the way through the wind and heavy seas. The ugly old boat proves her worth--no complaints from her--not even a creak. Twice more we run through heavy storm and rain, but nothing so bad as last night. The jetties rise out of the chop and we follow the channel markers back through the port, tie up at the dock. It's nearly dark by the time we get the gear off-loaded and into my car--lots later than I'd meant to be home.

Joel falls back in the seat as I start the engine. I turn on the wipers and the radio. The weather service has noticed it's raining.

Joel runs one hand through his hair. "God, I'm exhausted," he says.

"I don't know why," I say, "you've slept most of the day."

He gives me a quick grin, checks for music on the radio.

The rain's stopped by the time we turn into the parking lot at my apartment. We load up with gear, haul most of it up the steps in one trip.

"I'll get the rest," Joel says. He drops his load on the living room floor and heads back toward the stairs.

It's a while before I realize he's been gone too long.

I check over the railing, can't see him out by the car. Then I remember what he's been worrying about.

"Joel?" I call.

No answer. Shit. Nothing on the stairs. Nothing out in the parking lot. Dammit. Where else? Maybe the pool.

Sidewalk, grass, a chain link enclosure off to my left. Wet darkens the parking lot, rises in a faint, drifting mist. Wind and shadows tear at the clouds, mutating the familiar landscape into something eerie, threatening and strange.

I hear the voices first. And then I see something on the lawn, a hulking figure, half-distorted by darkness and a shapeless, flapping shirt. He's got something slung over his shoulder that gives him a hunch-backed, monstrous shape. Closer, there's a stench on the wind that turns my stomach, a reek of death and corruption that emanates from the man. The thing on his shoulder is a basket, misshapen and crusted with filth. The guy's got Joel cornered against the fence.

The kid looks frozen and desperate, spread against the woven wire.

"Joel!"

I sprint into the shadowy space between them. "Keep away from him," I say. "He's mine."

For a second I think the guy's going to take me on. He looms, towering over me, but somehow I still can't see him. He's made of darkness and the daunting stink of a grave. Black shards that might be eyes glitter at me from between wild dreadlocks and a wind-blown, flying beard. The man grows and swells, casts a shadow that's big as all of night. My knees are shaking. I feel a shudder run up my spine.

But the bastard doesn't know that. I grit my teeth and stand my ground. Dammit. I know if I give back an inch, he'll take both of us.

"*Mon amour...*" The monstrous shape sighs, spreads its arms with a lust that buffets like the wind. He clenches and unclenches his hands, reaching for me--for Joel--for both of us. "*Mon cher...*"

"No," I say.

"No," Joel echoes. He moves finally, steps up behind me, and I feel his arms go around my waist, his head tuck down against my shoulder. What he's done half scares me to death--if I should have to move away fast...

The wind gusts, the shadows shift...and there's nothing there in front of us at all.

"God, Joel," I say. I shudder and reach for his hands, suddenly stiff in his arms. "Let's get upstairs."

I slam the door and lock it behind us, peer out the windows. There's only empty, windblown darkness behind the blinds, the distant clatter of palms. Joel looks pale and sick. He falls on the couch, slides down and kicks off his shoes. I turn and search his face as he lies there.

"Shit, Joel," I say. "You might as well sleep in the bed."

He only lies there, closes his eyes. He sighs, and then somehow he looks at peace. "Okay," he says.

He goes to sleep right there. I throw a blanket over him, pace back and forth. Everything seems quiet outside, perfectly safe. Finally I relax some and get out a beer, check the messages on my voicemail. There's one from Paul wanting to know where the hell we are, and then there's the one from Gloria that I was expecting to find. She sounds worried.

"Your Macoute must be some kind of a haunt," she says. "Watch out for him, Anna. No record, but the Haitians around here are all scared shitless of him. They call him the soul-stealer--some foolishness like that. Let me know if you need any help. Okay?"

Well, maybe not. Maybe I've defeated the haunt all by myself. Just give it a while and we'll see.

ASCENSION

The winds buffeted, roiling with clotted snow, hurling knives of sleet that numbed his fingers and the tips of his ears. The storm was hardly formed, but Chyani knew he wouldn't be able to fly much longer. Soon the gale would dash him into the rocky moraine to his right, and already it was hard to negotiate the heaving currents. His wings were tired, aching in every sinew and bone, and he was getting scared.

The storm went up high. Unable to get above it, he had chosen to hug the ground, negotiating the worn, desolate crags of the badlands south of the ice. The ground lay only vague and half-seen below, close as he was. Hints and shadows of glacial till loomed in the eerie blue lightnings, and thunder crackled above the shrieking wind. Chyani was driven onward by more than one kind of desperation--Malesko would be furious at the delay--but there was only so much that muscle and bone and a quick mind could do.

He saw the danger, but there was no place to go--no way to fight backward against the storm. Below him the ground failed, sheared off into infinite space. Without any defense, he fell into a raging river of wind.

Agony seared through his pectorals and down his sides, and he nearly tumbled. The only possible refuge was down, and he plummeted into snow.

He lay there aching, heaving for breath, beaten by the wind--it was far too long, past the danger point, until he felt the cold lassitude of death creeping over him. Easy to let go then, to give in to it, but instead he roused himself.

He lay on the slope of a deep glacial rift. Bruised and trembling, he rolled to his knees, hunched as the wind gusted over him. His insulated suit had been warm enough for flying, but now it was soaked and freezing against his skin--no protection at all. He was light and fine-boned, not built for climbing in conditions like these--but he had to move. He started off, belly to the ground, and made his way up the slope, his breath burning--fighting the tendency to open his wings for balance, fighting the wind lift, even with his wings tight-closed. Aiming for a dim-lit mass, he found an outcrop that promised shelter from the gale, and found it hid something else as well.

He nearly turned and crept away.

The ice had dislodged henges, uncovered one of the tombs of the Ancients that dotted the abandoned lands. Most were already looted, or the contents corroded by time. But if this one wasn't empty, it could be deadly. The tombs had defense systems.

Worse than that. There were tales of old curses, viral hexes that could reach down through time to punish those who desecrated the tombs, so they died horrid, torturous deaths. Of Oracles that spoke from the sarcophagi, of omens of ruin and destruction. These were just tales from the nest, of course, but still they left a mark, enough so that Chyani slid down where he was to think about this, freezing or no.

The outer seal was already broken.

He huddled at the entrance, shivering uncontrollably, trying to convince himself he was suffering from superstition. He had to take shelter or die. The storm whipped his hair around his face, tore at his wings, stealing what warmth he had left. If he went on, soon he'd fall into the snow again, and not get up. The storm would have him then, and he'd never see the Loft again. And it was all he had--however doubtful his welcome there.

Chyani was young, and he wanted to live. He gathered his wings up tight, slid through the narrow opening and into the dark.

It was comparatively warm inside, though shafts of ice followed him in. He huddled in a corner, waiting, but nothing awful happened. When his eyes adjusted, he found it wasn't as dark as it'd looked from outside. Something like phosphorescence streaked the walls, caught the vague storm light in a chemical snare. The wall opposite the opening was the actual access to the tomb. This was only an anteroom.

Chyani stirred finally, tried to wring out his clothes. The entrance was an arch of coiled and sinuous forms, snake-fanged, and above the arc letters incised the stone. He sounded them out, whispering the archaic forms. Lilake Bat Zuge, it said, and as he stood before the inscription, a red eye flashed at him and the inner seal slid back.

"Come in," the eye said. "It'll be warmer inside."

He jumped the other way instead. The storm slapped him in the face, full force now, and he turned back, horrified at his choices.

"I won't hurt you," the eye promised. "Come on in."

Chyani found his breath. "What do you want?" he asked.

"Just some data. It's been a long time."

Chyani didn't like it. He stayed where he was, poised and breathless, ready to bolt. "What are you?" he asked. "A sentinel?"

"No," it said. "I'm the occupant. I'm electronically encoded and resident, and I'd like to talk to you. A small obligation, of course. You can spend the night here, ride out the storm. I'll even make it warm for you."

It was telling bait. He could feel the warmth already, issuing to snare him like the light. There wasn't any choice, he decided. Soaked and freezing as he was, he'd die here in the anteroom nearly as fast as outside.

He shoved the wet, pale mass of hair out of his eyes and stepped bravely through the portal, tried not to notice how it slammed shut behind him. He twitched his wings aside, leaned hard against it, but it didn't give. There was another of the red eyes inside.

"Are you Lilake Bat Zuge?" he asked.

The voice laughed. "It was a whim to inscribe that, but maybe it suits me, after all." The words were archaic, like the script.

The tomb was lined with banks of machinery.

"How's the temperature?" asked the eye. "I think I've got something you can wrap up in. Hell of a storm, isn't it?"

It seemed that he'd gotten an Oracle, and not one of the deadly virals. The voice sounded chatty and harmless, but still Chyani was terrified. He was suspicious of kindness.

"What's your name?" the voice asked.

"Chyani," he said, knowing he could safely give that much, but not the gene line and Choir.

He jumped as a panel in the machinery yawned wide, but it only offered wraps. Chyani approached gingerly, lifted some out and ducked backward against the door again. He pulled one around his shoulders, but the wet clothes kept him shivering. He'd have to take them off.

He dropped the blanket reluctantly, unsealed the quilted edge of his flight suit and tugged it down. His reflection mirrored from the silvery cowl of the eye, ivory-pale and honey-haired. The colors would lighten as he dried, dust his groin and the cloak of his wings with gold.

The eye had a voyeuristic bent.

"You're very...interesting to look at," it asked. "What are you?"

"What?" As he turned, the mirror caught his face, high cheekbones and violet eyes in a heart-shaped frame.

"I mean what do you call yourself? What species?"

"I'm a human," he said, surprised at its ignorance.

"Well, damn," the voice said.

"What?" he echoed.

"Nothing," it said. "Listen, I don't have any foodstuffs around here, but if you have something, I can heat it for you."

He had some water and food concentrate in his kit, and he passed those through the dilation. He wrapped in the blankets again, still shivering, but warmer already, waiting for whatever process made the lights flicker and play along the wall.

"Algae, huh?" said the voice, apparently having analyzed the mix. "Is that what you eat?"

The aperture opened again, revealed steaming broth in a cup with handles, and Chyani lifted it out with steadier hands.

"Yes," he said. "It's grown in the vats beneath…" He stopped, realizing that wasn't wise. The information might go nowhere, but if it got back to Malesko that he'd babbled about the Loft…

"Beneath what?" asked the voice. "A city?"

"I shouldn't say," he whispered.

"I want information," repeated the voice, and it had a hard edge to it now. "It's the price of your life."

Chyani winced, pushed down a stab of panic. The broth was too hot to drink. He held the cup against his chest and let it warm his hands, tried to decide what to do. He wasn't surprised at the sinister shift--and honesty seemed a possible solution.

"I could die for telling you," he said.

"Oh?" said the voice.

Silence then, that meant more than words.

"Well, don't then," it said. "Just tell me about your people. Does everyone look like you?"

It was less threatening, but still Chyani thought about it carefully. This felt like fencing--lunge and parry in a contest he was in no condition for now--with maybe his life a stake.

"More or less," he ventured. "The coloring varies, and mine's… unusual, I guess. Most people are darker." The broth was cooler now and he swallowed some, feeling it accumulate like a warm pool in his belly. He closed his eyes, letting comfort steal over him. He could have that much at least, before he died--if he did. He really had no idea how this would end.

"Do you actually fly?"

"Yes," he said. "I can do it easily, but some…can't." He didn't go into why, but the voice pried.

"Why not? Too heavy?"

"Yes," he agreed, and left it at that.

"What do the women look like?"

"Women?" he asked.

"The females."

"I don't know what you mean," he said, and there was silence again. A wrong answer, and he felt a flicker of alarm. He wasn't understanding this conversation--different from evading Malesko, or even the Opposition lords. The Oracle had ancient, mystical knowledge that he wasn't party to.

"How were you born?" the voice asked.

That was calculated. Chyani inspected the question from different angles, but he couldn't find the barb. After all, everyone came from the same process, whatever the Choir, and it should be safe enough to talk about.

"From the hatchery labs," he said.

"Labs?" it said. "Are you a clone, then?"

"A what?" he asked.

Conversation faltered again. It continued to do that for a while. The interrogation wore on.

Chyani thought he'd said nothing, but it was too much. The voice inferred things he'd never said, demanded things he'd never known. He was defeated before he'd begun. It was impossible to keep his guard up in the insidious dimness and warmth, and exhaustion weighed heavily on him. He should have been terrified, but instead he was numb. He lay against the door, rested his head against the ornate jamb.

"Why do you go back to him?" the voice asked, about Malesko.

"I have to," he said. "There's nowhere else--no other way to live." And of course, he used Malesko, too.

"Yes," the voice said. "I'd forgotten the climate, the changes. What were you doing out in the storm?"

I was given to a Warden of a different Loft, to spy on him."

"And you did?"

"I poisoned him."

"He died?"

"I'm sure he did. Please," he pleaded. "May I sleep now?" He couldn't talk any more.

It considered.

"Sleep," it said. "You've discharged your obligation."

Released, he fell unconscious. He heard nothing of the howling wind, the raging blizzard that blew through the night. And he didn't need any silks or cushions. Wrapped in the rough, odd-smelling blankets, he slept as well as he ever had in the nest. He only needed Tysell.

Finally a voice whispered into his dreams. "Chyani?"

He stirred, found himself belly-down against the door, with his head pillowed on one arm. He jerked up, remembering where he was, but there was only quiet and warmth in the tomb, soft lights playing along the banks of machinery, and the red eye watching him.

"The weather's cleared," said the voice. "The wind's died down. I thought you'd want to go."

He sucked in a breath and rubbed his eyes, ran fingers through the tangles of his hair. "Yes," he said numbly.

He hurt all over, rest or no. He shoved up and stretched carefully, found the muscles of his chest and sides still ached. Regardless, he'd have to fly. There was no way to walk home from here. He let the blankets fall and reached for his flight suit, found it was almost dry.

"There's some of the mix left," said the voice. "I'll make you some breakfast."

"Some what?" he asked.

"A morning meal."

"Oh," he said, awkwardly. He tugged the garment up over his shoulders, sealed the edges. "All right."

He was glad of the offer. The air would be frigid after the snow, and he'd need the energy. He rubbed his chest, trying to work the soreness out of his muscles, but the strain wouldn't go. Then he sat against the door and closed his eyes, wondering if it would open when the time came. He'd believe it when it happened.

He was more afraid of Malesko now than he was of the tomb. He could expect a beating, and probably some rough sex--if he got there early enough. Another delay and he was dead, whether Malesko loved him or not. The cup appeared in the orifice and he took it, breathed in the vapors.

"Chyani?" said the voice.

"Yes?"

"Listen," it said. "I have another deal to offer you."

Here it was. There was no place to fly. Until the door opened, he was a captive. He kept his eyes down, studied the swirl of the broth.

"Yes?" he said.

"I've been trapped here a long time," it said, "ages and eons beyond your count. There was a time when I was rich and powerful, and I want a way back into the world."

He waited, but the thing was waiting for him to answer.

"What will it take?" he asked finally.

"Your blood."

He started and gasped, thinking it meant to kill him then and there, but the eye caught his reaction.

"Wait," it said. "Not all of it. Just a sample."

"No," he said. His voice was shaking.

"You didn't ask what I can give you."

"What can you give me?" he asked.

"What do you want?"

"Let me go," he said.

"Chyani..."

"I have to get back."

Silence then, filled with the faintest whir and click in the machinery.

"Okay," the voice said then. "But kid, the offer stands. You can have my protection instead of his."

The door snapped back suddenly, and he nearly fell into the anteroom. Cold air dashed over him.

The red eye flickered. "Get going," it said. "You can have the damn cup."

Outside, snowfields stretched as far as the eye could see, crisp and still in the dawn light. The ground dropped away sharply from the liths to what might be an esker, iced over in the basin below. From above, the rift walls cast pink shadows over the snow, and the chasm stretched away on either side to a misty infinity, lined by sharp spines and the peaks of horns.

Yesterday he'd been following the channel of a hanging valley, and had fallen into the gorge. He could see the truncated edge from here, but he'd never be able climb so far. There would be few updrafts from the snow, but he thought the invisible river of wind still ran. He had only to open his wings to know. The canopy of ivory and gold lofted above him, and he fell forward onto the horse of the wind.

It hurt. He had known it would.

There was no help for it. Or for his lack of experience in living. He guessed at direction and headed north, riding the wind, following the path of the ice. Within minutes he saw the lavender glint of crevasses deeper than snow could fill. At the tip of the glacier, he had an idea now where he was. Relieved, he bore west.

It took nearly an hour to find a familiar way; he'd gone far off course in the storm. He hurt less with the activity, and then more. By the time he'd found the access, his sides ached constantly, and he was laboring. Sharp pains attacked him with every stroke. Still, it wasn't beyond bearing.

He signaled for the invisible sentinels, glided down through the winding approach path, and landed on a hidden ledge east of the Loft.

The sun lay well short of noon. Maybe it was early enough.

He hurried downward through the private corridors to Malesko's apartments, feeling the solid oppression of the mountain close over him like a weight. He tapped at the private door, waited. Old Nestor opened it finally, and Chyani slid in.

"Boy, what are you doing out there?" the man hissed.

"Tell Malesko I've come," Chyani said, and brushed past. He needed to bathe and dress, to be presentable, at least.

He slid into a tiled, scented pool, remembering as he always did the contrasts of his life--the luxury here in the upper chambers and the squalor below. He was frightened by the encounter with the Oracle, and disturbed, but he couldn't let it shake him. He had to deal with Malekso, and puzzle out meanings later on.

He only had time for the bath. He finished, pulled on a robe and headed for the bedchambers, shaking out his hair.

Malekso was already there.

The man stood like a statue cast in bronze. Huge, darkened by age and larger than life, he seemed to swell, and his rage charged the room like crackling flame.

Chyani flinched, seeing the blow coming. It grazed his cheekbone, still knocked him flat. He fell awkwardly, twisted a wing. A kick caught him square in the belly. Darkness gripped him then, and lack of breath.

He came to vague sense on the paillasse, felt cords bite at his wrists. Malesko jerked the knots tight through the head screen of inlaid fretwork. He shook Chyani until the boy gasped, and then the blows turned to caresses.

"Slut," Malesko whispered, "I thought you weren't coming."

Chyani made do with breathing.

Malesko gripped his damp hair, tugged his head back and kissed his throat. "Is the man dead?"

"Yes," gasped Chyani, finding the breath somewhere.

"How will they come to the games?"

"Through the north pass."

Laughter commenced in Malesko's chest, a rumble like an avalanche, spilled out like the fall of ice.

Malesko left him then. Chyani was early enough, and the hosts hadn't yet gone.

He lay on the satin cushions, resting, and let tension flow out of him. It had been a token beating. There would be more after the games when Malesko was flush with victory, but this was following a familiar and predictable pattern that gave him hope. Maybe he still had a hold on the man.

Chyani wondered how many flyers would die that day, caught by surprise in the pass. It lay on his own head this time, but still it was nothing. He had protected what he loved, and he might live through this, after all.

The cords that held him were silk. He could easily work out of them, but it would be taken as defiance, so he only lay there. Eventually he slept.

He wakened to a flare of light. Malesko caught him by the hips, yanked him to a kneeling position and penetrated at the same time. Half-asleep, Chyani gasped at the jerk on his wrists. Malesko smelled of blood and death, and he pushed in deeper, began to move, to thrust. He slid his hands down Chyani's belly and fondled his penis, squeezed his balls.

Malesko was a big man and it hurt, but Chyani couldn't deny it gave him pleasure. In a way he wanted Malesko, but he was terrified of him, too.

Chyani was nearing maturity, and he knew Malesko wouldn't bed him much longer. Sometimes the Wardens rewarded their lemans with wealth and position, but other times the lemans died. Chyani had used his master, and they both knew it. When Malesko began employing him in other ways, he'd thought he had a chance at something--life, perhaps. But now Malesko seemed to feel it was a mistake, and his dominance increased, as did his cruelty. It wasn't hard to see how it would end.

Malesko exploded within him, fell forward to rest on the silks. After a while the man stirred, slid a hand along Chyani's thigh and touched his penis again, stroking the slight erection.

"I've found your lover," Malesko whispered, and fell asleep.

So, things weren't as he'd hoped after all--deteriorated, in fact. They had sex again in the morning, and afterward Chyani lay in the tumbled wraps and cushions of the paillasse as if nothing were wrong between them. But after Malesko had bathed and dressed and gone for the day, he pushed up and hurried to the bath himself. He braided his hair and dressed as obscurely as possible. Then he bribed the door guard, hoping for secrecy, and headed downward through the maze.

It had been months since he'd seen Tysell, and weeks since he'd even had word. Malekso might only be torturing him--he'd done it before--but something about his tone was different this time--an exultation that meant more than threats. It was time Chyani checked into the status of things below.

It was a risk to go out. His complexion was hard to hide, and Malekso had a thousand spies. But he couldn't trust anyone in the Warden's service for this. Wealth and power, even reflected, could open doors for him--and buy a certain obscurity.

Chyani hurried down back corridors, dimly lighted, came out on the second level, and chose a herald at random. With his message sent, he doubled back and merged with a crowd in a main thoroughfare, slid into a weapons cove and out the other side. It was a convoluted path he took, aimed at losing any spies, but eventually he came out on the catwalk above the old tenth level storage vats. The tanks had been abandoned for years, and the walks were unrepaired, rickety and dangerous. At one time they had been popular for lover's trysts, other illicit meetings, but now they were seldom used.

Chyani slid into the umbra of a massive truss to wait. Below him the cavern floor yawned blackly, empty and must-scented, exuding a breath of cold. Within minutes Chyani caught a movement, a shadow out of place in the gloom. He tucked deeper into the shade of the truss, watching to see who it was. Not Tysell.

It was Kraften, one of the Opposition guard. Safe enough, unless the man had taken to doubling lately. He had carried messages before.

Chyani stepped out of the obscurity. "Here," he whispered.

Kraften's shadow stopped dead still, then moved toward him along the ledge.

"Kraften," Chyani hissed as the shadow neared. "What's news of the Lord Tysell? I need to see him."

"He won't see you now," said Kraften. "Too much trouble's brewing above."

"What trouble?" asked Chyani.

"With Malesko." He stepped so close that Chyani could feel the heat of him, radiating like a brazier in the cold. "You don't know, boy?"

"I can't spy on my own lord," Chyani hissed. "Tell me."

"Malekso intends to use his successes at the Games to challenge the Seraphim. It'll be open war. If he takes the labs, he'll execute the lords, install his own wardens. He's got the backing already, the scheme underway. The Opposition's trying to stop him, but the Wardens know they're going to fall this time, and the subs with them. It's foregone."

Kraften brushed against him in the dark, reached out to stroke the bruise on Chyani's cheek, caught by a shaft of light.

"Boy, we're all going to hell," he said softly. "And Malesko's going to send us there. I think you better give up the designs you have on the Lord Tysell."

It was rude, and his subtle caresses even ruder. But he could be wrong. There might be a way to stop Malesko--and a chance to save Tysell. Again.

Chyani feathered his wingtips and dropped among the henges. He found the opening and, exhausted and hurting, slid cautiously into the dark. In a trick of memory it seemed almost a haven now. Crouched before the eye, he hoped it was. Malesko would know he was gone by now; and fled, he could never go back.

"Bat Zuge," he whispered. "Are you there?"

The eye lit. "Chyani?" it said. "What do you want?"

It wasn't much of a welcome. Chyani suppressed a shudder of doubt, lifted his head and spoke to it directly.

"I need a weapon," he said.

"Is your face bruised?" the voice asked.

"Yes," he said. "Will you give me what I want?"

The portal slid beneath the dragon glyphs. He gave the eye the whole story this time, explaining the hierarchy and the Games, the coming upheaval--and he told it how he loved Tysell.

"Do you understand all this?" he asked.

"Yes," said the voice.

"I've used Malekso. But now I need a weapon to use against him. He'll take the Seraphim and the hatchery labs, and then he'll murder Tysell from spite."

"I can make you a weapon," said the voice. "But you may not like the results."

Despairing, Chyani spread his hands. "What can I do but bargain? I've got no power of my own--no way to stop this."

"I'm talking about destroying your world, the whole structure of your civilization."

He drew an uneven breath, dropped his head in his hands. "Will you kill Tysell?"

"Not if I can help it."

It was enough.

"I'll take your offer then. What else can I do?" So let the world fall in ruins. He was desperate, and he'd cope later on, in whatever way he could.

"All right," it said. "It's a bargain then--to be written in your blood." The voice actually laughed. "Give me your hand."

The all-purpose aperture gaped at him--waiting.

Chyani nearly panicked, staring into that void. But it didn't matter now what happened to him. The bargain was made. He held his breath, stepped forward and slid in his arm.

The aperture closed around it. Metal fingers clamped his bicep. He gasped as a needle cut the vein, leaned against the machinery, dizzy and braced for pain, but there wasn't any. The single cut was all. The panel dilated, released him suddenly.

There was a bruise in the crook of his elbow, a spot of blood. He hugged the arm against his chest, glad to have it back.

"Now what?" he asked the eye, and found his voice quavered. He was shaking.

"Wait, sleep. Whatever," it said, seemingly indifferent. "It'll take a day or two. Can I heat you something to eat?"

"Not now," he said, and swallowed a sudden nausea.

He lay on the folded blankets he'd slept in before, and the voice talked to him. About things he didn't understand, and some things he did. After a while it began to make near sense.

"I have a theory," the voice said, "about what's happened through the ages. The sun was yellower when I died--it's been that long--and there wasn't the ice then. The climate was nearly torrid instead, and male fertility was in a sharp nose-dive. I have to assume human survival came to depend on cloning."

"What's that?" Chyani asked. It was one of the words it had said before, that he hadn't understood.

"Making new people out of just a few cells."

"It's what they do in the hatchery vats?"

"I think so," it said. "So now all the power's vested in reproduction. Also, there's been a lot of genetic manipulation. You're not at all what a human used to be."

"How am I different?" he asked, curious.

"They didn't fly, for one thing."

It was a strange thing to imagine how the Ancients must have lived, trapped in their great, scalding cities on the ground. He was learning more from the voice than he'd ever learned from the Guardians of Knowledge. Certainly the eye knew more than all of them.

"Now the Earth's cooled again," the voice was saying, "but your culture's so far from the old one that no one's got any memory of how things used to be, or what the dynamics were. And of course, once the power's vested, no one wants to go back. It's a very limited, dead-end culture you've described."

"And the weapon?"

"Wait. It'll be ready tomorrow."

After that he slept in the faint, flickery light--and woke suddenly. It was the type of waking where all his senses came alive at once, with a clarity near psychic. All of them gave him a warning. There was someone else in the tomb.

He jumped up, gasped as he banged his head on a rack, came to rest against a wall. But there seemed no need for his fear.

He was looking at himself--naked. The figure mirrored his reflection, clear and true. The fair hair and violet eyes were the same, the ivory skin, the arc of wings brushed with gold. This could be his hatchmate--but there was a difference.

"What are you?" he whispered.

The creature laughed, plainly cynical. "I am the goddess returned," it said, "your weapon against the labs. I am a woman."

He only gaped at her then, but later on he understood.

SHADOWS

The old house was haunted, they'd told me in town. When I had looked at it that first time, I could see why people might think so. It stood at the end of a long, ragged drive, backed up against stark woods. Scraggly weeds obscured what must have been the lawn, and a good-sized oak tree had shoved over the garden wall. Heavy shadows darkened the house even at noon, and the sun picked out a morbid rot infecting the gingerbread trim. The inside was open to the elements, spider webs on the mantel, filth on the stairs. Bird's nests and bats' droppings cluttered the second floor bedrooms, violated through broken casements.

Retreated to my car again, I'd dusted my hands in dismay. It would need a lot of work to get rid of the rumors. Still, I needed a project just then, and an old house was certainly that. A money pit, didn't they say? Aside from my consulting, I had enough from Milo's life insurance to cover it. I had forgotten my hands were filthy then, and smeared dirt across my forehead and into my eyes.

The various workmen took care of the weeds in the yard, trampling over them with their tools and heavy boots. I did a lot of the yard repairs myself, as much as I could, anyhow. The physical labor was something I had needed.

Was this a personality flaw, my wanting to live in the past? Or did I just want to hide from my friends?

Whatever, I was moved in now. The finished house was staidly Victorian. Seen from the yard, it was a somber clapboard spine barely softened by the rounded, ornate porch. Leaded-glass windows cast a shifting, ghostly pattern on the pastel walls inside. The stairs had turned out mahogany, a convoluted swirl of patinaed wood and carved balustrades that rose into the dim glow of the second floor hallway. I'd furnished the place with period antiques and carpets to match, but still it was lifeless, because Milo wasn't there.

Well, hell. Standing there in that shifting, dying light in the upper hallway, it struck me all of the sudden--the effect of finishing the job--a terrible angst that had been lurking in wait for me all this time. Milo and I had always meant to retire here. We'd argued about it for years, put money away for the work. And now it was just me, coming to live here by myself--and sooner, rather than later.

I shuddered, wandering back downstairs and through the cavernous parlor, touching things, glancing over my shoulder now and then. Since I was here and solitary, the place had a questionable ambiance, as if I'd imported shadows with my things. Well, dammit, of course I had.

I fended off the urge to spend another night in town. For a while I sat on the new wicker furniture of the porch with my feet up, not sure I was pleased to see the sun disappear into the deep tangle of surrounding woods--this new barrier that insulated me from the rest of the world. Finally at dusk, I shivered briefly from the chill, and retreated from the mosquitoes to see what I could find to eat.

I was ravenous, just digging canned salsa and chips out of the grocery bags when a knock came at the kitchen screen. It was a man's shoulders that darkened the last of the twilight. I had an instant of reserve from recent city living. Still, it wouldn't be good to get off on the wrong foot with the neighbors, so I crossed to the door. Seen closer, he was a reassuring silhouette, youngish and not overly large or hulking.

"Come in," I said, and shoved against the door spring.

"Thanks," he said.

The world tipped as he came into the light, slid sideways. He didn't seem to notice.

"I was just walking in the woods," he said, "and I saw your lights come on. Didn't know anyone was living here yet."

"I just moved in today," I said, with a certain difficulty. For a terrible second, I had trouble getting my breath. I'd thought he was Milo--a ghost suddenly materialized outside my door. I got a grip on my nerves. "I'm Lora Stansic." I nearly choked as I held out my hand.

"Giancarlo," he said. "Also, Stansic."

I stared, forgot to take my hand away. He was indistinct with the light behind him, an inch or so taller than me, slender and dark-haired, dark-eyed. China pale skin, gorgeous in that chiseled, eastern European way that had first attracted me to Milo. He was wearing a navy sweater and jeans, nondescript boots, and he smelled somehow of earth, old woods and old houses. His hand felt wide and strong, very cold. Chill from the woods, no doubt. Or maybe it was my own hand that was cold. I let it fall, took another breath.

"I didn't know any Stansics still lived around here," I said and eased backward against the counter.

The house came from Milo's family, an older aunt that had died and left it years before. She'd been in a nursing home for years, and the house was already decrepit by the time she was gone. Milo had come up and taken care of things, sold her furniture--fallen in love with the house. Maybe I'd meant this as a memorial--I'd never seen it until after Milo was dead himself. Damn lucky the local kids hadn't vandalized it worse. But then, it had that reputation.

And now, here stood someone who could be Milo's ghost.

"I do," he said, answering my unasked question. "My friends call me Carlo."

A cousin--it had to be. His smile was faint, a delicate curve to his mouth. A darkness touched his eyes, a deeper dusk than the shade gathering within the house.

"You're Milo Stansic's widow, aren't you?" he said. "I'd heard he died, but not how."

His voice was a smooth tenor, oddly attractive. I turned away sharply, back to the groceries. "An accident," I said. "A car crash on the New Jersey Turnpike. Do you live close by?"

"Well, yes," he said. His eyes were opaque now. "Within walking distance, anyway."

"Would you like to stay a few minutes?" I asked. "Have some coffee?"

He looked at the cans spread over the counter, identified the jar of instant.

"I'll pass this time," he said, and flashed me a real smile to soften the refusal. He glanced at the clock above the sink, presenting an angular, dark-edged profile. "I should get going." His midnight eyes came back to me. "I just wanted to say 'hello.'"

Sudden panic shuddered through my veins. I wanted to keep him here. I wanted to ask him about the family, whether he'd known Milo. I gasped for another breath, choked, desperate, but then I pushed it all down. Don't scare the man away, Lora. There'll be other times.

I held out my hand again, hoping he wouldn't feel it tremble.

"Well, um, thank you for stopping by," I managed. "I'll have some real coffee next time."

A curious vapor was already rising from the woods, a breath of ground fog from earlier rain. He dissipated into it like mist himself.

Dammit, I thought, dammit, dammit--feeling the desperate loneliness crash down in his wake.

I opened a can of soup for dinner, ate in the kitchen alone. The rabbit ears on my TV didn't bring in much in the way of reception. High as the house was on the hill, there were higher ridges around me. I'd have to see about getting cable hooked up.

I drifted upstairs, stroking the banisters, trying not to think how empty and cold the house still seemed, trying to ignore the shadows that flitted away when I tried to look at them directly-

-another unhealthy symptom like staring at strangers and seeing someone else. Moonshadows flowed through the beveled panes upstairs, shattered into obscure patterns, nearly blood-colored. Tonight I didn't like the effect at all.

I showered and shampooed, rinsing off the sweat that I'd accumulated in the day of moving in. The tub was quaint and frivolous, decorated by claw feet and a ring of hanging plastic, ruffled outside with real lace. A big room, big windows, high ceiling. I'd lined half the walls with tile, left the rest with the original dark paneling. Naked in the full length mirror, I looked stark as a ghost myself, pale and frosted with moisture. I was reasonably slim, but not as thin as the norm. No gray in my brown hair. Too young to be a widow, and to sleep in a cold bed by myself.

I yanked a comb through my permed curls, blew them dry. Well, to hell with it all. The bed had nice carving, and I'd held out for an authentic feather mattress to make up for the lack of a husband's arms.

I woke from an erotic dream. It was a problem I'd had for a while after Milo died, but it hadn't happened to me recently. It was some time before the cool summer dawn. I'd thrown back the blankets during the night, and now I lay naked under the canopy, aroused, alive, quivering on the tremulous edge of orgasm. The dream had been confused, immediate, as if I had really felt a man's lips on mine, his hands on my breasts. Worse, I could feel where he had been inside me, fitted and tight against that throbbing, hungry spot that ached to be rubbed, to be mated and used.

I sighed. My skin tingled, ablaze with fire. I captured a quick breath, raised my hands slowly, slid them along my heated belly, over my breasts. The nipples were tight, hard from the chill air, aroused by that ghostly touch. I teased the points gently and stretched, enjoying the heat, the ache. Then I gasped sharply, groaned as the orgasm crashed down over me, triggered by the movement. I arched, rose with the tide of sensation, throbbed, peaked--slid down the other side into sweetness.

It was the best orgasm I'd had since...well. After a while I got cold, and felt around for the blankets.

Later when I opened my eyes in bright daylight, the whole thing seemed part of the same cloudy dream. But certainly the orgasm had been real. Checking myself in the mirror, I had tousled, satisfied look of a woman recently laid--only a few mosquito bites the worse for wear. I'd have to get some bug repellent the next time I went to the store.

I'd need different coffee, too. I poured most of the instant down the drain.

I wanted to get the computer hooked up today, my connection with the rest of the world. I intended to work from right here, so I'd set aside a room as an office, still had my files to unpack. I got off to a slow, difficult start, and by night my shoulders ached and burned with overuse.

I fell into bed, had the same dream again, but later this time, in the pale light of dawn--but not the orgasm.

That was unusual two nights in a row. Typically my needs, or maybe my hormones, built up, and then once released, left me alone for a while. Yesterday's mosquito bites had faded by night, but now they were back, dotting my throat and my breasts with red and angry welts. I checked the window screens, but they all seemed tight. Damn, I hadn't realized the things were so predatory.

The local paper had come this morning, its bright wrapper clear in the dawn. I sat on the shaded porch to read it, drank some of the godawful bitter coffee. There was a listing of clubs, a social page. I wanted to meet more of my neighbors, get involved. Still I had work to do around the house, plus a consulting job I'd done the research for and not wound up before I'd moved.

I folded the paper and laid it across my knees, leaned my head back to study the pattern of shade on the refurbished lawn. The woods loomed beyond, thick and forbidding. The roses I'd put in were blooming already, and the perfume seemed heavy, almost cloying on the damp, morning air.

A curious thing. Somehow the dream hadn't completely cleared this morning, and the erotic urge still nagged at me. Not quite an ache, but still a distraction, it was a warm need that resided in the nerves of my inner thighs, a teasing where my nipples brushed against my flannel shirt. I closed my eyes, breathing the rose scent again. Damn. It had been such a long time since I'd had a man. Was it the ghost of Milo doing this to me? Had I brought him along with me, his memory? Or was it something else, something that came with the house?

Whatever, this morning I needed to go to the grocery store. There was a ramshackle shop just a few miles down the road, a combination meat and convenience store with gas pumps out in front. Homely and old-fashioned, it had taken my fancy, and I was determined to shop there instead of making the longer drive into town.

The store proprietor's name was Bogart, I recalled, with maybe the faintest, aging resemblance to the star.

"Miz Stansic," he said, tipping a nonexistent hat. "What can I do for you this morning?"

"Coffee," I croaked, and then I tried to remember what else I needed.

It took me a while to gather up a few supplies and get back to the counter.

"Ma'am," he said. "You be careful out there in the woods by yourself. Don't you go openin' your door to anybody at night. Things goes on in the woods sometimes. And folks might take advantage of a widow livin' alone."

I had my mouth open to say certainly I was going to be careful, but instead I shut my teeth with an audible click.

Bogart didn't seem to notice. He checked out the groceries on his manual register, turning them over slowly to search for the prices and ringing them up one by one. I watched him, chewing at my lower lip. He'd gotten me to worrying about strangers, infected me with doubt.

"Mr. Bogart, I've been wondering," I asked. "Do any of my husband's relatives still live around this area?"

"No," he rumbled, blinking through half-glasses. "None I know of."

That confused me.

"None?"

"Not since Miz Edda Stansic died," he insisted. "And that was years back. Your husband's aunt, wasn't she? Last of 'em, as far as I know."

"Um," I commented.

He began to bag the groceries, set them up on the counter with a gesture of completion.

"Here you go," he said. Then his face changed, darkened to a frown.

"What's that?" he asked.

"What?" I said, almost startled.

"What's happened to your throat?" His voice had gone gruff.

"Nothing," I said. "It's just a mosquito bite."

Still, in the car my hand strayed upward. The bites didn't itch. Instead they felt tender, ached with a sweet pain that connected in some way with my dreams.

And it seemed Mr. Giancarlo Stansic had lied to me. Still, the way he looked bothered me--too much like Milo. He had to be a cousin. So where was the lie? That he lived around here? Maybe he'd just been in town for a visit, and I'd never see him again. Suddenly I felt the choked, desperate fear recurring that I'd felt as he went out my door--that I wanted to see him again, and I wouldn't. He was the first man I'd really looked at since Milo died. He was real, concrete--I had touched him that night. Or was he? Now I wasn't sure. Somehow the incident had gone confused too, lost in the erotic cataclysm of that next morning.

I was starting a headache, and my ice cream was beginning to melt in the seat. I started the car and drove on home.

A pair of aspirin killed the throb behind my eyes. I studied the marks on my throat in the bathroom mirror, found they were fading already. I dabbed on some Neosporin and went to work in my office, but by two o'clock I had to give up.

I couldn't keep my mind on what I was doing. My nipples itched with the slightest brush of the shirt; my breasts felt heavy and swollen. My jeans were too tight, the seams hard across my aching flesh. I'd never had anything like this happen to me before, nothing so sweet and full of pain. Not even when Milo and I had first gotten married and spent a week lusting after one another in the Bahamas. And this whole obsession was beginning to center on a face that wasn't Milo's at all. Panic surged through me when I realized that. I thought about masturbating. I thought about calling the sheriff and asking who the hell was masquerading as Giancarlo Stansic.

That would be downright dumb. People already whispered about the house.

I sighed and shut down the computer. In the end I didn't take either option. Instead, I spent the rest of the afternoon going through the old family albums that were something else Milo had inherited from his aunt. I dug them out of the boxes, leafed through the pages. The brittle sheets crackled over one by one, the sepia faces staring out from the past.

Nothing.

I don't know what I'd expected to find. The eyes, the jaw, the delicate line of his mouth. Or maybe the dark mole that had stood out on the pale skin of his forehead. And why was I so focused on Carlo's face? No idea. I had barely seen the man. I packed the dusty albums back in their box.

I was starving. I had forgotten lunch, and now it was late for dinner. I had something to cook tonight, made up some spaghetti and a salad, bolted a tumbler of wine.

By then my whole body was throbbing as I thought about coming night, and the dark empty hours of the morning. Pure lust. Was this something that could be captured and labeled like the wine? Maybe not, but still I meant to try.

I meant to stay awake. I lay there watching the slow march of moonlight across the walls, listening to the deafening rasp of cicadas from the woods. I counted off the minutes, the hours, and finally I felt a dark lassitude sweep over me.

With it came a tension, the ominous stabbing of fear. I didn't really know what the hell I was doing here--playing with the supernatural? Maybe I should have fled back to New York as soon as I realized something was...was...But then the thought was gone, sighing away on the shimmer of moonlight.

Something drifted through the screen like wind-blown mist, took shape, a darker shade in the cloudy darkness of the room. I lay, mesmerized, watching.

And something else materialized, as well. I'd known all the time it was there. It haunted me in the shadows of my apartment in New York, again in the gathering gloom of this house. The ghost of Milo stood between me and every man I'd met since he'd died, a dark, indistinct phantom that warned me away.

But not this time. The air sparked with electricity, exploded in swirls of white-hot cloud. Flames crackled along the ceiling, flaring, hissing where ectoplasms met. I jerked up in terror, cowered against the headboard, clutching the blankets with frozen hands. Wind battered at me, tore at my hair. Fire scalded my skin. A portrait tore loose from the wall and crashed across the room. The frame flew into splinters against an antique chair. A vase exploded with the next slash of fire, and thunder crackled through the billowing mist.

Stop it!" I screamed. "Stop it! What do I have to do, make a choice?"

Suddenly, just like that, everything was dark and quiet in the room. The house was empty, still--too empty. I huddled against the headboard, heaving for breath.

"Dammit," I shuddered. "Don't both of you go."

A shadow reformed, blocking the moonlight.

He shed the sweater, the solid boots and jeans. His body was paler than Milo's, taller, heavier about the shoulders and thighs. A breeze drifted the curtains. The bed gave, and then his arms went around me.

I sighed, turned my head slightly, felt the sharp edge of incisors within his kiss. His hand drifted over my breasts, and my nipples hardened and rose to meet him. He nipped my earlobe, kissed my throat, and already I hurt for him.

"He's gone" he whispered. "You had to let him go."

"Carlo..." I said.

"Wait..."

He caressed me in a way I'd never felt before, his hands like the moonlight, his lips the soft flutter of moth wings, with needles of fire beneath. Every touch inflamed me, until finally I couldn't wait any longer. I slid down flat in the bed, reached for him, and he shifted over me. I caught my breath as he went in--gasped at his first thrust into that heated, burning ache. Then I lay helpless and shuddering beneath him, clutching him, moving as he did, my face pressed tight against his ear.

He felt the tide rise between us, pierced my throat as it broke. I had never felt such an orgasm, but I had guessed at it, feeling the pale afterglow that first morning after he'd gone. I rocked beneath him and fell, lay there shuddering in the aftershocks, wondering how much blood he took each time.

I didn't care. I was young, hot-blooded--and dammit, I had the resources to spare. I held his cool body over mine like the missing blankets, breathing in the scent of earth and old houses that still clung to his hair. He stirred finally.

"I was afraid you were another ghost," I said.

He shifted to one side, nipped at my earlobe again. "No," he said, "but I do come with the house." Then he sighed into my ear. "It's been empty far too long."

Desperate Lives

Dedication

For Carlos Ann

Fear cannot be without some hope, nor hope without some fear.

—Baruch Spinoza

THE WHITE OWL

He was riding to his death. When they came out of the woods, Ash could feel the dark, hungry bane reach out for him. It enveloped the castle ahead of them like a sullen storm, swirling outward over the land like the fetid breath of a swamp, drifting and settling in the hollows like a phantom mist. Above the keep's towers it rose with the wood smoke of winter fires to darken the sky.

He had sensed this shadow all his life. As a child he had thought it was because of something he had done. Later he had known that wasn't so, but still it had haunted him, whispering to him from a distance. He had felt the tendrils of it twine more closely about him in the last few turns of the season, and he had known the time was coming when he would have to deal with it. Still it was a shock to ride out into the chill morning sun and feel an immaterial thing so close and real—so immediate—as if he could reach out and touch it like a living thing.

He sucked in a breath of winter air, cold and dry enough to hurt, and twisted his wrists against the cord that bound them to the saddle bow. There was no give in the bindings.

Ash had no real desire to be here on this horse, under this guard at this approach. He had been working, attending to a sick child, when the lord's men had found him. Given a choice, he would have avoided his fate a while longer. Still it was questionable whether the bonds were necessary. Once he was caught, he'd been fairly well resigned to the likelihood of his own death.

Of course, there was always the chance he could evade it. Somehow the feel of the winter air made him doubt it at this hour.

Horsemen rode on all sides of him, a close circle meant to keep him from bolting. Or maybe it was to protect him, instead. He wasn't sure which.

Harness jingled, and the salt, steamy smell of the horses rose as they began to sweat with the exertion of mounting higher ground. Now and then guttural words passed between the guardsmen, but none of them seemed ready to start a conversation this morning. They seemed as weary of the ride as Ash, and just as grim. Seeing the castle close, they kicked their tired horses into a gallop.

The horses thundered onward through the fields, throwing up clods where frost still glittered on the stubble of last year's weeds. They slowed at the rising motte near the keep as alarms sounded from the crenellated towers above them. Finally they hove to a stop at the massive, iron-bound gates. The horses shifted, blowing clouds of heated mist, waiting for the watch to let them in.

In the courtyard Ash waited for the lashings that held him to the saddle to be undone. He was clearly a prisoner, but dressed as he was in rough peasant garb, still the guardsmen treated him with respect. The guard captain waited for him to dismount, took cautious hold of his arm once he was on the ground. The man must have some idea why Ash was here. Likely more than Ash had, himself.

They climbed the steps of the central keep. Beyond lay a cavernous, shadowy hall, colder than outside. Ash shivered, glad of his ragged woolen cloak, but the chill wasn't from the season. Invisible darkness permeated the stone, ran along the floors, dragged and smothered at the guttering flames which burnt on the hearths, fuming as if the wood were wet.

The keep's lord sat in a heavy chair at the end of the hall. Anton Seine, this was. The man had been a terror in his prime, but now the raven gloss of his hair was threaded with snow, and his massive shoulders had bowed under the years.

The guardsmen halted in front of their lord. The captain left off his hold and stepped back, leaving Ash in possession of the floor. Or maybe it was to face this man alone. It seemed no one else wanted to share that gaze.

For a moment Seine said nothing, only stared. Ash stood half a head taller than the stocky southern men, and his features were sharp-cut. It was a face that was doubtless transparent to the man who searched it so fiercely.

With a flash of jeweled rings, the lord stirred.

"What's your name, boy?"

"Ash, my lord."

It wasn't the answer of a peasant. Perhaps the sound of it betrayed more than his face, but there was little about himself that Ash could conceal. Once here, his fate seemed out of his own hands.

"It's true. The rumors..." said Seine. "I hardly believed it." And then with more conviction, he said, "You're the man I've been searching for."

In answer Ash only lifted his bound hands.

Seine laughed harshly. "I know you're at my service, boy. After all, I'm lord of this keep. So it's true you're Meril Cane's bastard get?"

"I don't know, my lord. I make no claims."

"You've heard the curse he laid on me?"

"I've only heard tales and gossip, my lord."

"Well, it's all true," said Seine.

He pushed up out of the chair, and within two paces he had become a shadow against the bonfire on the hearth. His shade had a scarcely visible limp.

"Meril Cane was a great sorcerer," said Seine. "There was a time when he controlled these lands, regardless of the wealth of its lords. The man constantly plotted with one lord against another, and shifted loyalties at the drop of a coin--or a maiden's shoe."

Seine turned, and his eyes glittered briefly in the firelight. Then he paced again with his limping stride. His voice was low as an animal's growl.

We had a dispute," he said, "over the maid I took to wife. The man cursed me, and her, and the babe in her womb. It was to be the death of the babe, and the death of my line." Seine stopped short, staring at the fire. His shoulders twitched.

"We got a changeling," he said. "No human child at all. The creature was born fay, a bone-white monster with fangs and claws, and cold as death. As the midwife cried out that it was stillborn, it opened its eyes and stared at her with the red eyes of a demon."

Seine turned.

"The creature still lives, shut up in the north tower."

Standing before the lord, Ash shuddered. For a second he saw only blackness, as if the keep's dark shadow had passed over him. Sweat sprang out on his ribs, beaded his hairline. The room came back into focus slowly, and he swayed, abruptly faint.

"What?" he said, realizing Seine was speaking to him again. "My Lord. What did you ask?"

"I said, I want you to remove the curse."

Ash twisted his hands against the cords which still bound him, managed to find his balance. He took an unsteady breath.

"I have my mother's talents for healing, my lord--but if Cane was my father, I was scanted of his sorcery. I cannot remove the curse."

"You have to."

Ash shook his head.

"I can't. Whatever hatred that existed between the two of you will have to work to its own conclusion."

Seine's face darkened. "And that monster in the tower?"

"I have no control of it, my lord."

"Dammit. When it was a babe I had some hope. But now the creature hasn't a mind at all, only some terrible, ravening hunger that devours it wholly and completely." Seine strode forward and dropped into his chair. He closed his massive hands into fists, beat them like knotted hammers on his thighs. "My thaumaturge says it's a hunger for blood," he said. "The priest says it will devour life itself."

The man lifted his head. His eyes stared up at the fire-shadowed ceiling as if he could see through it into the dark tower hidden by the solid mass of keep between.

"The auguries says the creature should be destroyed," he said. "That it should have been slain at birth. Maybe they're right. What I wanted…"

"My lord…"

"I wanted an heir," the man insisted. "I was sure the curse could be undone. Now they say I should keep it from tasting blood at all cost, that once it does that, it will transform to some worse evil, to some unholy terror that's completely insatiable, something which will destroy us all."

His eyes came back to Ash.

"Remove the curse," he growled.

"I can't, my lord," he repeated. "If the curse is ever broken, it will be outside of my control."

Seine's eyes fumed like the fire.

"Into the dungeon, then, until I can think of a better use for you."

And that was that. The cold stone of the keep was no warmer nor sweeter for greater depth. But at least there was a slitted window, through which Ash could watch the sun arc and fall. Later, the moon slid down and spattered into frost along the ground.

The Lady Aestiva climbed the steps slowly, enveloped in a dim pool of light. A dark wind tugged at her, and her rush light flickered near the stair top. Regardless of her determination, she faltered on the landing below the tower.

Gods. At least the cell was quiet tonight.

Leaning against the stone, she sheltered a small flame of hope. She held out a fold of her robe to protect the lamp. The flame sharpened and steadied after a moment, and having caught her breath, she finished the ascent.

There was an additional soul within the keep that night, and she yearned for it to make a difference. It was a senseless longing, of course, an urge born of a lifetime of disappointments, an unspoken prayer she already knew in her heart would be denied. After all, the man she was praying to was dead.

She stood at the head of the stairway now. To the right a dozing guard jerked upright, waited for her to speak. But she had nothing to say to him tonight. The door lay before her, a solid oaken barrier, once locked to keep the occupant safe. Now she wondered who would really be at risk, should the door ever fail. The guard would be the first to know.

There was a barred window in the upper half, a slot in the bottom for sliding things through. Other than that the door told her nothing. She closed her eyes and swayed forward against the wood.

"Pavané," she said, and then started at movement behind the bars.

The fire in her hands darkened his eyes to the color of dried blood, colored his face to a flush of near humanity.

His voice was rough from screaming. "Mother," he said.

"Pavané..."

He closed his eyes, laid his face against the rough wood of the door. The pale glimmer of his hair shone briefly, a sharp contrast to the black iron of the prisoning bars.

"Are...are you well?" she asked.

"No. No. You know I'm not. Let me out, Mother."

"I can't."

She heard the convulsive slash of claws along the wood, heard a moan rise from his chest--a feral, animal sound. She turned her head away, knowing her son was caught in a cage of fate's making. It was far stronger than the cold iron bars could ever be, and there was no way she could reach him from where she stood.

"Pavané?"

There was no answer this time. He was gone from the door, disappeared into the haunted darkness of his cell--it seemed a rare moment he was lucid these days. Aestiva sighed finally. The guard pretended not to see her as she turned to descend the stair.

The cell was a measure of his life's worth. Ash had investigated its dimensions in a few paces, stumbled on moldering bones in the corner. Clearly, no one had bothered to remove the previous tenant. The test, he decided, would be in how soon he was fed.

It turned out to be fairly soon, and again before full dark had filled the single slit of his window--which was reassuring to a point. It seemed he would live for a while. Still, that said nothing of other plans for him.

Weighty darkness hung above him. The magics were oppressive, smothering him with their evil taint. He'd meant to rest during the day, but time and again he found himself pacing--panting, hardly able to breathe. He wrapped his cloak tighter against the chill, stopped beneath the slit of window in hopes of catching a clear, unfettered breath of air. He'd meant to be objective about this captivity, to keep his wits about him, but now he found himself gripped by an unreasoning panic. His hands trembled and his skin was damp. He shivered with cold, warmly dressed as he was.

His restlessness eased as night fell. Perhaps the curse slept with the darkening of human minds. Ash nearly fell asleep, despite the promise of rats, sitting huddled within his cloak in a corner. He started suddenly from what might have been the beginnings of a dream, searched for what had wakened him. It was footsteps approaching, a tentative sweep of skirts along the flagstones outside his cell.

Light flickered through the barred grating of the door. Ash waited for a summons, but none came. He heard a faint stirring of cloth, a slight outrush of breath--then nothing more. Ash pushed completely up out of the cobwebs of sleep. He got up from the bench, crossed to lean against the door.

It was a figure shrouded in darkness, holding a tiny flame in her hand. The woman turned her head at the sound of his step and met his eyes through the grating. She was richly dressed. He blinked, realizing who this must be.

"Are you the Lady Aestiva?" he asked.

She shifted the flame, which became a lamp.

"It's Lady Autumn now," she said. "My season has waned."

"Perhaps not so much, lady."

A faint smile quirked at her lips. She stepped closer to the door.

"You are well spoken, lad, and you flatter me."

"What do you want from me?" he asked.

Her eyes roved over his face in the lamplight. "Tell me what you think of us," she said.

He decided to be honest.

"Evil lies heavy on this place," he said, "as if hatred is engraved in the very stones."

"I know it," she said.

"And still you wanted my opinion?"

"Your tongue can be sharp as well as sweet," she said. "Who are you, boy?"

"My name is Ash."

"That's not what I meant."

"I'm a simple healer, lady."

"Where have you come from?"

"A village to the west."

"And your parentage?"

"My mother was a southern slave girl. She was freed for services rendered."

"I recognize the face you wear," she said. "Don't evade me, Ash."

"I don't mean to, lady. I was born at a castle north of here, and I have no knowledge of my getting."

"The lord wasn't your father."

"No," he said. "I think not."

"I can see Meril Cane in you," she said, "as clearly as my husband can. It's in your face, your hands—the shape of your eyes."

The woman paced, pivoted in a swirl of skirts, and her shadow moved along the wall. Her voice turned with her, rang back sere and bitter through the dark.

"I am the cause of the curse," she said, "the cause of this darkness which lies upon us. All those years ago Cane wanted me. In my innocence I wanted him, too. Perhaps I loved the man, or perhaps it was his power which enthralled me so completely. I was a girl then, and I had no idea of consequences."

"I...have no knowledge of it," Ash hazarded.

"Afterward," she said, "I heard it wasn't my fair face the man was interested in, or my sweet hand, but rumors that my mother's kin were fay." She laughed, a harsh sound that echoed along the stones. "Cane wanted to beget a line of sorcerer kings."

"Lady..."

"My husband took me by force, you know--to spite Cane, and without my father's consent. I can't complain; at least the man married me. But the results? There are easier ways to be damned."

She stopped before the barred door again.

"How do you know Cane?" she asked.

"He came to my mother to die," said Ash.

Aestiva's breath hissed out in a whispering sigh.

"You're not so much older than...than the demon is," she said. "His name is Pavané. It's eighteen years this past greening of the spring, and he suffers from...from...gods, I don't know what."

"The curse?"

"Yes. The thaumaturge now says we should feed you to him," she said. "That only you, as your father's son, can satisfy his lust for blood and death."

Ash caught his breath. "I?"

The woman stood rock still. Then the lamp glow shifted suddenly in agitation.

"No," she said. "Gods. It won't happen while I'm alive. That would only send us deeper into hell."

Her shadow leaped fantastically against the wall. The iron key twisted in the heavy lock. "Push against the door," she said. "I can't open it."

Ash laid his shoulder against the wood and shoved. The massive portal stirred, groaned open with a sound like mortal sorrow. The note cut to his very bones, echoed through the roots of the keep. Standing within the cell, Ash closed his eyes and hugged his chest, then started to find the woman next to him.

"There's an underground passage." Aestiva pointed. "That way," she said. "A tunnel surfaces near the wood. I sent a servant to wait with a horse."

The lamplight caught her face, turned her to something nearly fay, herself.

"Did you mean all the time to let me go?" Ash asked.

The woman bowed her head over the lamp. "I had thought of it," she said. "But I wanted to speak with you, to see if you were… were…ah, but never mind."

She straightened then, thrust the lamp into Ash's hands.

"Here. Bread and cheese," she said, handing him a bag, "and a flask of water." Then she sought within her clothing. "Take this with you, as well." It was a sword she had beneath her cloak.

"No," he said. "I'll go, but I have no use for this."

"If you're pursued…"

"Still, I'll have no use for it."

His refusal brought a thin smile to her lips.

"The healer," she said, "principled to the end."

"A live healer," he corrected. "Lady, I can't mix in the dealings of soldiers and lords."

"Go, then," she said, "with only my blessings."

Pavané dreamed of death. He knew it in the instant of waking, and then he felt the sharp pain of wounds. He had clawed himself in his sleep, left painful, bloody weals across his chest. He lifted one pale hand and touched a gore-tipped claw to his tongue. It gave him nothing; his own blood was empty.

The hunger was worse tonight than usual, more painful and more immediate. It had risen within him with the return to consciousness, flared to the level of torture. It clouded his mind at the best of times. Now he fell down into it, burning with pain, forgetting even the ache of his wounds.

He had been sleeping on a pile of rags on the floor. He writhed there, panting and moaning, clawing at the shreds of fabric that insulated him from the rough boards beneath.

He had torn his clothing to shreds the way he'd torn his skin, but still he didn't feel the cold. Nothing could warm him. Ever. Even in the hottest sun of summer, he always felt cold, as if it welled up from somewhere deep inside him.

Shadows flitted through his brain, instincts and urges beyond comprehension. It seemed some darker current fed them tonight, crossed time and distance as if they didn't exist. The hunger gained in power and urgency, but still Pavané didn't scream and claw the walls as he usually did.

He only had a fit of gasping and trembling. Quiet touched him, then. Wind flirted with the shutters. In more rational times, he would unfasten the panels sometimes and watch the stars turn. But tonight there were no thoughts in him. He clawed and tore mindlessly at the bindings until they fell away.

Like an animal he curled into the window ledge, struck the iron bars sharply with his fists. There was no give in them, but he didn't fight them now, didn't bruise his flesh against their obstinacy. Instead, he crouched still as death, waiting—wanting for blood. Only the flicker of his red eyes betrayed the life in him.

It came to him finally, a faint speck of warmth afloat in the dark cold of night. It fluttered and dropped erratically as he tracked it, sometimes near and sometimes far. Always it ventured closer to his tower, to the window, to the iron bars, and finally to the stone beneath.

It squeaked as his claws slashed down on it, struggled desperately within the confines of his hand. Sleek fur tickled his palm, thrust outward with the bones of delicate wings. A sharp pain cut at one of his fingers as the warmth bit him. He half-growled then, a rumble that died before it was formed, and snapped at the thing with his own sharp fangs.

The result was a flash of fire. He choked as it burnt down in his throat. It flamed through his soul, pumped through his veins, burnt to the very tips of his fingers.

With it came something—not reason—nothing so sweet and civil as that. Instead, it was a terrible, burning intelligence which flared in his brain. It was hunting instinct, a concept of prey. A red haze spread over his vision like the color of his eyes.

For a moment he leaned there against the stone. Gasping, confused by the sudden bloodlust, he shuddered, tangled his gory fingers into the long, pale strands of his hair.

The haze cleared suddenly. Pavané slid out of the window seat and crossed to the door. There was always a warmth outside this portal, similar to the flying thing which had come in at the window. The shape of it leaned there against the wall now, faintly visible in the vague starlight.

Pavané licked his swollen lips, felt the needle sharp scrape of fangs across his tongue. He released his claws from the wood, ran his hands down the rough boards. The barrier was a problem, but on some level he found the answer. He moistened his lips again, found his voice.

"Guard..."

The sound was hoarse, hardly recognizable. He tried again, managed to make it clearer, almost a human voice.

"Eh?" the warmth said. "What?"

"I...need...I need water."

The warmth stirred, produced a clanking sound and then a splash. Footsteps crossed the floorboards and then something slid, a bowl through the slot near the floor.

Pavané's claws slashed at the sound, caught in flesh. The warmth screamed--but already it was too late. Fangs had followed the claws, caught the bright spurt of life. Soon the warmth was less so, and lay very still.

The flush of fire was stronger this time. The door was still there in his way, but again the answer rose from somewhere. Pavané stretched on the floor and reached through the opening, felt along the guard's leather harness. His fingers closed on a ring of keys. He tried them in the lock one by one, fumbling through the window grate until one of them worked. Then the door set him free.

Ash never found the servant with the horse. He surfaced from the underground passage into a storm. It was a damp, cold wind which blew from the eastern sea, and tonight it carried cold sleet on its back.

Ash tasted the wind and decided he needed to find shelter more than he needed to run away. He crossed the fields, and by the witch's hour had found a sheltering log in the wood. He was shivering with cold by then, heat robbed from him by the clawing, ice-tipped wind. He wrapped his cloak around his shoulders to conserve what warmth he had, and with the winter howling in his ears, sank into a restless sleep.

The wind billowed. The sleet turned to snow and covered the log, drifted across the fields and through the wood like a white, downy fog. A white owl formed from the snowfall, rose upward on silent wings. It ghosted across the wind, soundless as the snow, a red-eyed, phantom creature with hooked beak and cruel, bloody talons, seeking through the night.

It found a weasel too far from its hole. The owl dove and the weasel screamed, twisted to bite, but the predator had broken its back. The owl spread its wings for balance, and hot blood sprayed across the snow.

Ash started awake. He couldn't breathe, couldn't see. His heart thundered in his chest, and the weight of eternity pressed on his back. A storm, he recalled. It was only a storm, and he was sleeping safely in a log, in a wood. The weight on him was only snow, and not death at all. He tugged at his insulating cloak, dug himself out of the snowfall.

So. There was to be no easy escape from the keep's dark bane. Now it would follow him. He would have to move, daylight or no.

Actually it wasn't that long until dawn. Ash had hardly walked long enough to lose the heat of waking when he saw the sky's first light through the trees. He shifted his course and began to climb, stopped on the bare, rocky ridge of a hill to look back. The keep stood there on the next ridge, but there was nothing to see but the lowering clouds, still pregnant with snow and glowering with a murky light. The owl followed him regardless, as sure as the cold that blew in his tracks.

Ash had meant what he said to the Lord Seine about not inheriting his father's gifts of sorcery, but he had not been completely honest, either. He did have a way with earth and dream—a witch's strength he could call on. He couldn't change his actual essence, but with the earth under his feet, he could blur the shadow he made on the ground.

He had never really tried something like this, a pressured, critical deception, but his mind slid into it easily, like changing his cloak. He breathed, and the shadow of a hart formed on the earth beneath him. Silent, swift of foot, it lifted its hocks over the depth of snow, disappeared easily into the shade of winter hollows.

The journey eased, at least for a while--the shivering, and the fear. The snow left off in early afternoon and the wind picked up again, flirting across the drifts. The sky lightened. Ash looked down and found his shadow had changed to that of a man.

Caught by surprise, he stopped short. He jerked against a tree, scanned the sky. There was nothing above him, no raptor plummeting—only the dim, gray nimbus of unshed snow.

He steadied against the tree. The hart had failed somehow. Stripped away from him? Perhaps so, but he had other forms.

Ash shifted his mind along the wind, giving it wings. Where the man's shadow had been, a hawk now flew. The white owl beat muffled wings on his back trail, soft as the wind. It defeated the hawk as easily as the hart.

But a real dusk blurred his man's shadow this time. Ash hid himself in a cave, had a meal of bread and cheese from the lady's pack. It was a demon that followed him into dreams that night, fanged and red-eyed in a shroud of darkness.

"Cane," it whispered. "Where are you, Cane?"

"Cane is dead," he said. "My name is Ash."

"Who is that?" it said. "Who? Who?"

Ash woke in the cold and shuddered, wondering if he could walk through the night as well as the day. But he needed the rest, even if the thing hunted him through his sleep.

Gods. It seemed he'd lived his whole life in this same nightmare, cowering in his father's shadow. The man had left him nothing but a resemblance, and with it, this legacy of evil. Did it help to know that? Ash thought not.

The day dawned, and the white owl took flight, searching for a hare. Leaving the wood now, Ash took the thought and turned it. Like the hart and the hawk, this was a comfortable shape. It was something he'd always done, becoming invisible. This time it seemed to hold.

Still uncertainty plagued him, and a growing fear. That night he dreamed a creature of ice and winter wind—the white owl hunting. It was a red-eyed horror that dogged his footsteps through the snowfield—in whatever form he chose to walk.

Day dawned again. Ash stumbled through the hours, dozed in the snow where he fell, leaving only a hare's confused track behind him. He was only a rabbit, invisible, headed home. But then he felt the white demon, and his shadow changed again.

Something was wrong. Ash was sure of himself in the small magics of hart and hawk and snowshoe hare. But still the white owl followed him, and his own images altered and twisted about him at every turn.

It became a sere, cold waltz with death. The evil took no clear form in his dreams, continually altering and sliding away from him—from owl to demon to shadow wind, and then flowing back again. There seemed no way he could grapple with it--an ephemera—a wanting, a need for prey. There was nothing else.

Somehow Ash finished the journey in safety. Three days it took, and then as dusk scoured the snow to a whiter pale, he came finally to his own stronghold. The house was a simple hermit's hut, built on a hill above the sea. Ash climbed the last grade numbly, cold and weary, stopped to gaze at the homely dwelling. It was hardly visible against the massive summit behind it.

If there was any place he could lay a trap for his father's curse, it was here. This place was his own hearth and home. He had built it with his own labor, his own sweat. He had shaped the rough beams with his own hands, laid in the magics of serenity and balance. He had leveled the floor, caulked the piled rock of chimney with mud and horse's hair, laid the firebricks of the hearth. He had gathered the aromatic herbs which hung from the rafters and lined the walls in hand-shaped jars.

He rested against the door and stroked the lintel post, felt the peace of the earth seep into him. If he were going to die--or worse, be dragged down into hell--he meant to have this place about him when he did.

His mind cleared gradually. A hush filled him, as if he were coming to himself. When he felt that, Ash straightened, and set about laying a fire on the hearth. The way it burnt was reassuring--upright and blue-edged, the way fire should burn, untouched by any darkness within himself.

The hiss and crackle of the new fire steadied into the steady burn of heartwood. Ash stripped off his cloak and washed, found a clean set of clothes to wear. He set out dried fruit and dried fish to eat, and put on water for tea.

It was little fortification, but it was all he had for tonight. When he had finished the tea, he sat in front of the fire, watching it burn down into coals.

Night had fallen outdoors, and the chill wind rose slightly, flirted with the eaves. In the song of it, Ash could almost hear his failures of the past few days. Something was wrong with his assumptions, he thought. So what was it, then?

He was truthful in his insistence to Lord Siene and his Lady that he could do nothing about curses, but he knew his death was coming for him tonight. He needed to deal with this.

So what was it? Had his father made this thing which followed him—or had he raised a creature from hell, instead? Ash had been thinking this was something of his father's making, a wisp of malicious bane—but the thing was no cipher. It had altered and changed his own magics, deep and earth-linked as they were. So it was more than it seemed.

The fire bent beneath an invisible wind. The flames sputtered and died. Ash rose to his feet. He reached into the rafters for devil's bane, tossed the herb on the coals. For a second that revived the flame, but then it only smoldered again. The pungent scent of the herbs died with the fire, filling the room with smoke.

And in that second Ash knew what was wrong. This creature wasn't a shadow at all. It was real.

Wind whipped around the cottage suddenly, dashed against the door. Ash turned sharply as the panel crashed inward. A demon stood in the doorway, with eyes that had stolen the fire. Ash reached out with all the strength of earth and sea to embrace it.

The creature launched at his throat. He fell awkwardly, felt the slash of fangs, the tearing of his flesh. Wetness pumped over his chest, and he fell into darkness.

Ash woke in the wan light of early morning, working his way through layers of unconsciousness like rising from the depths of the sea. He found he was alive.

The world felt still and silent around him. Ash lay with his eyes closed, listening to the hush. Somewhere an icicle broke and fell with a muffled crack. Nearer, a faint breath stirred at his ear.

He turned his head, felt a dart of pain stab down his throat. It was a slight, half-naked boy who slept against him. A sheer veil of white hair half obscured his face. White lashes lay curled against the pale arch of cheekbones. The sharp points of fangs dented the full curve of his lower lip.

The boy lay with his head on Ash's shoulder, one arm thrown across his chest. A stain of dried blood darkened his lips. Ash searched, found memory not too far away.

This was the white owl. Ash had never seen a clear reality in his dreams. He would have thought the boy dead, except for that breath against his ear. Ash reached up to touch the wrist, found it cold as the snow outside.

The boy stirred, jerked upright suddenly.

"You're not dead," he said.

"No."

Ash sat up, too. He felt a sudden weakness, fell against the solid wall behind him. The boy closed his eyes, ran pale hands down over his own bare chest.

"What did you do to me?" he asked.

"Nothing," said Ash carefully.

"Yes, you did."

"No. I…"

The boy leaned close. He was still frightening with his sharp fangs and garnet, glittering eyes, but this morning he seemed washed clean of any threat. He only ran one pale finger down the half-healed scar on Ash's throat.

"I meant to kill you. Tell me what you did." The boy drew a breath. "Was it sorcery?"

"Not mine." Then Ash said what he thought. "I'm only a healer. You're the sorcerer here."

"What?"

"From your mother, I'd guess. Don't you feel it?"

The boy looked confused. "No."

"Well, it's there, regardless." Ash sighed. "I've seen sorcery before."

"What?" asked Pavané.

"Do you know about the curse?"

"The one that Cane laid?"

"Yes," said Ash.

"Of course." His brows drew into a pale line. "He changed me from a human into something else."

"Bound you in some ways, doubtless. That was the result, but it wasn't the curse. What was it, exactly?"

Pavané closed his eyes. The memory of it was there when he looked for it, clear and uncolored by blood-lust, or any hunger at all.

"Death," he said, "and no more heirs."

"That's right."

Ash waited while he thought about it.

"So the question is…why aren't I dead instead of only a monster?"

"Yes. That's it."

The pale hands lifted. "I don't know."

"Because you defeated him."

The garnet eyes opened wide. "What? From the womb? But I couldn't have..."

"Of course you could," said Ash. "And he must have known what you did to him, too. Gods. You took everything he had, all his power. He broke so many men, but he died broken, himself--for that one attempt to murder an innocent babe."

The red eyes narrowed.

"And you're not..."

"What? Looking for revenge? No." Ash stirred, shook his head. "The man was never a father to me. I've lived my whole life in his shadow. He had his own passions, his own conflicts, and he brought ruin on himself. No one could save him from that. I couldn't, and neither could my mother. All he left was a curse to hang over us."

"A curse?"

"You. I knew you were coming."

"To kill you? How?"

"I've felt it all my life. More so in these last few months. I don't have my father's powers, but I do have my talents."

Pavané reached out to touch the scar on his throat again. Ash hardly flinched this time.

"You broke it," he said.

"I don't think so. Maybe you took what you wanted from me. I don't know. My talent being what it is, maybe I've healed us both."

"And you knew you could do this?"

"No." Ash closed his eyes. "I thought you'd kill me."

"And still you waited?"

"This is my home—my own hearth. I wouldn't run any further."

Pavané stared at him.

"Well, what else?" asked Ash. "With the scent of my father so strong about me? How long would I have lasted?"

That provoked a tentative smile. Pavané dropped his head, ran his long fingers through the milk-white strands of his hair.

"So what do I do now?" he asked.

Ash stared up at the smoky beams above them.

"Whatever you like," he said.

"But the curse…'

"It's gone." Ash hesitated. "Are you hungry?" he asked. "I can make breakfast."

MOONSHADOW

Shadow, I flee before the dogs. Nightshadow, moonshadow, for the moon is full. Mist lies on the moors tonight, rising ethereal like the ghosts of men long dead. It touches the moon's face with unholy splendor—delusion, born of earth mated with the moon. My feet are delicate, but light, and I flee like a wraith through the world. Clothed in the mist, I am the hunted, tonight, but hunter, too; and I laugh with the wind.

The cloud is mute. Within its shroud, I hear my own breath labor. But I have distanced the pursuit, baying still far out on the moor. I have gained the forest, arched cathedral, seductive maze, and I lay a trail of confusion for the dogs.

A playful chase, diverting, but dawn nears, and shortly I will seek my rest. The moon falls, sinking, before they find me. There are two, a final diversion. I shiver in anticipation at their man-scent; while the mist caresses my bare skin, sets dewy beads in the pale, shining fall of my hair.

I flush before the dogs, with a wail of terror. When they see me, they haul at the leashes, curse at the dogs, kick them into submission; while I sob, kneeling beneath the moon. The taller one comes to me, but I cower beneath his touch.

"Help me, please sir!"

"Mistress, how in the world…"

"Please sir, my family is wealthy. I've been kidnapped, but escaped. My father will give you anything if you help me to get home….a reward…anything."

He takes my hand and helps me rise. Though he means to be kind, he cannot help but stare at the nakedness of my body as I shake back my hair. Virginal I stand in the moonsilver, but chill has rounded my breasts, teased the nipples.

He conceals me with his coat. But it is short, and hardly covers. His companion is rougher, sly, and licks his lips.

So easy. They argue, and I must only cling to the taller and weep. The seduction of wealth and woman do their work, and soon he lies dead beneath the knife of his fellow.

"Come here, girl," commands the sly one.

I whimper, hesitant, but come to him.

He pushes back the jacket, caresses my shoulders, arms...

"Please sir...a favor."

"What?"

His voice is harsh. He aches for me.

"I'm afraid. Give me your cross."

He laughs.

"This little thing?"

It is silver. Still holding me, impatient, he breaks the chain with one hand, holds it out.

I cannot take it. I dash it from his hand; and as the moon, my magic, touches the dawn, I change, wereform, to sink my carnal fangs into his throat.

ARTIFACTS

The hologram shimmered, the laser interference pattern gradually settling into consistency. It drifted on the dais, like a performer on a stage, as near to concrete as the past could be.

The image was a child from the valley of the Nile and the New Kingdom of Thutmosis III, and the chiseled features and full lips of royalty were softened by youth. The application endowed the image with suitable clothing of the period and social class, an apron and headdress, and provided a readout of pertinent information. A separate screen showed the results of the nondestructive analyses, the ESR dating and DNA assay. Of course, it was possible to have only the data printed out, but the value of the system was in the image, the way it could make the past actually live for a while. It took the data and the dry analyses and made them into a three dimensional figure that could be seen and studied, or saved for incorporating into the museum displays.

Christine Eisler tapped the escape key. The image collapsed, telescoped into nothing; and she smiled slightly, turned to the man who had been watching beside her. The lights came up automatically on rheostat.

Although the dais was a stage for the splendors of ancient civilization, the rest of the room, revealed by the cold fluorescents, was pretty mundane. The computer equipment spilled its guts, cables really, out the side panel. Thick coaxial bundles ran to the scan chamber and the projector. Shelves lined the walls, cluttered with audiovisuals, littered with tagged samples and boxes of journals. Offices opened off the perimeter. A hallway ran to the side exit and from there down to the museum proper, where completed displays resided in all their ancient glory, pressed under glass.

The man sitting there was sandy-haired, casually dressed in slacks and a knit shirt. He lounged beside her in the control station in a careless slouch, his foot propped on the console.

"Well?" she asked.

"It's um...nice, babe" he said. "A pretty good show."

"It's a really powerful tool, Jerry," she said, propping her chin on one hand to study him. Then she sighed. "Though I do have to admit it's a better show for the public than all these desiccated mummies and old bones." She smiled abruptly. "You saw what it actually is yourself, there in the scan chamber."

He had seen the bones that lay in the polycarbonate cylinder before they started, but clearly he was more interested in looking at her.

"I'm impressed," he said. "And you...developed it?"

She glanced at him sideways, piqued by the obvious flattery, but ambivalent, too. "Not by myself, of course. We applied for the grant, and I helped develop the software. We contracted out the hardware."

He glanced back at the dais. He was in business and something of a jock, not historically inclined at all. Sometimes she thought she would enjoy him more if he didn't try so hard to pretend he enjoyed what she did when he clearly didn't.

"Does it work every time?" he asked.

"Usually." She frowned. He had touched on the very subject annoying her tonight.

"Huh?"

"Actually, that's why I wanted to get an early dinner," she explained. "So I could come back to work. We got in some samples that I'm having trouble with."

"Chris!" he complained, and she laughed.

"Now Jerry, don't sulk. It's not like you own me."

He studied her face and managed a grin, but still his irritation showed. "Of course not. I only want to." The honesty must have slipped out. She laughed again.

"Well," he said. "If that's it, thanks for the show, anyway." He took his foot down from the equipment.

The shimmer of the hologram refused to form up. It seemed as if it were about to, sometimes, but the image always fractured and scattered, just as it produced the specter of shape, the ghost of features. It fled into stubborn nothingness, and the readouts fluctuated wildly.

At first Christine had thought this particular sample was mixed, with more than one subject represented. But she had eliminated the possibility now, removed everything from the chamber but a single fragment of bone, and still the system wavered, unable to make up its damn mind.

Marcus Borland even stopped to watch her fight with it a while, intrigued away from his scrolls and digital enhancements.

"What's wrong?" he asked, adjusting his heavy, dark-rimmed glasses. He blinked at it, looking owlish, with his untidy hair standing up.

"Oh, damn. I don't know," she said. "It's screwed up."

"Screwed up? Your machine? Do you mean it has a bug?"

"No. I'm sure the programming's all right," she said. "It's been working fine. It's got to be the system." She looked at the controls in aggravation, the spill of cables.

"Why do you think so?"

"The way the readouts are fluctuating." Then she had a thought. "Maybe the current's variable. Do you suppose the surge protection is bad?"

He only reiterated the obvious.

"You're sure your sample's singular?"

"Yes. I thought of that."

"What have you got?"

"Human remains for sure—probably European. It came in from the British Museum, in a mixed bag of uncatalogued stuff they found in their back room, from God knows when. They sent it for us to analyze and sort, in case there was anything of value in it. This is a piece of jawbone, a couple of teeth. I took everything else out. It's not much, and in bad shape, but we've synthesized from less before."

"Well, you're the expert." He gave it up. "If I could help troubleshoot it for you, I would. Just don't stay all night."

She gave a short laugh. "I won't if you won't." He was famous for staying in his little cubicle until well into the morning.

"Right," he said crisply, turning to go. His red cardigan had a hole in the back.

She gave it up for a while and went on to some of the other samples, all of which seemed to assay perfectly, with only a little engineering. It was just the one stubborn bone fragment that seemed to go wrong every time. It was almost nine o'clock, and she had finished everything but that. She got it out again, turned it over in her hands. It looked like it had been burned, evidence of char, and maybe that would affect the analysis, but there was no reason, really, that it shouldn't assay. She put it into the scan chamber and set up the tests again.

The whole system went down, including the lights, and briefly, power in the building. It went down like it was going to brown out, then collapsed into total blackness—the work station, the background lights—everything. She sat there in dismay, but it was only a few seconds, really, before the fluorescent tubes in the hall flickered and came back on, and the console hummed to life, beeping as the system rebooted.

"Christine?"

It was Marcus.

"Yes. I'm still here."

"Did something happen?"

"Just a power blackout, I guess," she answered, already shutting the equipment off. "But that's it for me. I'm not going to sit here in the dark."

"I'll have to stay a while," he said. Then, plaintive, "I lost everything I've done tonight."

"I'm so sorry," she said, sympathizing. She got her jacket and purse from her office off the computer room, took off her lab coat and smoothed her skirt. Putting things away could wait for tomorrow, she decided. She turned out the lights, headed for the side door and her taxi.

She wasn't expecting to meet anyone, looking in her purse for her keys to lock up—they were always at the very bottom. But in the murky computer room, barely lit now from the hallway, she ran right into somebody.

It surprised a yelp out of her. She jumped back, her initial surprise whetted with disbelief, a glimmer of fright, at contact with naked skin. It was a man's body she had felt, and now he was a dim ghost against the wall, dark-haired, light-skinned.

She caught her balance, ready to run, but he said something she didn't understand, in a voice that sounded so unsteady that she hesitated.

"Are you all right?" she asked, and caught her breath, hearing the tremor in her own voice.

He didn't answer, but crumpled and fell, and she heard his head strike the hard tile floor. She ran for the hallway.

"Marcus!"

It was eleven o'clock when she got home to her apartment, after all the excitement. She and Marcus and the two security guards had milled around for a while, covered him up, tried to decide if they should do anything more. In the light he was pale as death, but his pulse seemed steady. He was medium-sized, not more than thirty, and the dark hair was long, about shoulder length, framing a face with high, broad cheekbones that looked vaguely Slavic. After the paramedics came, they tried to decide where he had come from, but it remained a mystery. He didn't wake, and the paramedics took him off to Mercy Hospital.

Christine thought of it again once she was at work in the morning, and it kept nagging at her. About midmorning she called the hospital to ask about him, and they said he was still unconscious. She frowned at that, and worried a little, she decided to check again later. Curiously, trying to put things away, she couldn't find her bone sample today.

Dhanis Neftaly woke to coolness and quiet. He lay for a while before he opened his eyes, becoming gradually aware of serenity, and the painless rise and fall of his own breath. Awake, he searched for an intimation of eternity, a trace of transition, but there was nothing, as if there had been no lapse at all. There was nothing in his memory but despair and anger, distanced now; and then a brief flash—how long ago?—of a woman's voice.

There was no indication of how long he had been here. But it must have been at least a day. The room was in twilight. He had awakened in a bed with white sheets. There were white draperies, white walls. A window let in the fading light. He seemed to be alone, and unrestrained. When he moved, he found he was connected to a machine that hummed and blinked, but the connection was only stuck to his shoulder, and came loose easily enough when he pulled at it.

When he sat up, he still felt all right, only a slight headache, and he found he was dressed in a short tunic that was open in back. He sat for a moment, just breathing, before he tried standing up. That worked out fine, too, without any dizziness, and he looked around the draperies to find someone sleeping in another bed. It gave him pause, but the other seemed sleeping soundly, so he went carefully on, looking around the room.

The other man's curtained area was cluttered, in contrast to the bareness of his own. There was a vase of flowers, slightly wilted, books and papers, cups and plates, and something that looked like little cakes, wrapped in clear paper. The scent of them caused a hunger pang like a stab, and he got one out, glancing at his roommate as the paper rattled, but the man continued to sleep soddenly.

One door opened onto a broad hallway, lighted, but he only glanced out. He checked the other door and found it led to a tiled bath and apparently a toilet. The plumbing was unfamiliar, barely identifiable. He looked at it carefully, tried experimenting. It took him a few minutes to sort it out, and he wasn't sure he had it right then, but the toilet was fairly obvious, and he got the water to run in the sink.

Back out in the room, he ate another of the cakes, checked through the cupboards. His own was empty, but the roommate's had clothes and shoes in it. It took him a few minutes to sort that out too, especially the fasteners. He put them on, found they were loose, too big in the waist. But then, they were available.

It wasn't until then that he went to look out the window. The twilight was deepening to dusk, and he was looking down on the street lights from a long way up. It took his breath away. In a second of vertigo he leaned against the frame.

But of course, it only meant the building was tall, like a tower. A shadowy skyline suggested others similar. But there was no question of going out the window and avoiding the lighted passage. Actually, he couldn't see how to even open it. So he crossed to the outer door, hesitated, and came back for the package of cakes.

The passage was fairly deserted. The walls were white there, too, the floor something smooth that wasn't wood or stone that glistened softly in the diffuse light. The light seemed to come from panels in the ceiling, and he looked at them curiously, but couldn't decide how they worked.

He stood in the doorway for a few minutes, watching and listening to see what went on in the hallway. Of course, he could stay in the room, wait for someone to come and look for him, to check, perhaps, to see if he were awake. But he didn't really like the idea. Regardless of his lack of design, he felt like an intruder here, illegitimate, and he might not be especially welcome.

There were voices from a little way down the hall, a constant two or three people. Other's came along periodically, walked out of or went into this room or that, and he studied them, their clothing, the way they acted. He decided they would be fairly safe and easy to imitate. He had nothing to lose, after all. So he went down the hall, stopped as he came around a corner face to face with the voices. It was a desk.

One of them, a man, said something to him, but he only smiled and shook his head. Stopping had been a mistake. He walked on by, and they seemed to think nothing of it. Just past the desk, a set of doors slid back and a woman stepped out of a little room. A man was apparently waiting, stepped into it. He paused, looked out at Dhanis and said something, an invitation. So Dhanis stepped in, too, waited as the other touched labeled plates, and closed his eyes at a sensation of falling. He felt off balance briefly, but when the doors slid back again, they opened onto a large room that gave onto the outside. It was what he wanted, so he followed the other man out, paused at the top of low steps to look around at the city.

Christine forgot to call the hospital, but remembered she had meant to on the way home. So she went by instead. It was very little out of her way.

She already had the room number and stopped at the desk in the lobby. She had only meant to ask if he was okay, but instead she found herself asking, in some Freudian mistake, "Is the gentleman in 1020B accepting visitors?"

The woman wasn't paying attention really, busy working at a keyboard. She glanced at a list and said, "Sure. You can go on up."

The room was dusky, and Chris hesitated, wondering abruptly why she was here, why the brief encounter in the night had stuck in her mind. She should have called from home. It was safer, impersonal. She started to go back to the nurses' station to ask about him. But that was dumb. She didn't have to give him her name, and for some reason she wanted to see his face again.

A stranger was snoring in the first bed, so she tiptoed past, checked the second. It was empty.

She stood there a second, looking at it, the empty bed, the monitor blinking by itself, glanced around. The bathroom door was open. He just wasn't there.

Then she went down to the nurses' station.

"What happened to the man in 1020B?"

"Nothing," said one of the nurses, checking his list. "No change. He's not awake yet."

"He must be," said Chris. "He's gone."

That caused a little flurry of activity as they looked for him. They woke the other guy, who knew nothing about it at all, scurried back and forth checking rooms nearby. Finally, back at the nurses' station, one of the women hit herself suddenly in the forehead, struck by a thought.

"That was him that walked by a while ago, wasn't it?"

The other nurses looked at her, and finally one laughed, shame-faced. "You're right. Whose clothes did he have on?"

The roommate's, of course. And his chocolate cookies were gone, too.

Apparently she had just missed him. Chris decided it was best to leave the staff with their own problems, and faded away. But in her taxi outside, she laughed, too, feeling cheated, and instead of giving her address, she said, "Just drive down the street, will you?"

It was a long chance; the light was getting bad. But it worked. She picked him out after only three blocks, the shoulder-length dark hair notable even in the crowd. He was watching an animated window display, apparently absorbed, and looked reassuringly normal. Briefly, she wondered why, studying him from the taxi.

But personality and a certain amount of character must show, even in borrowed clothes. And maybe she was intrigued. She got out and paid off the driver.

She thought at first he was going to run from her. She stopped next to him and said, "Hello."

He swung around in startlement, and she could see it in his eyes. But she put out her hand and said, "Wait." And he did. The eyes were dark, too.

"We met last night," she said, "but I didn't get your name."

He cocked his head a little, re-composed already, listening, but he didn't say anything.

"My name is Christine," she went on. "Do you know how much you've upset the hospital staff?"

He said something this time, but it wasn't English.

"Oh." She had forgotten. She hadn't understood what he said last night either.

She wasn't exactly a linguist, but she tried a few words of Spanish, a few of French. He blinked, so she tried it again, remembering the cookies.

"*Hambre?*" No response. "*Affame?*"

That did it. But what he said was different.

"*Ad fames?*"

He said something else, and she realized he had changed languages, too. At first she thought it was Italian. She had taken Latin in school, and it sounded similar. But he didn't look Italian. She stared at him, vaguely frustrated, and then decided to pursue it. She took him by the arm.

"Come on," she said. "Let's go for a walk."

He went along, as requested. There was a book store just down the street, and she took him in there, stopped at the row of paperback language dictionaries. It was Latin that he picked out.

Odd. She bought it for him, and took him to a restaurant.

By then they had arrived at his name, Dhanis, but not where he had come from. He told her when she asked, in her rusty Latin, but it didn't mean anything. Communication was slow, and took a lot of looking through the dictionary.

The restaurant was Italian, and she ordered spaghetti for him, an empirical test. He didn't seem to recognize it, but ate it all with a passable imitation of her table manners.

Then she had a dilemma about what to do with him.

Obviously he had no money, no identification, and only stolen clothes. He didn't seem worried.

"Where are you going to sleep?" she asked.

"Outside."

"No. You can't. You'll get mugged. Or arrested for vagrancy."

She worried about it, through dessert and coffee, and found his face still haunted her. As if she had seen him somewhere before. She kept glancing at him but couldn't figure it out, and toyed with the idea of taking him home.

It was a stupid idea, of course; dangerous to take a stranger to her apartment. But he didn't seem threatening, and she hadn't answered the questions he posed. Maybe if he stayed for just for one night, then she could find somewhere else for him to stay tomorrow.

She could take him back to the hospital, of course.

She felt her mouth quirk in a smile, wondering how long they'd keep up with him if she did. Not until tomorrow, probably.

"Will you come home with me?" she asked finally.

He had to think about it.

"All right," he said.

They took a taxi, and he looked at it like he'd never been in one before. It was the same at the apartment. He glanced around the living room, waited for her to tell him where to sit.

She sat down too, propped her chin on her palm.

"You can sleep there on the couch where you are. I'll get you out a blanket."

Looking at him, she thought she should return the clothes to poor Mr. McKay at the hospital, and smiled again at the thought. They were too big, but Jerry's clothes should fit him better. And it might be good if someone else knew he was here—just in case this did turn out to be dangerous.

So she called Jerry and had to explain. Of course Jerry didn't like it. Still, he dropped some things off in about half an hour. Sulky and antagonistic, he glared at Dhanis, looked as if he wanted to fight about it.

"You could keep him at your place instead," she suggested.

"Fat chance."

"Okay, then. Don't complain. Thank you very much, Jerry."

She got him out the door, came back with a sigh, dropping the bundle of clothes and toiletries on a chair.

"Sorry about that," she said.

Actually, she had been reassured at his response. She had thought of the awkwardness too late, would have expected an answering animosity from him, a competition between males if nothing else. But Dhanis had only looked uncertain and wary, aware of it no doubt, but low-key; and when Jerry was gone, he seemed to forget it, as if the problem didn't extend beyond the moment.

She yawned, found it was later than she expected. "I'll have to go to bed soon. I have to get up and go to work. But I'd like to watch the news, if you don't mind."

She had an entertainment center in the wall, and touched a button that exposed the TV, turned it on. When the news was over, he asked what it was.

"You really don't know?" she asked, staring at him anew; and he shook his head. She told him it was a television, or TV, and then he asked how it worked. She pointed out the remote, the switches, the cable and the electrical cord, and still wasn't sure he understood the whole thing. Once in bed, she lay awake, wondering about it.

She had left him studying the dictionary, found him asleep in the morning; she hadn't awakened him stirring around. Mr. McKay's clothes were folded in a neat stack on the chair, as she had asked. She wanted to tell him when she would be back, so she touched him on the shoulder.

"Dhanis?"

She was already used to his composure, and the response was a surprise. He started awake violently, jerked away from her, at least a foot, in the instant of waking. She jumped too, and for a second she read something frightening in his eyes, but then it was gone.

"Sorry," she said. "I...didn't mean to startle you."

He pushed back his hair, rubbed his eyes, and hugged his knees.

"I'll be back this afternoon," she said. "Will you stay here?"

"Okay." He had already picked up the word. She hoped he'd understood what she said, went on to work and left him there.

After the woman left, Dhanis lay back down, but he couldn't sleep again. Fright had wakened him, flashing through his veins like fire, and it still throbbed in his pulse, his temples. He took a breath, his face in the pillow, trying to flush it out, but it was a useless effort. He wondered again at the persistence of terror, the immediacy of recall, over the span of time. It was real, more than an abstraction, even though he didn't know if he really had anything to fear here and now. But of course, probably he did, and it was only a matter of when. Still, he wouldn't worry about it. He sat up.

Since she had left him here alone, apparently he could do as he wanted, so he got up and poked around, exploring the rooms. She must live here by herself. He found a bath, still warm and steamy, the tub easier to identify than the place last night. He tried it out, found one knob provided hot water, the other cold, and another, a shower of water from above. The hot water was a wonder.

The bath opened off a bed chamber, with an amazing supply of women's clothes in the closet. Back in the other room were chairs and small tables, the couch where he had slept, all arranged in a semicircle. There was a minor clutter of belongings, books and papers. Odd paintings hung on the walls. Off to the side was a table and chairs for dining with dried flowers centered on the table, and an area with cupboards that must be the kitchen.

The rooms seemed full of machines, but nothing of the kind he was afraid to find. Perhaps the time and place were neutral, after all.

He decided to bathe, as apparently that was what she had done, and when he was finished, he put on the clothes the sulky fellow had brought last night, a pair of pants and a long-sleeved shirt, finely woven. They did fit better.

Then he checked the kitchen for something to eat. He had to look a while before he found anything he recognized. Everything seemed packaged so he couldn't tell what it was. One of the cupboards was a machine that was cold inside, with cheese and milk, some fruit in a drawer. He found a loaf of bread and a knife, but the bread was already sliced.

He looked out the windows for a while, absorbing the view and the traffic, well above the street again. Then he found the button she had used to work the TV last night, sat down to watch it and study his dictionary.

Chris returned the clothes after work, managed to get away without having to offer an explanation. She had left work early to allow for it, and to get home early, assuming he would be there.

But he wasn't. He had left the door unlocked too, the slippery son-of-a-bitch.

She dumped her purse on the dining table, irritated. After having gone to a lot of trouble to talk Marcus into keeping him, now she would have to call and say he was gone. Still, there wasn't anything to do about it, and nothing seemed missing. So she changed her clothes and made dinner, sat down to read.

He tapped on the door about eight o'clock, hesitated when he saw her frown.

"And where have you been?" she asked, with her hand on her hip, surprised a little at her annoyance, and also her relief at seeing him there.

He probably didn't understand what she said, but he read the lack of invitation easily enough, started to turn away.

"No. Wait," she said, hastily, seeing how easily he would go. She reached for his arm. "I'm sorry. Come on in."

He reassessed her expression doubtfully, but she tugged at his sleeve, and he came on inside. His pockets were full of money. He emptied them out on the table.

"Would you help me count this please, Christine?"

"Dhanis," she asked, with her mouth open, "you didn't steal it, did you?"

"No," he said. "Would you show me how to count it please?"

He sat in one of the chairs to stack it up neatly, and she sank into another. It turned out he didn't even know how to read numbers. She went through a brief arithmetic lesson, and he seemed to get the idea, counted it up. It was more than a hundred dollars.

"So how did you get it?" she asked.

"I'm a magician," he said, and seemed to watch for her reaction.

When she only looked doubtful, he tossed up one of the coins and made it disappear. He showed both hands, made it reappear with a flourish, out of his sleeve, no doubt. It was a smooth and accomplished trick. She laughed, and he grinned, briefly.

"And?" she questioned.

"I saw people performing on the street, in the park, and getting money, so I thought I could do it, too."

"Well, I guess so," she said. "Did you work at it all day?"

"Only the afternoon," he answered. "How much will it buy?"

"A fair amount. If you make that much every day, you'll be able to live, modestly, at least. You'll have to pay taxes, of course."

He wrinkled his nose. "Taxes?"

She laughed again. Obviously he knew what that was. He smiled responsively, his eyes amber under the light, warm and unclouded. His Latin was already sprinkled with English. He was quick.

"Dhanis," she asked, as her curiosity surfaced, "how did you get into our computer room?"

"I don't remember," he said, easily enough, folding the bills. She blinked, having gauged him as straightforward, but for some reason she thought now he was lying.

She didn't have a chance to pursue it. He seemed to think about what she had said. "What is your computer room?" he asked.

She explained about the museum and the scanner and the synthesis program, but it was hard going, and she ended up doubtful he had understood it.

"I'll show you, if you like," she offered. "We can go down tomorrow evening."

"I'd like to see the museum," he said. "Thank you."

She had thought about her atlas today, and got it out, hoping he would show her where he was from, but he didn't identify any of the maps. She decided it must be Eastern Europe anyway. Otherwise, she would recognize the language he spoke.

It was too late to call Marcus and change her mind still again, so she got out the blanket for him to sleep on the couch. He was really strange, she thought, awake in her own bed, thinking of him asleep in the living room. A collection of ambiguities and inconsistencies, an opportunist, obviously; naive, but learning fast, and still a mystery.

He watched the Egyptian assay as if mesmerized, and when she shut it off, he blinked, startled at the way it disappeared. She waited for his reaction.

"It looks alive," he said, "like the child's soul, but it doesn't feel that way." And she wondered if she had understood him correctly. "It's really only the machine?" he asked.

"Yes," she said. "What do you mean 'it doesn't feel that way'?"

He hesitated, with a glance at her, shrugged. "It's only an empty vision."

"Well," she agreed. "You're right about that. It's called a hologram."

"What it shows is true, though?" he asked, curiously. "What the child was really like?"

"Well, I hope so."

"It's wonderful," he said, "to study this way, and to honor the dead in your museum."

She studied his profile, found herself comparing him to Jerry, who had sat in the same chair not so long ago. It was a curious comparison, she thought, and striking that Jerry came out second best to someone apparently indigent, and with amnesia— or whatever was wrong with him. Dhanis wasn't exactly a flashy personality, but he was compelling in a way, with something—a quiet intensity and self-sufficiency, perhaps—that Jerry was flagrantly missing.

They had stopped on the way finally, gotten him a haircut and real clothes of his own. Pleased at his choice, she thought he looked respectable in a dark shirt and twill pants, though his hair was still a little long. She wondered again where he had come from, and why she was intrigued, but not why she enjoyed his company.

"Dhanis," she asked suddenly, still looking at him, "do you like yourself?"

"What?

She smiled at his reaction. It had taken him by surprise. "I don't mean to pry, I just thought you did."

He looked at her, typically collected. "My self? No. Not usually. But I have to put up with it." His mouth quirked to an answering smile, a little wry. Then he glanced back at the dais, dead and still now, around at the machines, the laden shelves. "May I touch your samples? Do you mind?"

"No, of course not," she said. "Go ahead."

He took them off the shelves, one by one, turned them over in his hands, deciphering the tags, and kept himself occupied for another hour until Marcus was ready to go.

He had accepted the transfer easily enough, once he had met Marcus. She thought he had hesitated when she mentioned it, and expected he would resist, but there had been no problems.

The two of them went out the side door, but she had a few things to finish up, so she lingered. The Egyptian child had to be copied on disk for a display set to open next week, so she brought it up again, keyed in the commands. But finished, checking it, she hesitated, touched by the figment now, seeing it from another viewpoint. It shimmered, and cast a transparent, ghostly light—an astral soul captured on disk, stolen from eternity.

She studied the perspective, remembering the glow mirrored from the man an hour before. And memory, contiguous, bore a whisper of intimation, a glimmer of where she had seen his face before. She shivered, as ghostly fingers touched her spine.

Metaphysical, it had been another shade of hologram that had refused to form, that shattered and fled--and her sample was still missing.

It was impossible, of course, but it kept bothering her. She called Marcus as soon as she got home, wanting to talk to Dhanis, to reassure herself he was substantial, perhaps. But it turned out to be useless effort.

"Sorry, Chris," Marcus reported. "He's not here."

"Oh no!" she said. "What happened?"

"The guy took off before we even got started," he explained. "I thought we were getting along fine. I wanted some Chinese take-out, so we walked down a block."

"And?"

"We were waiting to cross at the corner, and I looked around and I was talking to myself. He was gone."

She could almost see him shrug, push up his glasses.

"For no reason?" she asked, frustrated now, not wanting to accept it.

"No reason I could see. I didn't do anything. Nobody else did anything. There was just the usual traffic, maybe a couple of guys down the street."

"Well, damn," she said, and then sighed. "I hope he'll come back."

"Maybe the guy's crazy," suggested Marcus.

Jerry thought so too, but he wasn't so kind about it. He came over to pick up his things.

"You take in strays, babe, you take your chances. You're lucky he didn't rip you off, or rape you or something."

"Oh, Jerry," she said. "He wasn't like that at all."

But Jerry's attention had already wandered. He stood close, wound a curl of her hair around his finger. "Want to go out?"

Another time she would have been pleased that he asked, but now she felt cross, dissatisfied with everything.

"I don't know, Jerry."

"Babe, you're not going to work all week-end are you?" he protested.

"No. Sorry. I'm just out of sorts. Could we make it tomorrow night?"

"Okay, babe. Seven o'clock?"

Her week-end went all right, except for a certain angst, but Monday morning was a jolt. Someone had broken into the museum the night before—vandals probably—and had ransacked the computer room and the offices and smashed several of the displays up front. Mr. Sullivan, one of the security guards, had heard them, but he was in the hospital with a concussion, and couldn't describe them at all, apparently. He said they glowed, which was odd, and probably only the concussion.

The museum was closed for two days, cluttered with insurance adjusters, before the staff could even begin to clean up and reorganize. It took forever to sort out the mess in the computer room again, and some of the sample tags had been lost. The ones that had been assayed she could match up with data in the computer, but the others left her in bewilderment, trying to identify the artifacts from memory alone.

Then someone broke into her apartment. It was on Thursday while she was at work—only luck, probably, that she wasn't home. But she had the same mess to clean up there--closets ransacked, drawers emptied, books scattered. A few things were broken, but again, oddly, nothing was missing.

Jerry was sure it must have been Dhanis, and she considered it, almost gave his name to the police. But it just didn't make sense.

She was jittery all week-end, expecting them to come back, jumping at every sound, and that same tendency continued into the next week. She tried not to stay late at the museum, though Marcus was there every night as usual. Waiting for her taxi, even in daylight, she looked over her shoulder, kept away from the shadows.

Nothing happened, but still her nerves got worse, as she imagined someone watching her, shadows at the edge of vision, furtive shiftings. But when she turned, there was nothing there, of course. It wasn't only on the street, either; it also happened in the computer room.

On Wednesday Tasha Flauros stopped by there to talk. Tasha ran the gift shop and qualified as a friend, but she was moody and strange sometimes, and today she only made things worse.

She slipped in, watched the hologram incorporate, an assay in progress, and her breath whispered out.

"Those things are so freaky. They haunt me," she said, and Chris looked around at her. She was a black orchid, delicate, darkly dressed as she often was. She faded into the dimness so her pale face seemed to float like a reflection of the hologhost, a few feet above the floor.

"Tasha," Chris warned, "if you're having one of your moods, I don't want to hear about it. Things have been weird enough around here without you pointing it out."

The image displaced, smiled softly, settled into the extra chair.

"I apologize," she said. "It's difficult to keep all the pessimism to myself, sometimes." Dusky-eyed in the gloom, she seemed to study Chris. "I'm not having a mood, though. Don't you feel like you're being watched?"

It caused a shiver that Tasha put her finger on it like that, as if she were psychic. Chris stared, and Tasha took it as answer enough.

"I saw your friend, Dhanis," she said, cocking her head.

Chris was startled. "Where?"

"Outside. I think he watches you leave in the evenings. From the library."

She thought about it, as Tasha went on. "He just watches. And maybe he follows you. I don't know. He's not said anything to you, has he?"

"No," said Chris. She sighed abruptly, rubbed at her face. "The library?"

"Yes. Right out front, on the steps. I saw him Monday, and he was there again last night."

"Okay. Thank you, Tasha."

It was a dismissal, and Tasha, sensitive to such things, got up to leave. "Sorry," she said, "but I thought you should know."

"Yes. Thanks."

The building across from the side exit was a law library. At one time it had been a public building, and it remained with a grand approach, the steps guarded on either side by crouching lions. Instead of going out the side tonight, as she always did, Chris

206

went out the front and walked around to where she could see him there on the steps.

He was sitting in the space between lion and building, unobtrusive against the stone, where she wouldn't have seen him if she had gone the other way. The space was shadowed, but she could see him well enough from this angle, and she expected him to look different somehow, guilty. But he didn't. He appeared still himself, composed against the granite as if he were perfectly valid, perfectly legitimate in waiting there.

But he wasn't. He couldn't be.

She meant to walk right up to him, catch him without any possibility of escape, but it didn't work. He snapped his head around when she was still yards away, warned by some subtle sense, and leaped down from the steps, ready to run. She sprinted to intercept him.

"Dhanis," she said, and he stopped.

He turned sharply, and he *was* different. His eyes were different, encumbered by darkness that wasn't just a color—a reflected shade of something, a risk, a danger in him now. Maybe she should have called the police, after all.

"What are you doing here, Dhanis?" she asked, carefully keeping her distance. "Are you watching me?"

He didn't dissemble or deny it, only said, "Please, Christine. I don't want to talk to you now."

Whatever was in his eyes, it seemed no threat to her. His response was disarming, only confused her. "Why not?"

"I can't. Please."

"You won't explain?"

"No. Just let me go."

Then she only stood there, wondering what the hell was the matter with her—and him—as he turned and walked away.

But at least he hadn't disappeared into thin air.

She decided to relax and quit looking over her shoulder so much. And the lack of vigilance left her prey to the very thing that had been hanging over her.

She went on home, and the next night was back in the computer room, recopying disks to repair the displays, while Marcus worked on damaged artifacts up the hallway. Out of residual caution she had him wait with her at the door for the taxi, and when she saw it, she said, "Thanks, Marcus," and ran for it. He was already turned when she was struck by dizziness, before she reached the car, and thought she was fainting. But it was too late to call him back, and she fell forward into terror.

A rushing in her ears, an aurora that pulsed and grew. She didn't quite wake to consciousness, but came to awareness. Someone was talking to her and she was answering. It was a hard voice, an accent she didn't know, and it compelled. She had a vague impression of faces, figures—gray-clothed—and the taste of blood.

She started abruptly to clarity, though she didn't know why. She found darkness and quiet, and still the taste of blood--but stale now. Her mouth was bruised, but she couldn't remember hurting herself. She lay still, managed to discern a glimmer of light, heard nothing but the clamor of her pulse, the pounding of her heart. She seemed alone somewhere, lying in a chair. Ambiguous shapes of furniture lay around her, boxes, a flow of air. She felt a growing dismay. Horrors crowded the dark, and dread. She pushed up and managed to get to her feet.

There was movement behind her, a presence, and she started, too late. Still, it was only an ordinary assault this time, nothing surreal or eerie. An arm caught her and a hand closed over her mouth. She struggled and dragged at the hand, thinking he would smother her, but a voice whispered against her ear.

"Don't scream Chris, and I'll let you go."

She lay against him for a frozen instant, her breath shuddering, and he was good as his word.

"All right," he whispered, taking her hand instead. "This way is a passage out."

She couldn't identify the voice, whispering as it was, but the Latin was hardly usual.

They emerged on a street she didn't know, with little lighting and less traffic.

"Dhanis!"

"Are you all right?" he asked.

"No," she said. "Dhanis, I want to know what's going on. If I'm in danger…"

"You haven't been, really," he answered. "You're not. Just wait, please, until we're away from here, and then you can talk."

She grew more indignant as her fright waned, in proportion. They found a place to stop, finally, and he asked her to call for a taxi. Then he drew her into shadow again.

"All right," he said.

"What do you mean, I haven't been in danger?" She had a challenge ready. "It feels like it to me. My office has been broken into, my apartment's been ransacked, and now I've been kidnapped by these weird people, dragged off to a dark hole. I want to know what the hell is going on."

"I think they'll leave you alone now. It would be better if you didn't know anything."

"What do you mean by that?"

"Safer."

"I thought you said I wasn't in danger."

"You weren't. I knew where you were. And I could have sent someone to get you any time. But it would have frightened you, so I waited and came myself."

She stared at him.

"Who would you send?"

"Someone from your museum."

He touched her chin lightly, turned her face to see the cut on her mouth, as headlights turned the corner.

"Where are we going?" she asked, glancing at the taxi.

"Wherever. To your apartment, if you like."

"I should go," he said. "If I stay, I will cause you this same kind of trouble again."

"I still want to know what's going on," she insisted.

In the warm light of the apartment, the strangers seemed far away. He was dark and alive, with emotion closer to the surface tonight than usual. He didn't quite pace, but he moved about, restive, touching something now and then—a book, a framed photo.

"Even if I explain," he said, "you won't believe it."

She sighed. "About now, I would believe anything. Please try me."

He hesitated, studying her face, her resolve, perhaps, and finally sank into one of the dining chairs, where the light turned his hair to gloss and outlined his reluctance.

"All right," he said. "Maybe it's better that someone else knows."

Still she had to prompt him. "Yes?"

"The men you saw were from the future."

"The what?"

"The future."

"I don't believe it."

"I said you wouldn't."

She looked at him, but he seemed perfectly serious, direct and uncompromising, and she was conscious of disorientation, suddenly, a dislocation in reality, as if through a sudden warp in space and time, it could be possible. She took a deep breath, tried to remember she had asked to hear this.

"How do you know?" she asked carefully.

"Because I've met them before, of course," he said simply. "They're not harassing you without reason. They're looking for me."

"Are you from the future, too?"

"No. The past."

She winced, closed her eyes against memory; his face composed in a shimmering hologram. "Assuming that I believe you, when?"

"I don't know. I can't find any point of reference."

"When do you think?"

He shrugged. "After Christ and the Catholic Church, but a long time ago. How long since anyone really spoke Latin?"

"You're right. A long time." She hesitated. "Why did you come here?"

"I had no intention to."

"You are a time traveler, though?"

"Yes, I suppose so."

"How did you get here?"

He hesitated, unsure.

"I think you provided me an avenue with your machine."

Her eyes widened. "Are you saying it's a time machine? That it will actually transport people?"

He considered. "Transport? No. I don't think so."

"Then how..." she began, but he only shook his head.

"I knew they would come," he said. "I had hoped to have a while to orient before they did, but it wasn't much. I have to thank you for helping me."

"Did you ask where you were, that night? When you came?"

He looked away, laughed sharply.

"I asked if I was in hell."

"Why?"

"It's where I expected to be. I thought I had committed mortal sin."

"Oh." She tried to evaluate his response, couldn't. He was really serious. The darkness in his eyes was transmutable, coloring her judgment, her dislocation. Finally she managed to form another question, "Where did you meet these...men from the future?"

"In my own time."

"How? Will you tell me about it, please?"

He was still reluctant.

"A machine brought them. A time machine, you called it?"

"Wait." She had to interrupt. "Did you actually see one?"

"Yes. But of course it does more than just that," he said. "You saw the aura of one tonight. It glows."

She stared at him.

"Anyway, they came for an evil purpose. At first no one noticed or saw what they were doing; but afterward there were tales of demons that stole men's souls. I've never been..." he took a breath, "afraid of demons," he said, "and I didn't believe it. But finally they hurt someone I loved, an old man, a priest that...had helped me, taught me..." He seemed to say it with difficulty, looked away. "It made me angry, so I watched them. I saw they were only men, really, for all their different ways, and their magic was only a machine. So I took it. It was the time machine, I suppose, but it was the thing that stole men's souls, too."

"Why should they want men's souls?"

"I don't know," he said. "I haven't understood it yet. Maybe they want to put them into a...museum, like you do. Or maybe they're vampires of some kind and need souls to eat." He shook his head.

"Ah." She hesitated. "But it doesn't make sense, Dhanis. If they're so powerful," she began, "and someone from so far in the past would be totally naive of...I mean how could you...?"

She floundered to a stop, found he didn't seem to have reacted. His hands lay in his lap, and he turned them over, stared at the palms, flexed the fingers.

"Dhanis?"

He raised his eyes.

"I'm a magician," he said. When she only stared, he went on. "You don't believe in magic, do you?"

"I..." She took a breath. "No. I don't think anyone intelligent does now."

She bit her tongue too late, expecting it to offend him, and he saw her embarrassment.

"It's all right," he said. He quirked his mouth, but it was hardly a smile. "It's best that you not believe it. I've never had many friends. Once people know…" He shrugged then. As if it were real, as if he really didn't care.

"The things in the park are tricks, of course," he went on, studying his hands again, watching the fingers flex and tighten. "I haven't any power over inanimate things. I could take their machine only because it was alive."

Surprised from her disbelief, she started. "What?"

"I don't know how to explain it. At first I thought it was magic. In a way it felt like the machines you have, the ones that think, but in a way it felt alive, too."

She frowned, searching for the concepts, less difficult to believe than magic. "A computer? Bioengineering?"

"You know what it is, then?" He looked at her sharply. "Perhaps I'm not so far from their time after all."

She only stared.

"Anyway," he went on, "you're right. It was stupidity, and arrogance, to take it. I'm wiser now; I didn't realize at all what they could do. They caught me, threatened death and torture if I didn't give it back."

She waited, but there was no indication he was going on. "And what?" she prompted, finally. "Did you give it back?"

"No." He stopped. "I don't have it now, but I still know where it is. And so it's dangerous for you to be around me, for me to be here at your apartment."

"Are you going to give it back?"

His face hardened, and his eyes went very black. "No."

She rubbed her face.

"How can you fight them?"

"I won't underestimate them again," he said. "I've touched your samples," he said. "The ones in the museum."

"I don't know what that means," she said.

"It's important that you respect the danger," he answered. "And keep away from them."

She only stared at him, doubtful. But that seemed to be it. He didn't seem ready to persuade her further. He didn't even look at her. Composed and grave, he picked one of the dried flowers out of the centerpiece, a rose, turning it over in his hands.

She tried to force the story into her system of reality, but it didn't assimilate readily, even after what she had seen tonight, though perhaps only something so far-fetched could explain all that had gone on in her life just lately. She was too pragmatic, too rooted in Western rationality to admit the supernatural, the stuff of occult scandals and pulp magazines.

She sighed, giving it up, but not wanting to tell him she didn't believe it. If he did, maybe he was crazy after all.

"Well. What kind of magic is it you do?" she asked.

He looked up at her.

"Necromantia," he said, and he held out his hand, to offer her a living rose. "Your samples will provide me servants of the dead."

ENTWINED

He was her obsession, it seemed, and she came increasingly between him and anyone else. Between him and Cynthia, somehow, though Cynthia should have saved him if anyone could.

She followed him, a wraith of mist, an exhalation of autumn breeze, from apartment to apartment over that year. (He didn't stay in any one place too long, constrained as he was by the vagaries of university support.)

He found her breath beside him, restless in the dark predawn, as he drank black coffee in his efficiency kitchen; found her walking with him in the humid nights after the evening class he taught on sociobiology, oblivious to the presence of others under the trees, along the university sidewalks. He caught the glimmer of her form in the river of car lights flowing down the hill at Tennessee Street, the filmy outline of her shadow in the fluorescent lights as he worked late in the library, researching his thesis that spring.

In his dreams she lay beside him, and in the mornings he remembered the long curve of her back, the soft pointing of her breasts under his hands. Sometimes he woke, sweating in the summer nights, his penis throbbing with her embrace, with the familiar hint of her lips, the caress of phantom hair over his groin, or the illusion of breath in his ear.

Sometimes he lay alone (she didn't always come), decanting sense of her like wine. She poured out of nothingness like white sauterne, crystalline and prismatic in the sun, ghostly by the moon, and left him helpless, drunken, with yearning for her growing like an ache. He drank of her, and found her cool and satisfying. But she sapped him of life; and at last he tried to protest, lying in the dark of his bed. Watching the ghostly reflection of her on the ceiling, he found she was winter after all, and that he was her own.

The autumn before, the cold had come down quickly, without warning, after a long, soft October at the university. He was at Apalachicola then, his first visit to meet Cynthia's mother (a symptom of how their relationship was progressing—though he wasn't sure how he liked it.) The drive from Tallahassee down to the coast was dull, the long, flat roads lined with live oaks and rotting Southern cracker shacks, each with its cluster of rusting car hulks, pickup trucks and pit bulls chained in the yard. Spanish moss hung from the trees where the shacks were interspersed with cypress swamp and mosquitoes, wispy and parasitic as the leeches that swam in the black, scummy water.

Cynthia's mother was delicate and sallow. She evoked decadence, the plantation South, the over bred aristocracy in their high, clapboard mansions overlooking the slaves. Her hand was moist and flaccid.

"Cynthia's new friend?" she breathed. "From New York." There was almost disapproval in her voice. She sighed. "I declare, the world is so full of Yankees these days." Then she smiled slightly, like Cynthia, undermining the stereotype, so that he wasn't sure of her any more, or whether he had her disapproval.

The house moldered alone at the end of a long sandy drive, paint peeling in the constant brackish wind, with the faint miasma of river on the one side and the restless tide of the Gulf behind. The river was a real presence, the dark water turgid, muddy with tannin, flowing imperceptibly towards the savannah and the tangled dunes and sea oats of the beach. It was overpowering, and he felt restless already the first day, smothered by the damp house and the musty river.

It was humid and almost hot that morning, while they sat in the ancient parlor with its stained sepias and strained conversations. In the afternoon he had to get out of the oppressive house, into the sun, at least, so Cynthia walked with him to explore along the dappled river bank, on an old road that was just a track now, like the rutted drive.

Feeling his discomfort, Cynthia was too bright, too sunny, chattering along in her jeans, clutching his hand and pointing out the ancient oak hammock overgrown with palmettos and wild vines, while he listened, impatiently, with only half an ear.

Then she stopped suddenly. "We can't go any further," she said. They had come perhaps five miles, but the road continued on, crowded by live oaks and scrub. He couldn't see a reason to stop.

"Why not?"

"There are stories." Cynthia didn't laugh, though he did, and when he looked, her face was serious.

"Stories?" he asked. "What about?"

Avoiding him, her glance slithered away to the shadows, the bleak contrast of light and shade. "Vampires," she whispered.

"What?"

"It's an old legend. The trees come alive that cast their shade on you."

"You really believe that stuff?" He laughed again.

Resentment darkened her eyes then, at his tone. Her eyes flicked back, caught his in their black embrace. "I guess it's just stories," she said. "But remember, I grew up here."

"What's back there?"

"An old house," she said. "A graveyard."

It sounded the most interesting thing yet on this dreary trip. "Let's go," he said, and when she shook her head, he took her by the shoulders, kissed her chidingly. "Come on, Cynthia. You're not really scared are you?"

She wouldn't go, and finally he walked around the road himself to chart the shadowed ruin.

The house was a gone, only a jagged foundation left in the slanted sun of afternoon. It was an old plantation that had burned, marked by crumbling, blackened chimneys and broken slave houses under the trees. He stirred through it, found the ground slanted sharply beyond towards the river. He slid past a faint retaining wall of coquina stone and into the family cemetery below.

The tombs were cracked, blackened, lichen-covered, overgrown by something, an evergreen with red fruit, a yew, he thought, standing in the shade. A legend touched him then, an eerie whisper of ephemera.

He walked back along the road. The river began to smoke, fog lifting in the sharply cooling air, and the cold crashed down on him like death.

Mist and hoarfrost now. Silence. The gravestones lean, defying the will of those who set them, falling to the twin debasements of gravity and time. Ageless, the winter exhales from the tombs.

He has come. He knows her finally, advances to meet her, the yew with her bloody fruit and her vampire roots, entwined forever with the dead.

SURVIVAL

The Security Commission meeting hadn't gone well. It had been a bad morning all around, and now it was getting worse. Andrea Forbes-Carlson knew she was in trouble when her escort lost the fire fight. The limo had been flying through the policed corridor between domes, and they were half-way to New Richmond when her pilot suddenly recorded pursuit. Andrea braced herself for the maneuvers, and suddenly claustrophobic, she brought up the sensuround. She was sorry right away—what it showed wasn't something she really wanted to see.

Kidnapping was a well-established method of political extortion within the northern domes, but one glance showed her this wasn't going to be an extortion—likely not even a kidnapping. The fire was deadly.

One of the fighters exploded on the port side with an eye-searing blast. Andrea flinched sideways, gasped as the vista skewed and dropped, then caught sight of more gunships zeroing in from the east. Her flyer was armed, but the pilot was concentrating on evasion, on getting them out of the line of fire and running like hell. For a second it looked like he might succeed, but then one of the attackers broke suddenly through the reeling line of defense, and it was all over.

The screens blinked out of existence, leaving Andrea blind to the sickening fall that followed. The pilot was hit, but he still managed to control their trajectory. The limo leveled out, almost gliding in, but it was too close to the ruins below. It clipped the edge of a building and spun around, crashed with a flash of sparks inside that settled immediately into near darkness.

Andrea didn't quite go unconscious. The safety webbing had automatically protected her from the shock. Still, it was hell of a jolt. She groaned and thrashed, knowing she needed to get out of there--her predecessor had died of political assassination just this way when the downed flyer exploded. She found the webbing release suddenly, dropped awkwardly to the bulkhead below.

Disoriented, she searched for the hatch, shoved at the emergency release. It gave slightly, but then in the middle of her confusion, she remembered the pilot. She crawled back over the jumbled equipment and caved-in panels, fell into the cockpit. Dim light showed her the man slumped over the controls. As far as she could tell, there was no sign of a pulse.

"Dammit," said Andrea, and lurched back through the dimness again, headed for the hatch.

It hurt to shove it open. The numbness she had felt at first was going away, and her side hurt. Sharp pains ran from her right shoulder down to her fingertips. Still she braced herself and heaved desperately, found it was only gravity holding her in. She panted, hoisted herself out into filtered daylight and tumbled down the crumpled side of the flyer.

The crash had apparently impacted a wall, cracked dry masonry into scattered heaps that were spotted with an ill-looking, leprous growth. Andrea rolled to her feet and managed a staggering run through the debris. A kaleidoscope of sky wavered, smudged and gray above her. Cracked pavement stretched beyond the shattered wall, lined with ruined towers. Broken masonry sheared at impossible angles here and there, punctured by the shafts of twisted trees—all of it overgrown by wild vines. She distrusted the strange vegetation, but it still offered cover. She tripped on a creeper and fell flat, then rolled into the shadow of thorny canes to catch her breath.

It seemed the wreck was indeed burning. A column of smoke rose behind her, but she didn't know if it was just the fuel that had caught, or if the fighters had come around again to fire at it. Panting and dizzy, she lay there on her belly, hoping the smoke had covered her escape.

But what the hell was she going to do now? She had lost her pad, didn't have a way to call for help. Likely she should stay near the downed limo, but they had been run off course. More likely she needed to get back to the policed corridor between domes, where she'd be located by the right security squad.

She eased out into the open, then jerked sideways at a sudden rush overhead. She glimpsed something diving after her with leathery, claw-tipped wings. Sharp teeth snapped in a gaping beak--but the creature shrieked and sheared off, unable to get to her as she lunged back into the canes.

It was an atavism—a throwback to some godawful terror of the past. The monster reminded her that there were more dangers here than just the flyers overhead. Around her the silence turned instantly ominous and threatening—the empty streets, the shattered buildings, the dark column of smoke billowing upward. She shuddered, wiped her face with a sweaty hand.

Among other things, the Commission Andrea headed monitored conditions outside the domes. For the last year, there had been increasing demands that the ruins should be "sanitized" because the residents had become so dangerous. So now she was here, gathering experience first-hand.

She'd only taken the chairman's position last year, and the big surprise was that she was already prominent enough that she'd attracted assassins. Lying there on the filthy pavement, protected only by sparse, flimsy brush, it was an honor she could do without.

She took stock. Her side ached, lanced sharply when she breathed. Broken ribs? Maybe. Her shoulder had settled down to a sharp throbbing, likely only a huge bruise, but maybe strained muscles, too. She fumbled for what was wrong--she wasn't used to feeling pain or diagnosing its cause. The nanobots in her blood would already be cleaning up the damage, as well as taking care of any random virals she was picking up that might affect her genes, but still she felt ill. The bots couldn't insulate her from the shock.

The air moved, rattled the canes above her faintly, shifted the acrid, poisonous smoke in her direction. She coughed, found it was a poor idea with her damaged side aching the way it was. There were other things here under the bushes, too—nasty insects collecting that might have a poisonous bite. She needed to move, whether there were still dangers in the sky overhead or not.

Andrea shoved forward and crouched, looking through the canes for a path that would lead her away from the wreck--she needed a better place to hide until someone came to look for her. She would have to cross a brief open space, but then there was a larger outgrowth of brush near the ruined buildings off to her left.

She made the run successfully, felt a little better protected once she was hidden in the heavier brush. She sat down to rest, wondering how long it would take before she was rescued. The pilot had called in a mayday, so New Richmond had to know about the attack.

After a while she heard something, moved cautiously to look out through the brush. She jerked back at a clatter off to her right.

She had heard the reports, had seen holos taken from a distance, but that did nothing at all to prepare her for reality. There were five of them, hunched and ape-like, brute-faced, wrapped in tattered rags. They slunk forward, stopped. One of them grunted inarticulately, waved an arm at the smoke. The others answered with squeals and howls, jumping around.

Andrea eased back deeper into the brush, but the traitor wind turned, carried her scent to them, and they wheeled around, snuffling the air. One of them turned its face upward, tracked the hungry bird still circling. The wind fluttered, and Andrea flattened closer to the ground, then jerked suddenly as an insect stung her. It was enough to rattle the brush.

The half-men crouched, circled like the predators they were. One of them darted forward and snatched at Andrea' ankle through the brush. Another jabbed at her with a stick, and she yelped at a sharp pain in her already damaged side.

That produced a savage outcry, more beating at the bushes to knock them aside. Andrea cringed backward, but the next hand caught her squarely by the arm, dragged her out of hiding. She knew she was going to die then, and she struggled for all she was worth. They beat her with their fists, pinned her down with their weight. One of them sat on her legs, while two others gripped her arms and held her flat, still shuddering, for the pack leader to look her over. The leader was huge, dark-featured and ugly, and his eyes held a look of pure ferocity. He ran his hands over Andrea' body, felt of her hair, her clothing, her breasts.

Andrea jerked at that, and the man made a sound like grunting laughter. Their faces, their bodies, weren't that far from Andrea' own, she could see—just filthy, shaggy and unkempt. Still they were horrible—their stink, their savagery, the inarticulate sounds they made. They were called muties within the domes, and they were atavistic, like the claw-winged bird—only more horrifying because they had once been men.

The leader discovered Andrea' jacket pockets, dug out the items inside and turned them over one by one, grunted as he inspected her data band and ID case. He grinned at the booty, showing pointed, animal fangs.

Her captors hauled Andrea along with them. They shoved her, beat her with the sticks, made her walk—but they really didn't show any of the boisterous triumph she expected. Instead, they ranged along behind the leader, checking the wind, their eyes darting constantly back and forth. They seemed to be watching for some danger that didn't appear.

Degenerate or not, they had definite skills. They tied Andrea up with scraps of leather thong, threw her into a ruined, roofless building and piled ruined furniture against the door to close it up.

It seemed a well-used den. The room was filthy with trash and rotted scraps of God knew what. Confused, sore and exhausted, Andrea lay on the mat of stinking garbage and tried to remember details from the Commission reports—anything that could help her now. Damned if she could recall very much. Only one fact really stood out: these creatures were supposed to be cannibals. Likely they'd been out hunting, and she was their prize.

After a while a sharp discomfort penetrated the fog of shock in her brain. Her damaged shoulder ached persistently, and her ribs stabbed her with every breath. She rolled and squirmed, looking for a more comfortable position. She didn't find it, but she did locate a scrap of rusty metal under the litter. About four inches long, it was probably dangerously contaminated, but still it retained a sharp, ragged edge, and she thought maybe it could be used like a knife. After a couple of awkward tries, she fumbled the thing into position and put it to use, sawing at the thong that held her wrists tied behind her back.

It took a long time, and she had to rest between efforts. She gasped in surprise when the trick actually worked. She lay there for a while, letting the pins and needles of returning circulation wear away, and then she got to work on the tie that bound her ankles.

The little bit of freedom made her feel more in control, but that was all it did for her. She was still trapped. She pushed to her feet and limped around, exploring her prison, found it was just that. There were no other exits, no way to climb the shattered, eroded walls. Weakness took over, and she sank down on a step. There was nothing she could do but wait.

Chilly, filtered daylight penetrated the ruin, cast shadows along the walls. Without her data band, Andrea couldn't tell what time it was, but eventually she heard a commotion again outside the door. She jerked to her feet, desperately searching for somewhere to hide. The step was part of a stairway to nowhere, but she ran up as far as she could go, flattened against the wall, meaning somehow to defend himself to the death.

Her captors were digging the trash away from the doorway, but it wasn't to get to her, as she'd expected. Instead they threw in another captive.

The creature landed heavily, awkwardly, but it wasn't dead. It moved, curled slightly, lay still. It looked like another of the muties.

Andrea stayed where she was for a long time. The domes protected the best, the last of humanity, and Andrea was one of those, herself. Though she was just beginning her political career, her family was powerful—she rubbed her fingers across the ID chip that said so, embedded in her wrist. This was a terrifying situation, but still, with all their wealth and influence, her family prided themselves on their humanitarianism. After a while Andrea had worked through the issues, and decided maybe she should check to see whether the mutie was bleeding to death, or not.

She eased to her feet, limped down the steps, moved in closer. This one looked slighter than the others, though he was still big enough. With the shapeless, ragged clothing they wore, it was hard to tell. The creature lay face down, didn't move, didn't respond as she moved closer. Andrea sank down, reached out a careful hand to touch the bound shoulder.

"Excuse me," she said, "are you okay?"

The creature came to life suddenly, jerked away. Andrea jerked backward, too, nearly fell. The two of them stared at each other. Dark, suspicious eyes glared at her from a bruised, snarling face.

Andrea let out an uncertain breath, rocked back to her feet. "I'm sorry," she said. "I was just wondering if I could help you in some way."

She retreated carefully to the steps. The black eyes impaled her, followed her every move. When she sat down, the mutie's head fell exhaustedly to the floor again.

The confrontation was somehow almost as disturbing as the manhandling she had received from the others. Andrea leaned against the wall, careful of her sore shoulder, and tried to determine why. It was the rebuff, she decided, the implied threat in the bared fangs and the suspicious eyes. But there was something else, too. The face had surprised her. The other muties were typical of the atavistic representations she had seen, rough-skinned and savage-looking, with wild, tangled hair and flying beards. This one seemed a little different.

Andrea sat there watching as the sun began to slide toward evening. After a while she got up. She caught the quick jerk of the mutie's head, the flash of eyes following her through the mass of hair. She walked over and scooped up the sliver of metal that she'd used to cut her own bonds and tossed it toward the mutie.

"Here," she said. "It's how I got loose."

That was really stupid, she thought. But she remembered how tight the thongs had been when they were jerked around her own wrists, and how much they had hurt.

The mutie rolled back slightly as the shard landed near him. It was a controlled move, though. The creature was wary, but he had accurately judged the trajectory and realized it was no missile. He wasn't slow in making use of it, either. He scooted and writhed, had his bonds loose in a fraction of the time it had taken Andrea to cut through hers. Then he sat up, flicked his hands--to restore some blood flow, she thought. He stared at her for a moment, then dropped his head to his knees, sat that way for a while. Likely he was hurt, Andrea thought. She was bruised and aching himself.

But the creature didn't rest for more than a few minutes. He shoved up suddenly and crossed to the doorway, set his shoulder against the barrier that blocked it and heaved sharply.

He didn't really succeed in moving the load, but it did shift, and some of it avalanched and crashed on the other side.

"Hey, what are you doing?" said Andrea, lurching up. "You'll make them come back."

The creature didn't look at her, didn't respond except to grunt with effort as he shoved at the barrier again. He heaved again at the debris, tore fiercely at the obstruction from the inside.

Whoever was outside had noticed, and they set up a howl—but there was only one voice. The mutie had made enough of an opening now to see through, and this time Andrea caught meaning in the quick flick of her companion's hands. It was some kind of sign language, she realized, directed at the guard outside.

Threats, maybe. He heaved at the blockage again, and the howl outside turned more savage. The barrier fell suddenly, and Andrea' companion lunged through the opening.

Andrea hesitated, frozen for a second, but then she ran for the hole. She arrived in time to see the last of the encounter. The hulking guard outside held a real knife, but his smaller opponent was quicker, more agile. The rough shard of metal Andrea had given him slashed across the guard's wrist, and then across his eyes. The howl turned from anger to pain.

He fell, and the smaller mutie kicked him in the face. Then the noise stopped altogether.

Andrea climbed over the remains of the trash. The mutie seemed to be going through their things.

"That was..." she breathed.

The guy wheeled on her, crouched and low, the bright flash of the guard's knife like flame between them. Andrea reeled back, felt the wall come up hard behind her back. She hung there, frozen, thinking again she was going to die. But finally the mutie stepped back. Watching Andrea all the time, he rummaged quickly through the debris on the ground, then turned and disappeared like a wraith into lengthening shadows.

Andrea let out her breath, closed her eyes and let her head fall back against the cold wall. She understood what the mutie had figured. Most of the wolf-pack of brutes was out still hunting, and there had been only one guard all the time. It was unlikely that Andrea could have overcome him at all, but at least now it was done--and she would be a fool to wait here until the others came back. The outside was terrifying. She was unarmed, hurt, starting to feel cold and hungry. In the darkness she wouldn't be able to tell friend from foe—God knew what horrors stalked the ruins at night.

So what then?

She made her decision, pushed away from the wall and followed quickly in the footsteps of the mutie. At least the creature was going somewhere other than here.

Andrea caught up within a few seconds. She caught a glimpse of the other, saw the quick flick of eyes over the mutie's shoulder. The creature was aware of her, then. But the other continued straight on without any attempt to lose her, walking quickly and silently along what looked like a foot path through the ruins. Andrea kept a careful distance, not wanting to lose sight of him. She closed it up a little as the light faded and shadows began to form, feeling insecure.

As dark closed down completely, Andrea found herself abruptly alone. She started to panic, knowing she was lost in the wide, empty darkness by herself. It was terrifying to see the real sky, the bright, frosty spray of stars spattered across the heavens. With no protective dome above her, they were terrifyingly cold and sharp. Andrea shuddered with chill, looked around.

The mutie hadn't fallen into the earth. He had to have gone to ground somewhere close by.

Andrea had just walked through what had been a narrow alley way, come out onto a wider stretch of broken pavement. She turned and retraced her steps, feeling along the broken walls, and found a crack half-way back on the left-hand side. She slid through the opening, felt her way along, caught a faint flare of light off to her right. She circled and approached carefully, found it was a fire.

The mutie she'd been following had just lit it. The place was carefully chosen, sheltered and baffled to keep it from being seen. The mutie sat on his heels beside the tiny blaze, feeding in sticks of splintered wood. His eyes flickered up before Andrea had gotten anywhere near the circle of light.

Andrea thought about staying where she was, lurking at the edges of the firelight. But the guy didn't snarl at her this time, didn't flash the knife—he just went on about building the fire. So Andrea edged forward and sank down, still at a little distance, and leaned her weary back against a wall.

The mutie ignored her.

Andrea watched dully. She was too far away to feel any warmth from the fire, but still it was a comfort. It flickered, highlighted the mutie's face: wide, prominent cheek-bones, a high-bridged nose. He seemed to be completely beardless, and his hair was thick, glossy and black, held back now by a rag tied around his forehead. Seen from behind, his hair had been surprising straight and long, falling almost to his waist. His eyes were strange, too. They were almond-shaped, not like anything Andrea had ever seen before.

Lord knew what it was. Populations within the domes were tightly controlled, the genes carefully monitored. All the genotypes were similar and resulted in a uniform phenotype as well—light brown to blond hair, pale skin, a little variation in eye color, a strong, compact build. The gene pool outside the domes was God-knew-what to begin with, and damaged and mutated like crazy after that.

The creature took out what he had stolen from the other camp, what looked to be two rusty, cylindrical cans. Andrea winced as the guy opened them with his knife, thinking he would break it. The blade didn't snap though, and the mutie only glanced opaquely across at Andrea, set the opened cans in the fire.

It wasn't until the smell started to circulate that Andrea realized they contained food. Her mouth watered, and suddenly her belly growled with hunger. She started up, settled back again at the quick stab of the mutie's eyes.

Andrea wasn't used to doing without food. She'd eaten a light breakfast, expecting to have lunch on the limo. She hadn't had anything substantial since yesterday's dinner. That seemed a long way in the past right now, the opulence of the setting, the rich fare. Maybe tomorrow she'd be sunk to fighting for food like the wolf-pack they'd left behind, but for now she'd wait. At least this meant the guy didn't mean to have her for dinner.

Andrea twitched and stirred as the mutie lifted the hot cans out of the fire with a wadded rag, set them aside to cool. After a minute the guy lifted one, scooped the food out with his fingers. He ate, carefully watching Andrea all the while, his black gaze pointed and sharp across the fire.

When he'd finished, he wiped his hands off on the rag and tossed the can into the shadows. Then his fingers flickered and wove into intricate patterns. Andrea was surprised at the complexity. Whatever the guy had signed at the other camp had been much shorter and sharper.

When Andrea only sat there, the guy frowned at her, shifted to simpler signs. He pointed to the can, and then to Andrea. He didn't have to offer twice.

The mutie slid away as Andrea approached, faded into the shadows like a wary animal. But once Andrea was occupied with eating, he slipped up again. Andrea didn't notice it until she felt the guy's hand on her sleeve. It was a light touch, hardly palpable. Andrea jerked in surprise, though, nearly cut her hand on the can. The guy jumped, too, snaked away.

Doubtful herself now, Andrea shifted a little so she could watch the mutie while she ate. Maybe it was an overture, but likely not. The guy kept his distance once Andrea was watching him. Still, the touch was evidence of something different. After a while Andrea decided it was just plain curiosity. The mutie pack leader had been a lot less polite about it, exploring the synthetic fabric of Andrea' business clothes—and her body under it as well.

The can was a sparse dinner. Andrea wanted more to eat, but there didn't seem to be anything else. The mutie watched her as warily as a wolf. Eventually he moved, though, apparently picking out a spot to sleep. The flames flickered and died to coals, like warm eyes peering through the darkness.

During the night water fell from the sky. Andrea vaguely recognized it as rain. She'd seen it on the sensuround, in holos, but never felt it. Damned if it wasn't uncomfortable. She got up and found a more sheltered spot to rest on the other side of the fire. Still, she hardly slept. She shifted back and forth, trying to find a comfortable position on the hard flooring. Several times during the night she thought she heard flyers, wondered if they were searching for her. Eventually she dropped off to sleep, woke to daylight and a cold mist. When she moved, she hurt all over.

The mutie was sitting up and watching her.

Andrea rubbed her face, wondered if there was anything for breakfast. Probably not. Instead, the guy seemed to want to talk to her this morning. He tried the intricate flow of hand signs again, frowned in frustration at her lack of response. His face was surprisingly human, the lines, the expressions. Actually, Andrea could read him without any trouble after he went to the simpler methods of pointing and looking like he wanted to know something.

"Andrea," she said. "My name is Andrea."

She was surprised at the signs, the quick, graceful movements of the guy's hands. The muties were called that because they couldn't talk, of course. Speech was the first capability they'd lost when the degeneration began after the bio wars of the last century. With it they'd lost their humanity—their ability to transmit ideas, their cultural knowledge. But now she was surprised to see that maybe speech wasn't completely necessary. The guy made himself understood well enough.

He pointed to the sky, made a shape like the flyers with his hands, pointed to Andrea, looked questioning. The meaning was plain.

Are they looking for you?

"Yeah," said Andrea. "I guess so. I just can't tell who's a friend and who's an enemy. Some of them may want to kill me."

The guy showed her sharp teeth, gestured back the way they'd come last night.

"Those are your enemies?" asked Andrea. She propped her chin on one hand, caught a sudden insight about different territories here in the ruins, different populations.

Yes. And yours, too.

"Yeah," Andrea agreed. "I guess so. Did they want to eat me?"

They guy wrinkled his nose. Then he made a dome shape with his hands, pointed to Andrea.

Are you from the domes?

"From DeeCee," answered Andrea, "north of here. I need to get back to the corridor so my security can pick me up."

She had no idea how much of it the mutie caught, or if the guy meant to help her. If you'd never heard speech, how would you understand it? Still the mutie seemed to listen intently. Then, when the fog had thinned, he seemed abruptly to have enough of it. He got up and stripped off his clothes, began to wash in a puddle of collected rainwater.

He had a beautiful body. It was long, lean and hard, the wide shoulders swelling over a flat belly, with tight buttocks and rounded thighs below. Like his face, his body was nearly hairless, lithe and graceful, and his hair hung in a sensual curtain over the curve of his back. Somehow he didn't seem so degenerate just then, only strange and exotic.

He glanced around at Andrea, his eyes appraising. Whatever he thought, though, he kept to himself. He swept the wet off his skin with his hands, dressed in his rags again, and then they seemed ready to go.

The guy stopped before they climbed back out through the cracked wall, and Andrea saw the flutter of his nostrils as he checked for scent on the wind. Down in the alleyway, everything seemed clear. Pools of mist still lay in the hollows. A fine haze hung over the pavement from the night's rain, but not thick enough to hide anything. Andrea thought they headed west. Within a half hour the mutie had her by the wrist, tugged her into hiding, waiting while yesterday's wolf pack passed upwind.

Competence was relative, Andrea decided. Within the domes she was someone to be reckoned with, but here she would never have survived the day. It was a sobering thought--and exhausting to be hunted. As the morning wore on, she started to appreciate her companion's survival skills more and more. His nostrils quivered constantly, tracking the deadly pack that trailed them. And that wasn't all. Search craft without logos moved intermittently by overhead. More than once the man caught Andrea by the arm, dragged her under cover before Andrea had even heard the oncoming drone.

Finally they huddled in the dimness of a fallen arch, and the guy ran his thumb over the chip in Andrea' wrist, gestured meaningfully at the planes.

They're tracking you.

"They can't," insisted Andrea. "It's a private band, and it sends out a scrambled code. Only my own security can track it."

The guy stared at her for a moment, his eyes liquid and quizzical in the dimness. Then he huffed out a breath and let his head fall back against the shattered concrete of the wall.

Andrea collapsed and rested, herself. She ached all over, her injuries nagging at her, the bruises stiffened with cold overnight. She was healthy, and relative youth was on her side, but hunger, thirst and the need to run were wearing on her. Still she had faith in the security organizations—and in the domes, themselves. Someone would come to get her.

They didn't rest there nearly long enough. Within a few minutes Andrea' companion was up. He checked the sky outside, shook Andrea by the shoulder. Andrea groaned and pushed up, wondering if they could find a rain puddle anywhere to drink from now--she was quickly losing her inhibitions about water quality. They seemed to have lost the wolf pack of muties, but in the afternoon they encountered a worse danger.

The overcast sky above had developed streaks of blue by then, and the cold wind buffeted sharply, moving the vegetation. They had just started down a hill into an open space when the mutie stopped suddenly, grabbed Andrea by the arm and jerked her backward into solid cover. They crouched there in a growth of tangled vines that shrouded a wall.

Nothing happened.

Andrea stirred, meaning to ask what was wrong, but when she moved, her companion clapped a palm over her mouth. He lifted a hand to pull at it, but the man's fierce eyes stopped her from struggling. In another second she heard it—a faint crunch, the misstep of a heavy boot. The mutie had heard it with his sharper senses when she couldn't.

Below them a squad of black-clothed men was advancing into the open. They carried assault weapons ready and held to a tight group, quick and alert as they searched through the ruins. Their helmeted heads turned like hooded cobras from side to side. They wore visors which could switch to infra-red—it was equipment meant for tracking.

The mutie hissed through his teeth, watching them, and then his eyes slid over to Andrea. Andrea wouldn't have been surprised if the guy had taken off right then—it was a little different from being hunted by a pack of primitives. But he didn't go. As the squad disappeared into the brush across the clearing, he caught Andrea by the arm and dragged her obliquely off into a deeper wilderness.

The guy circled and evaded, somehow keeping the trees and solid masonry of the ruins between them and the trackers, keeping ahead of them. It was a contest of wits— clear indication he'd had some experience with this kind of hunt before. Still, by dusk the two of them were slowed and limping. Andreas was hurting, and apparently the mutie was tiring, too, losing his alertness--they turned a corner and ran right into one of the commandos. The mutie ducked instantly, rolled aside.

"Halt!" the trooper yelled.

His eyes flickered after the mutie, his attention divided for a second. Then he focused on Andrea, leveled his gun. Andrea had started to run, but it was too late. She stopped, frozen.

The mutie had the knife, and attacked from the side. A slash of red appeared along the trooper's ribs. He tried to bring his gun around, squeezed off a charge. Andrea dashed in, kicked at the weapon, heard the gun slide. She wheeled to go after it, but the mutie had her by the shoulder. Andrea had a quick flash of the downed trooper's transmitter, crushed under the mutie's heel, and then they were running. She had another impression of black uniforms rounding the corner behind them, near phantoms in the dusk. The mutie dodged, sheared off to the side, dragging Andrea with him.

Andrea's legs felt like lead, and sharp pains darted through her chest as she ran. When they stopped, she slumped against a wall, heaving for breath, felt her heart hammer like it would jump out of her chest. She would have liked to die right there, but the mutie wouldn't let her. Within minutes the guy was prodding at Andrea to go on.

"God," said Andrea. "Just a minute, will you?"

But the guy was right again. The squad was right behind them, and with the infra-red they could see in the dark. Lurching through the shadows on wooden, aching legs, Andrea wondered if the mutie was right about the chip in her wrist after all. Maybe somebody in the government had sold her out.

It was well after nightfall when they got to a place where the mutie was willing to stop. It was a hidden den approached through a crawl space, and inside was a cache of food and water caught in a cistern. It must have been where they were headed all along—they had only come a long, hard way around.

Andrea collapsed on the floor in exhaustion, oblivious, while her companion laid and lit a fire. The flare of it lifted the darkness, highlighted the man's strange face. He looked finely drawn tonight, with dark circles under his eyes, but still he didn't seem to need rest right away. He prodded Andrea with his toe, handed her a battered cup of water. Then he opened several cans and set them in the fire. Finally he slid down and flung one arm over his face.

They both must have slept. Andrea was roused by the sound of liquid sizzling in the fire. The mutie was up immediately, rescuing their dinner. It was nearly enough tonight to fill Andrea' belly, and it left her almost comatose.

She lay a little distance from the fire, dozing and watching the mutie clean his knife. It was a worrysome, surreal vision—the flickering firelight, the flash of the knife as the man rubbed it against a stone, tried the point against his thumb. He inspected the edge with a resolute gaze, wiped the blade carefully, then held it in the flames.

The fire snapped, and sparks flared upward. Andrea roused, startled, suddenly aware that something was going on.

The mutie hit her. It was a solid shot, right to the jaw, and for a second everything went dim. Andrea tried to focus, felt the live weight of the guy fall on top of her. She panicked, tried to fight. They thrashed, rolled, and the guy hit her again. Dazed, Andrea went limp, felt the man's heavy weight, the grip of his fingers as he yanked at her sleeve.

"Don't..." she protested.

Does it define who you are?

The guy hissed at her—the flash of teeth was venomous. Andrea felt the slash then, the probe of the knife in the flesh of her wrist. She jerked, made a choked sound instead of screaming. It was over in a second.

Still astride her, the mutie pushed up, framed against the light. He turned the chip in his bloody fingers, inspecting it. He swayed in a lithe arc then, tossed it into the fire. Then he slid down again, lying on top of her.

It wasn't a surprise. Andrea had felt it all day, ever since that morning when she'd watched the guy undress—as if the mutie had caught her own interest and reflected it back. Like an electrical charge, it had jumped between them.

Now the scent of the man swept over her. It was a primal, natural scent, undisguised by colognes or perfumed soaps—and mixed with the scent of blood. The guy flexed his belly, rubbing against Andrea, and in spite of the pain in her arm, Andrea felt the rush of blood to her own groin, the leap of instant arousal. What followed was inevitable.

Afterward, they lay together in the glow of the fire, and finally the guy reached over and tugged the tangle of their clothes up over both of them like a rough blanket. It seemed he meant to sleep right where he was. That was okay with Andrea. She lay there on the edge of the firelight, warm and comfortable in the curve of his arm.

"Dammit," she murmured. "I don't even know your name."

The answer came to her as she poised on the verge of sleep, where the possibility of supporting hand signs was completely non-existent.

Cree, it whispered. I wish you could stay here with me.

It jolted her a little, hearing something like that out of the darkness. But then it was only a dream. She stirred and sighed, realizing that, and fell heavily into sleep.

The worry came back to her, though, on the rescue plane headed back for DeeCee—the mutie had been right about the chip. They'd lost the commandos and rescue had been fairly prompt once they made it to the corridor. Someone had given out the chip code—it meant there was a traitor somewhere in her own organization.

It had taken Andrea a while to find the information on the flyer's data link, deeply buried as it was. The face wasn't a recent mutation, as she'd thought, but a very old one instead.

"Minorities," the link recited, "bore the brunt of the war damage, and so were not well represented in the original gene pool of the domed cities. Those of Asian extraction were first and most profoundly affected because of particular susceptibility to the viral agents employed."

Andrea rubbed her forehead, achingly tired, still hurting. So what did it mean, she wondered? That the domes were wrong, the careful efforts to conserve purity of the human genome? Historically, evolution took place under pressure, where you died if you didn't adapt. And what was the adaptation for loss of speech? Telepathy?

Andrea snapped off the data link, sighed and rolled her head sideways to check the sensuround display, watching the silvery cap of DeeCee's dome slide into view below her.

The hell, she thought. What was she going to do about him?

POISON

She lay in the darkness, wondering how long it would take him to die.

The place she waited was hoary with age. It was the summer palace, creaking with unseen footsteps, sighing with unheard voices. The intrigues of centuries were recorded on the ectoplasm that haunted the corridors, and they whispered at night into the silences, eerie replays of bloody acts and metastatic intents.

The intrigues transcended reality, even. The breakdown of predictability, the twisting of absolute time and space in the event horizon used to reach this place, had no hold on subjective experience.

Kendrick had said about four hours. Fifteen minutes for the reaction to catalyze—long enough that the taster wouldn't detect it--and then it would be virulent, ready to work. Conversant had tossed back the whole thing, the whole cup of poisoned wine. Shelly had been standing there by the table, holding the crystal service, still waiting for the butler to dismiss her.

Lying there now on the narrow bed, she held a case watch in one hand, worried the chain. It was pewter—not gold. That wouldn't be appropriate for a maid servant. Slouched against the wall, she felt the bioware whisper it was improper to sit that way, but she lay there still, the long skirts crushed under her legs. In her other hand she held a stiletto.

She would have run already, from herself as well as death, but Kendrick had said she had to make sure of this. So the darkness was a necessity—mandatory. Knowing that from another vantage point this place was unreal and indistinct didn't help to lessen her guilt. She sat there quietly, listening to the unseen footsteps, the unheard voices, waiting.

In person Kendrick was immutable, cold as poly-steel, with the chiseled profile of a military robot, the same empty eyes. His voice could have been synthesized. Sometimes Shelly had imagined it was.

Her hands were cold, sweating.

"Just frigg off," she'd said, hoarse and sullen.

Kendrick stopped in front of her. The man's face didn't change. The cabin around them was drab and militaristic, banked with cabinets of machinery. The pilot's back was turned; he was involved with the interface. On the screen to the right, the cargo ship Shelly had been on was already disappearing.

"You have no choice," Kendrick said.

"The hell..." Shelly began.

"Theriac," the man cut in, "do you really want to spend the next ten years of your life in a Federalist prison?"

Shelly stared blankly at him then, chilled by the man's personality. It was like a dark radiation bleeding out of him, toxic and poisonous--the arrogance of absolute power.

"You've lost control of your life," Kendrick said flatly. He turned back to a leisurely pacing. "You made a mistake, and now I own you. Your only options are prison and cooperation."

Shelly grimaced. The mistake wasn't the smuggling, or even getting caught. The mistake had been thinking three years ago she could leave the Company's service once she'd signed on and begun the training. Shelly had lost all her options then.

The instructors had been impressed by her drive. She was top of her class--or close, anyway—tough-minded, perfect for the Company's service. The problems had turned out to be philosophical. There was a limit to her drive they'd never realized—hidden principles. Once in, she didn't like what she found, and so she'd taken off.

Afterwards was a downhill slide. The Company, and Kendrick, had played her life like a game, and all the time Shelly had never realized it. She was down and out now. She hadn't any friends left to even wonder where she was.

"We need someone with your phenotype, who's capable and looks young," Kendrick was saying. "And you nearly finished your training. I was sure you'd be available."

Shelly stared at him, but the man's face registered no trace of sarcasm. He paced. Shelly pressed into the couch, gripping her elbows hard, knowing Kendrick was right, for all her sullen mouthing off. There wasn't anywhere she could go that the Company wouldn't find her.

"This operation is important," Kendrick said. "We've been trying to implement it for nearly ten years." He stopped then, stared down at Shelly. "I assume you'll do it." His eyebrows may have moved a micron.

"Everyone's a damned whore?" Shelly spat, and then she added, "You too, I'll bet."

It struck a spark. Something flashed in the man's eyes then, a crack in his composure—but it was nothing Shelly could catch on to—it was gone too quickly. Kendrick's voice didn't change.

"Theriac," he said, "Fifteen years from now this won't mean a thing to you."

"Bastard," Shelly answered. But she could hear surrender creeping in. From that moment Shelly hated the man—almost as much as she hated herself.

Kendrick's eyes didn't change, either. He'd already accepted the victory as given. Likely he destroyed people every day.

He had the briefing data already up, he'd been so sure of her. Seeing it started another wave of helpless fury along her nerves, and she shook, trying to contain the gut reaction. Kendrick turned, gestured, and the virtuscreen expanded. Graphics ate the void where the cargo ship had been, built a colored chart.

"The assassination of a major determinant," he said, "will radically change the probabilities in our favor."

The Company's favor, he meant. One of the nodes on the future chart was flashing yellow, a hot spot of shifting change that signaled converging realities, a threat—a point where their position was at risk.

"We haven't much time to complete it," he continued. "The node is close to us already."

"Why'd you let it go so long?" Shelly asked, assessing the chart for herself. She knew how to read it—and well—but she had only a glimpse of the final layout. It flashed out of existence the instant it formed.

"We've attempted it before," Kendrick said. His eyebrows may have shifted marginally again. "It has been difficult to set up." The video scrolled, the images involuting, stopped. "Here is the target," he said.

It was a blurred likeness, taken from a distance, a boy in vivid contrast—dark hair and pale skin, outfitted in opulent dress. He lounged in a chair too big for him, sulky and bored. The view opened to a public square. The images didn't sink in at first, then sickened, set Shelly's skin to crawling with horror. She looked away.

"Presiding at public executions," said Kendrick, "the final agonies of a rebel group against the hereditary succession. It was taken ten years ago."

A series of relations paraded, court figures, a woman regent, supposedly retired by the coronation, who looked nearly as cold as Kendrick. Another image of the man appeared then, older, heavier, less distinct than the previous shot. The computer enhanced, showed a face with clean, elegant lines. The expression ruined it though, corrupt and degenerate.

"His name is Kerristan Ingwarsen Conversant, fifth of his royal line. The family has been unusually successful at maintaining their grip on the throne. Kerristan has no heir as yet, so he's carefully protected. He was wed at sixteen, and his consort became pregnant, but she was murdered before the child was born. Since then he has not appeared in public, and we've been forced to extend our operations into the court. We've lost two agents so far in attempts on his life."

Views followed from around the capital city: ground cars, gothic deco architecture, pedestrians in ornate costumes.

"The monarchy is totalitarian and cruel," Kendrick said. "It controls a broad region of the continent. Despite archaic and decadent social institutions, the technology is reasonably advanced. There are quite efficient arms and engineering, good sanitation, and an effective market structure."

"Why is Conversant so important?"

She was moved finally to ask—she wasn't sure, but it seemed something flickered in Kendrick's eyes at sight of him. Fear? Personal hatred? It was odd. But Shelly's probe deflected.

"We have no indication," Kendrick said. "You know our technology only identifies nodes, determinants and probabilities. There are no details. Still, the longer he lives, the stronger he looks in the paradigm. It's mandatory we get rid of him."

Herself on the virtuscreen now: Pale hair, pale eyes. The face wasn't beautiful, or even especially pretty. It was full of sharp bones and strong lines that extended down to her body—small-breasted, capable and physically effective. The screen split, featured her twin, or close enough, on the other side.

"The girl's name is Argent Iodice," said Kendrick. "She has been procured for service within the royal quarters. You will take her place, and implement the assassination."

That was all. The briefing was minimal. Most of the important, vital information was in the resource bioware, a cartridge to fit the jack above Shelly's ear. It was loaded with language and behavior patterns, and it would guide her in and out. She'd had the socket implanted when she signed the Company contract, and left with it still in place. She should have wondered why.

They put her in a cabin. When she tried to leave it later on, she found the door was locked. It was only another prison.

God, she hated Kendrick.

They fell into a black gravity well, a time stream of branching probabilities: lives, colors, histories, flowing along the event horizon to the other side. The shuttle emerged into different reality, a different universe.

Seen in person, Conversant was like the photo stills, and then again not. There was a grace to him, and a vicious quality that hadn't come across on the screen. His face was marred by dissipation—a puffiness around the eyes, a dullness to the skin that hadn't quite yet broken his health. The kitchen staff whispered he was drinking himself to death, and surprisingly, that he was ineffectual—the regent hadn't fully given over the reins of power.

That meant nothing. Whoever held the power, it was a reign of terror, and the staff whispered for good reason. It was easy to die of torture here, to become a public exhibit for only minor infractions—lack of loyalty, if nothing else. People did it every day.

Iodice was still in training, a good thing, because the bioware was superficial, and of course it didn't provide all the fine points. The gaps were nerve-wracking. Shelly knew she was expendable, knew Kendrick would cut her loose the instant she screwed up. Still, it was only a few days that she had to carry it off, until the assassination was done.

The adversaries had dinner together that night, Kerristan and the ex-regent, Tiberia. She was his mother's sister, childless herself. Shelly cursed silently when she heard the plans, but it turned out no problem to get the poison into the right glass after all—a minor slight-of-hand.

It was late, nearly nine when they served dinner on the salon balcony. It was a gaslit theater, overhanging the gardens. As a maid-in-training, Shelly had only to accompany the butler, carrying the crystal wine service. Rigid and careful as Iodice, she was invisible. Two maids and the tasters were just as nonexistent.

"This had gone on long enough, Kerris," said the woman.

He had been drinking steadily all day, and hadn't touched his food.

"What do you mean, Auntie dear?"

"You know very well what I mean."

The lamps flickered. He smiled sweetly, bored, dilatory, in the face of her arrogance. The contradictions of his face made him look capable of nearly anything.

"But I'm sure I don't," he answered softly.

He was baiting her. Framed in dark velvet, he was her antithesis in the firelight. Soft-voiced, indistinct, burnished, he lounged in his chair, fingering the wineglass. His eyes were derisive.

Twice his age, she resembled him somewhat, dark-haired and dark-eyed, a frigid beauty disciplined in silk moiré. She flushed in anger, put down her tines, recovered quickly.

It was surprising that he could snare her so easily, half-drunk as he was. But he was adept. It showed in his anticipation, his visible amusement at her anger. He must have practiced for years.

"The girl has everything we require," said Tiberia, "breeding, virginity. Plus there would be a political advantage in a consort from Yocasta, an additional clamp on the nobility."

"But I don't care for her, Auntie." He pouted now, the sulky boy from the photo, just older, darker.

"No one will give a damn. Just impregnate her."

The pout thinned.

"No."

"It's not wise to provoke me, Kerris," she threatened. "I've had enough."

Anger showed in her rigor, her paleness. He laughed softly in the face of it.

"Stalemate," he said. "You're nothing without me, Tiberia."

She jerked up, nearly upsetting the maid who was laying the course, and swept away in a rasp of silk. The staff fell back briskly to let her pass.

There was a second of hesitation. Kerristan only sat there, staring at the wineglass.

With her exit his laughter had gone, too, and his face smoothed out, the petulant child departed. For the instant he seemed dispassionate, only himself perhaps, reflective and uncolored.

The butler cleared his throat gently. "Your Highness…"

He glanced up, realized they were waiting. "Never mind, Linus," he said. He flicked his hand at the dinner. "Take it away."

Draining the wineglass then, he set it on the table, rose and strode away in Tiberia's wake.

The time was up—a full four hours—and the bioware whispered. It led Shelly through a secret passage from the servants' quarters to the women's, and from there a branch to the royal suite.

She opened the panel cautiously. The spring caught, but she worked it, got it to release on the second try.

She knelt at the opening, feeling her muscles tighten. The room was shadowed, cavernous, dark with heavy furniture, cloaked in tapestries. The windows were open; the draperies sighed, billowed slightly, letting in the night wind. A shaft of moonsilver lay across the canopied bed. The hanging curtains stirred there, too, ghostly quiet.

Conversant lay on the tumbled coverlets, half undressed, and Shelly could hear his breath rasp, harsh and labored against the quiet of the room. He was still alive.

Crouching there in the darkness, Shelly rubbed her face, swept back her hair. Revolt stirred in her again, and her lips curled back from her teeth. Of course it had to be like this, up close and personal, something bloody she had to handle himself. It couldn't be easy.

Dammit.

She had to do it. She got a grip on her nerves, slid through the portal. Conversant's face was hidden in shadow, his skin smooth and luminous, pale with the moonlight. The arc of his ribs expanded and fell in a strained rhythm.

He seemed unaware. But as Shelly raised the dagger and let it fall, the man came alive.

Shelly was agile and trained, but still outclassed in weight. They grunted, thrashed. Conversant hit her with something, the brass clock from the bedside. She saw stars, lost the knife. The man was surprisingly strong, considering how much poison he'd drunk—and the fact he should have been dead already.

He hit Shelly again, pinned her quickly. He snatched a cord from the curtains and looped it around her wrists, tied it off to the bedpost. Another for the ankles, and then he turned up the lamp. Panting in the gaslight, he knelt in the featherbed, hugged his chest. He was ashen pale, his bare shoulders backlit by the lamp, sloping sharply to his waist. His skin had felt clammy, cold with sweat, but his eyes were bright and feverish—electric with excitement.

"A girl this time," he breathed. "And I've caught you myself." He laughed, but there was a catch in it.

Shelly panted, too, as the world stopped spinning. She twisted her wrists against the cord, but Conversant had jerked it so tight it hurt. The strands didn't give at all.

Conversant studied her deliberately. "You're the new apprentice, aren't you?" He didn't seem to expect an answer. Shelly lay with her eyes closed, helpless, half sick.

"It was in the wine," the man said.

Shelly had to look at him then.

"I was ill, and I vomited." He laughed again—harsh and breathless. "I had planned to lie here quietly and see if it would pass, but this will be more fun." The viciousness came out in his eyes. "I'll risk the dying," he said.

Shelly turned her face away, sick, cursing him and Kendrick and herself all at once. She gasped for breath, hiding her fear, knowing it would only make the man hurt her worse.

Conversant sliced open her clothes with the dagger, cut the stays of the cummerbund one by one, slashed through the pleated skirt. When Shelly's body was exposed, he trailed the blade over her chest, down across her tight, ridged stomach. She twisted at the cords again, but they only bit deeper into her wrists.

"Shall I cut you?" Kerristan asked. "The servants are so carefully screened," he went on. "How did you get in here?" Shelly couldn't help jerking as the man stroked the cold blade over her thighs.

Conversant didn't cut her. He played with her body as if he had all the time in the world to make love to her. The man kissed her sensually, the taste of poison bitter in his mouth, stroked her breasts. He laughed when penetration was easy.

He was heavily aroused already, thrust quickly to a climax. He managed to finish, but when he tried to move away, he couldn't. He collapsed still half on top of her.

She thought he was unconscious, and she let tears of pain form silently, flow down her cheek. It was too soon, and the man felt it, reached up to stroke her face.

"Is that for yourself?" He didn't laugh this time.

"Maybe dying's not so bad after all," he said. "Maybe you've given me what I really wanted, and I should thank you." Later his hand moved on her flank. "I won't though," he whispered. "I'll see you in hell."

That was all. His breath grew harsher, heavily labored. Shelly's circulation was going. Her arms felt numb. She jerked against the cords in earnest, but she couldn't break loose. She was trapped.

She tried not to feel anything, tried to insulate himself from the man's pain. But she couldn't. Finally Conversant's breath caught—a final spasm. The man struggled against it, and then

Shelly was sure he died. But later she thought he breathed again. She couldn't tell.

Daylight came too slowly. She yelled for help as soon as she heard anyone stirring, and she didn't have to pretend her horror. Someone cut her loose, jerked her aside. Someone ran for the physician. Chaos filled the chamber, a babble of voices, total confusion. They worked over Conversant feverishly, but the limp body seemed unresponsive.

Someone had called the guard. They dragged Shelly out and threw her in a cell. She thought they'd leave her there naked, but a filthy blanket came flying in, too. The room was dank and frigid. Bruised, feeling used all the way around, Shelly wrapped the rag around her shoulders. Huddled on the single bench, she shivered, cursing, thinking there couldn't be any worse misery. She just had to hope she'd die soon.

Kerristan dreamed Tiberia was there in hell, shaking him. She was shouting, as she often did, angry and abusive. He groped after the dark. It eluded him, but still he must have touched it, because for a while he was suspended in limbo again, where nothing could find him, or cause him pain.

Eventually the dream recurred. Tiberia seemed gone, but still there were others. For a while he refused to answer, but realizing it was no use, that there would be no peace, finally he stopped his drifting and let consciousness take him. He opened his eyes.

It was only a glance, enough to see he was in his own chambers and not in hell after all, but it was enough that they left him alone. They were afraid to touch him then.

He lay there, slack and barely breathing, feeling sensation washed out of him, as if he'd been scoured. It was life he had sensed recurring, not a dream, and with it came a vague surprise.

Emptiness, and the world tended to spin in a reeling vertigo. A glimmer of lucidity touched him, a trace of understanding. He realized then why it was a surprise to be alive. In the night he had embraced what others fled—death. He had wanted it.

He let the bed hold him then, the life inside him frail and delicate, exploring the thought. In a moment he had found the reasons: boredom, acrimony. There was no excuse for the abortive caricature that passed as his life. Existence was a cosmic joke that had to be endured, and he wondered if it was always that way--a trap for the unwary, thinking they had something better to live for.

After a while he decided his head ached, but not much worse than other mornings.

He roused slightly. It was effortless, with only a trace of rawness, an afterimage of pain. He sighed gently.

"What happened to the girl who was here?" he whispered. His voice sounded faint and rusty to his own ears. It was hard to form the words.

A stir. Whispering. There was no answer right away. But they had heard him, and he waited.

"In a cell, Your Highness."

"Safe?"

"Yes, Your Highness."

He felt a smile touch his lips, a cruel satisfaction.

"Make sure she stays that way."

Revenge was all he had. He followed it down into real sleep then, as vitality crested, and maybe prevailed.

It seemed a long time before anyone came to check on Shelly. The hours crawled by like roaches in the stinking cell—light passed, then darkness, then light again—it was too much time to think. Restless, cramped by cold, Shelly quickly gave up the bench. She tried pacing instead, still muffled in the blanket, but it only circulated her blood a little, and didn't deaden her brain at all. Once a flask of water and a chunk of bread fell through a slot in the door. She had been dozing on the bench, started awake in a convulsive jerk. The bread was moldy. Shelly wondered how long it would take before she was hungry enough not to care. The water tasted of sulfur.

The light came through a high slit in the stone wall. At least she'd be able to tell the time, and roughly how many days passed before she went insane. But as it worked out, there wasn't enough time for that. Late on the second day, steps crunched down the unseen hallway, stopped by her door. Clutching the blanket, she waited.

It was the guard that unlocked the door, but they didn't do anything to her—not yet, anyway. They didn't beat her, didn't treat her roughly, didn't even leer. One of the officers reached across and gripped her arm, waited while she decided it was better to walk than be dragged down the hall.

They didn't go to any kind of review, or to the torture chambers, as Shelly half expected, but up to some private room. She'd been gathering her courage to die, or at least to rot in the damned cell for the rest of her life (while Kendrick shrugged coldly, and went on to another victim). Instead it seemed she was expected to take a bath. There was even a maid to assist her.

Filthy, Shelly welcomed the bath, but she did wonder what the hell was going on. It wasn't long before she'd figured it out, with depressive fatalism. She cursed quietly. She hadn't been presentable for whatever trial she was going to get.

The clothes were a surprise, though. Bioware whispered they qualified as evening dress. There was a green bodice and matching skirt—a little conservative, still they were velvet and silk, unusually flattering. The maid dried and brushed her pale hair, put salve on the bruises at her temple. The guard was waiting.

It was nearing the late summer dark by then. They strode through the warren of hallways, past windows that framed the fading sky. Her silks rusted, and Shelly's heart beat in her temples, measuring a tempo of mounting terror. When they arrived where they were going, she stopped short, nearly choked.

It was Kerristan Conversant who sat there waiting, on the same balcony where Shelly had given him the poison. He turned his head and smiled, but it didn't touch his eyes.

The guard urged Shelly forward. She stumbled into a quick curtsy, fell into a waiting chair. She ducked her head, tense and still, and the staff began to serve.

Damn. She'd been sure Conversant was dead—that it would be Tiberia, instead. It was hard to tell which was worse. When the dishes were laid, Kerristan waved the staff away.

"Go ahead and eat," he said. "You must be hungry."

She was famished. But Shelly's stomach flamed with acid. Her face felt hot, then cold. Afraid to disobey, she reached for the tines slowly, picked at the plate.

"Look at me," Kerristan said.

Shelly did. The man looked transparently pale and weak, fragile in the chair's supporting arms. He hadn't bothered the food, only held the wineglass. His pupils were dilated, mocking, alive with perversion.

"You're name is Argent?"

It sounded light, conversational. Shelly dropped her head again, sure the lie would show.

"Who sent you to kill me?" Conversant asked.

Shelly groped for a direction.

The man leaned forwards abruptly, caught her chin with fingers that hurt. "I could have you tortured to death for my pleasure," he hissed. His face was terrible, white, rapt with anticipation.

Shelly closed her eyes. Terror must have showed on face. Conversant tipped his head sideways to inspect her bruise. He laughed, dropped his hand.

"Aren't you going to eat?" he asked.

He didn't, himself. When the maid cleared the dishes, his were still untouched. The service staff was rigid tonight. They must know Shelly had been in his bed, but none of them so much as twitched.

Conversant had left the wine untouched, as well. Linus was waiting, and Kerristan hesitated, finally pushed the glass away. "Not tonight," he said. "My stomach's raw."

He lay back in his chair then, slack, his eyes closed. "You may go," he said to Shelly. But then he smiled faintly. "I'll see you again tomorrow."

The guard took her back to the private chamber. The room was luxurious, but the door was locked. Another damn prison, only nicer than the last.

Dinner felt better in Shelly's stomach than she'd expected. She paced while it settled, restless, inspecting the room, the drop from the windows. It was too far. There was nothing to use for a weapon. She didn't doubt there were guards stationed in the hallway. There was nothing else to do, so finally she went to bed. Then, cradled in the featherbed of a gentlewoman, she stared at the ornate ceiling and felt her perspectives rearrange. Of course Kerristan was playing with her. This was just another form of torture, likely a prelude to worse--but still the forbearance was a relief, however brief and deceptive it might be. It freed her mind to work for the first time since she'd come off the cargo ship. She'd only responded to stimuli since then, reacting. It was time for something else.

What she thought was sacrilege. But what the hell kind of loyalty did she owe Kendrick, anyway?

And in the morass of terror that had been corroding her wits, she'd located a curious pang. Maybe it was the battered principles trying to resurface. They whispered she deserved whatever she got from this. And she damn sure owed Conversant something.

Shelly lay there thinking about that, feeling it threaten to haunt her. It was only after midnight that she fell, finally, into oblivion.

She wasn't required until lunch time. The clothes today were cut for afternoon. The bodice hugged her chest tightly, low-cut, a peachy velvet splashed with gold embroidery. A pale blue chemise with puffy sleeves matched the skirt. Shelly didn't much like the effect of the velvets—she looked like a changed woman.

The guard came to escort her to a different balcony this time, on the east side, a terrace with steps descending into the garden. More organized today, she kept her eyes under control, managed to curtsy and sit without stumbling.

"Did you sleep well?" Kerristan asked.

Shelly glanced at him, the set of his shoulders, the casual flick of his hands. He looked better this morning, a shadow of strength returning. Shelly risked a brief nod.

"Oh?" the man responded, acid and burning. "Then perhaps you're not aware of your situation. You have nothing left but entertainment value."

Shelly had to wince. The staff was still serving, and she waited, gripping the napkin tight.

"Eat," the man said, and Shelly picked up the tines, toyed with the food.

Conversant ate a little this time, fingered the wineglass indecisively, and took his hand away again. Seeing it, Shelly realized he was completely sober, and unimpaired.

"Will you tell me today who sent you?" Conversant asked her.

The silence extended, palpable.

Shelly wondered viciously how long she had, how long the man would torment her before she died. She didn't really give a damn. Raising her face abruptly, she met Conversant's eyes straight on, and took the leap into sacrilege.

"His name is Kendrick," she said.

Conversant blinked when she said it, and his face grew still. Shelly glanced towards the salon, where the staff and the guard had disappeared through the glass doors.

"Could we walk in the garden?" she asked—afraid of how Kerristan would take it. She was on dangerous ground. The bioware shrieked with alarms.

Kerristan only glanced toward the salon himself, studied her carefully. "Will you try to kill me again?" he asked.

His black eyes were full of irony. Of course it'd be reckless for him to trust Shelly alone. She felt herself flush, shook her head.

"All right," Kerristan said, abruptly. He threw his napkin on the table, got up, and Shelly did, too. Shadows stirred within the salon. Shelly glanced behind them, going down the steps, but the staff all stayed out of sight. No one followed.

Kerristan walked with more grace than she'd expected, though he seemed restrained. Only his colorless face, the residue of ash in his skin, gave away any weakness.

"A secret?" he asked, smiling coldly again, intrigued. They were away from the veranda, screened by winterbloom.

"Yes," Shelly said. "But you deserve to know."

Kerristan halted, looked at her. Shelly stopped, too. The bioware screamed, but she ignored it. Kerristan appraised her carefully, as if seeing her for the first time.

Shelly took a breath, ready to go on.

"My name isn't Argent Iodice," she said. "It's Shelly Theriac. I've come from a different place...a different time," here was the hard part, "an alternate reality."

She expected Kerristan to laugh, but she'd surprised the man.

"You're crazy," Conversant said flatly.

"No." Shelly shook her head desperately, afraid Kerristan would cut her off before she'd said it all. "Listen," she insisted. "The man Kendrick is with a company that deals in imports from different alternate realities. It's got no competition from anywhere, no controls. It exclusively owns the technology to chart and reach the different time streams. Plus—I don't think anyone really knows what it does."

The mockery was gone out of Kerristan's eyes. He looked at Shelly impatiently, glanced back along the walk they had followed. Distress showed in his face, and he shifted, faintly unsteady.

Shelly saw it, reached out and grabbed his sleeve. "No," she hissed. "Don't go back there. You have to listen to me."

It was *lese majesty* to touch him, but Shelly's didn't care. Her insistence carried them along the walk to a bench. Wisteria shrouded the trees in privacy. Water gushed from the mouth of a gargoyle relief in a retaining wall, poured into a basin.

Resting on the bench, supported by the wall, Kerristan studied her with more patience, but derision had crept back into his eyes. He wiped a faint glaze of sweat off his face with a silken scarf.

"Your story's much too fantastic," he said. "You have to be lying."

Here was why no one ever told what was going on. Of course it was too fantastic—so the fucking Company got away with the damned immoral things they did. Shelly stared at the man sitting there, glanced away, swore under her breath. But she'd come this far, and she needed to make the man believe it. Both their lives depended on this. She reached up into her hair, flicked open the pseudoskin cover, unplugged the bioware chip and held out the cartridge in her hand.

Conversant's eyes widened, and he jerked back against the stone. The hardened shell of his contempt had shattered in a second.

Shelly expected him to shout for the guard, to have her locked up as a witch—or worse. But the man only stared, waiting for her to explode or transform or otherwise mutate. When Shelly didn't--only sat there soberly, waiting—finally Conversant looked down at her hand, reached out gingerly to take the cartridge. He examined it, turned it over in his hands, asked something.

Of course Shelly couldn't understand him now, couldn't speak the language.

"I can't talk to you without it," she said, and Conversant handed it back. Inserted again, it provided the speech patterns

Shelly needed. She rubbed her face with both hands, suddenly drained. "What did you say?" she asked.

Conversant gazed out at the garden, tightened his lips. When his eyes returned, they seemed darker.

"I asked what it did."

"It gives me the language, the standards of behavior. Your customs are different, and I wouldn't know how to pass for Argent, otherwise."

"What happened to her?"

Shelly looked away. "I don't know."

Kerristan was still shaken and white, his face unusually readable. He took a breath, steadied. "How did you get here?"

"On a ship that flies through space and time. We...fell towards a dead star mass, a black hole, and came out here."

"And you came to kill me?"

"Yes."

He accepted it this time. "From another...reality?" he asked. "Another time? Why?"

"The Company has a device that reads the time streams, calculates the alternate realities. It shows possible avenues and dangers, gives probabilities that juxtapositions will happen one way or the other. They use it to chart a path for their own progress." Shelly paused, plucked at the silken cloth over her knees. "I was taught to read it, but I haven't had a chance just lately. Kendrick said you were a major determinant."

Kerristan frowned, midnight in his eyes.

"A what?"

"He meant," Shelly said, "that you were a major influence in the paradigm, the progression scheme the chart outlines—a danger to the Company. The chart showed a juxtaposition of the two realities, not far away. Kendrick was adamant you had to be assassinated before then, but I don't know any details of their plotting. The chart might give me some, but I didn't get to study it." She stopped, staring at the water. "They've tried it before. To kill you, I mean. Kendrick's sent other agents before me."

That seemed to rouse Conversant. He got up abruptly, paced. Shelly got up too, more slowly, at the bioware's prompt. She clenched her hands in the pale pleats of her skirt, watched the man stalk up and down.

"Listen," she said suddenly. "I'm sorry about the poison." She needed to apologize. Her guilt had prompted this whole exercise. "Whatever happens..."

Kerristan glanced up, moved suddenly to shove her against the wall. The impact jolted Shelly, and she caught her breath in surprise. She stared across at Conversant, found the man's eyes were veiled again, dark and opaque. Coupled with the physical assault, it was a warning.

"Tell me more about the Company," Kerristan said softly. "What is it?"

"A...a trading company that deals in different realities," Shelly said. "It's registered as the Trans-Real Shipping Corporation. Everyone just calls it "the Company" because it's so...dominant."

"What does it do?" Kerristan insisted. "What does it trade?"

"Fuels, gems, gold—whatever. And...other things too, that aren't so well known." Shelly felt her face stiffen as she put her knowledge into words. "What amounts to slaves, though slavery's illegal where I come from." She was likely caught in that herself, she thought. "Drugs—other things."

"You don't like it?" Kerristan asked.

"The Company?" Shelly shook her head. "It's corrupt as hell. It victimizes people that haven't any way to help themselves."

Kerristan's eyes narrowed. He studied Shelly's expression, her face. "The trade's not regulated?"

"Political connections."

"Why do you work for it, then?"

"I don't," Shelly said. "I mean..." She stopped, took a breath. But she had to face this. There was no excuse. "It was ambition," she admitted, "pure and simple. I sold my soul. The Company looks attractive from the outside. After I found out what was going on, I tried to get out, but I couldn't. Kendrick has a hold on me, and he won't let go." She closed her eyes. "God, I hate him."

She wondered if Kerristan really understood what she was saying, or even gave a tinker's damn. Still, she wouldn't succumb to self-pity now.

"Part of the hold is their investment," she explained, "my training. My father died broke, a failure—and I wanted some kind of security in my life. I signed on as soon as I was old enough. My dad had a little shuttle business, a couple of ships, and I had a background as a pilot, in shipping—just what they wanted. They taught me to fly their reality shuttle, to handle the systems, and to be more, too—an agent, because I had the aptitude and the capability. But I never meant to do anything like this. It was just finally the lesser of evils." She glanced at Conversant then, at his pale face and night-dark, burning eyes. "Then too," she said, "I didn't plan to get caught."

"Of course," Kerristan said, gently. "I can kill you still. Did you consider it? It's the obvious way out—for you to die."

He felt Shelly flinch, studied her. Shelly held her chin up with an effort, met the man's eyes, waiting.

He let go abruptly, turned and stopped a meter away, watching the water splash into the pool.

"Do you hate me?" he asked suddenly.

Surprised, Shelly stared at his back, his careless shoulders.

"Don't lie," the man said. "I want to know."

What Shelly felt was muddled, ambivalent. It included terror, but also a certain respect. "No," she said.

Conversant's voice didn't change. "How were you planning to go back?"

"The shuttle's not far away," Shelly said. "I have a signal in Argent's room that will call the pilot to pick me up. The rendezvous point is in the woods, west of the palace grounds."

"Your door will be unlocked tonight," Kerristan said. "Take your device, send your signal and go."

"What?" It was a shock. "But why...?"

Kerristan turned back to face her. A flicker in his eyes could have been anger—or only mockery. He was baiting Shelly again. "You don't want to go?" he asked pointedly. "You want to stay here?"

Shelly flushed. "They'll try it again," she said.

Kerristan stepped up suddenly, took hold of her shoulders and kissed her, surprisingly, on the mouth.

"You are dismissed," he said, stepping back. "You may return to the servant's quarters."

The curtain of bored derision had fallen over his eyes again, and it obscured him from view. The glimpse of the man underneath was gone—so brief Shelly hardly knew she had seen it.

The bioware prodded. She curtsied deeply, pivoted sharply and strode off up the walk. As the path wound out of sight, though, she turned and glanced back. Somber, solitary, Conversant was a shadow against the stone, staring at the gargoyle face that vomited water onto the pool.

Darkness shrouded the palace again. The signal was sent. It was late enough that no one was likely to see her, and Shelly left Argent's room wearing boy's clothes that were comfortable again. She slid out cautiously, without much trust, but the hallways of the servant's quarters seemed deserted, her way completely clear. Maybe Conversant was grateful, after all. Maybe he really would let her go. She'd almost begun to believe it.

The night outside was heavy with jasmine, rife with cicadas. One of the moons was set and the other wouldn't rise for an hour yet, which gave her a full window of dark. Crossing through the garden, the woods, furtive and careful, she wondered what Kendrick would do to her for failing. It felt idiotic to go back. Kerristan had been right, had seen her ambivalence.

But she wouldn't take death as a solution to her problems. Even if there was no place to go, no other way to live but through

Kendrick and his sorry predation, she'd take that. With no flaw in the Company's rotten paradigm, likely she'd remain Kendrick's slave, body and soul. Her sacrilege was empty then. It felt like failure, and it left a bitter taste in her mouth. Still, as long as she was alive, there was a chance.

The shuttle was there in a stand of hemlocks, invisible, hidden by energy fields that faintly blurred the starlight. Shelly signaled, received a coded answer that located it exactly. The hatch opened as she approached, and the gang deployed. A glow made it sharply visible, highlighted the trees. Silhouetted by the lights, she cursed as she ran up the incline and ducked inside the hatch. The damn pilot hadn't even bothered to kill the lights.

It was the same one who had brought her in--Bruno, his name was—and Shelly swore at him in person, too.

"You want to make sure we're seen?" she hissed, jumping down into the broad cockpit. "Damn you. And thanks a lot."

Bruno swiveled his pilot's chair around. "Who's going to see us, kid?" He was cocky; he'd heard how Kendrick forced her into this. He smirked, appraising her. "Did you get the bastard?"

Shelly felt her face freeze up.

"No," she said, shortly.

"Then what'd you come back for? Kendrick's going to bust you good." Bruno laughed, arrogant and sure of himself. It was a taste of what her life would be like now.

"I'll make any reports directly to Kendrick," she said. But Bruno wasn't listening. His eyes had moved past her, and his mouth fell open wide.

Shelly pivoted, sucked in her breath.

"Oh, crap," she breathed.

Conversant was crouched in the hatchway. He must have run to catch the gang, and he looked pale as death. He was panting, gasping for breath, but his eyes were intense, alive, hotter than Shelly had ever seen them.

"Don't move," he said. He poised, held an ornate firearm aimed and ready.

Called Wind and Fire, it was a short-range pistol, shot an incendiary needle on a compressed air charge. This one was unusually frivolous, inlaid with platinum and gold, and Bruno underestimated it--or maybe he misjudged the man.

He lunged up, jerked at his laser weapon, and Kerristan shot him dead. The ampoule exploded his chest and he fell, burning, stinking, his blood smoking on the deck. The inlaid muzzle twitched over.

"No," Shelly said. She kept her hands still and visible, held her breath.

But Conversant wasn't going to shoot her just then. He got up carefully, stepped down into the cockpit. The bore of the gun didn't waver. He glanced down at Bruno.

The velvet was gone. Dressed in dark, practical twill, somehow he still managed to look decadent. There was a touch of warmth in his face now, from running—or murder. Shelly couldn't tell which.

She eased in a breath. "What are you doing here?" she asked.

"I followed you, of course."

"Damn you," Shelly said. "What do you want? I thought you were going to let me go."

Some of the electricity went out of Conversant's eyes, and he looked her up and down, taking in the clothes, the differences.

"I wanted the shuttle," he said.

"The shuttle?" Shelly stared. "But it's the Company's."

"No," Kerristan said. "It's mine now." He hesitated, went on casually. "And yours, if you want."

For a second Shelly didn't understand, couldn't believe what he'd said. She only stood there with her mouth open, while Conversant watched her face, waiting.

"Well?" he prompted.

"What are you planning?"

Conversant smiled, sweetly. "To get the hell out of here."

"But what..." Shelly stuttered. "What about your crown?"

"I hereby abdicate," he said. "No one will miss me but Tiberia." His smile turned venomous.

"Things will be a lot different, elsewhere," Shelly insisted.

Conversant sobered slightly. "Without the crown, you mean? I think I can handle that." His voice turned reflective. "I never thought of just leaving."

She moistened dry lips. "And what do I have to do?"

"Anything, nothing," Conversant said. "Just fly it."

It hit her then, all at once. A finger in the Company's face, in Kendrick's, for whatever it was worth. A chance for a final defiance, maybe.

"You said you didn't hate me," Kerristan reminded.

He studied her a moment longer.

"Will you do it?"

"All right," Shelly said.

Bitterly, she laughed, becoming in a second an outlaw that took what she wanted. She was giving up everything in exchange for dignity—and a chance to save her soul.

They went back, penetrated the black gravity well, pierced through to the bright-hot flare of the galaxy core. Kerristan watched the viewscreen spangle in awe, lounging in the co-pilot's seat, one boot propped on the instrument panel.

"This will be tricky," Shelly said. "They'll be onto us right away."

Kerristan just didn't know. This was stupid, senseless. But still Shelly felt her life surge hot and bright, leaping with the ship, searching for leverage, a way to make a difference. The interface played along her nerves like fire, augmentation answering to her slightest touch, boosting her reaction time. It couldn't help but affect her.

"This ship," she said, "is latest cutting edge. I think I can evade them, at least for a while. And we're armed. Maybe. Just maybe…"

They had hardly jumped free of the core when Kendrick came up on the screen, blighting a circle of stars. He took in the situation, and surprisingly dense, began to threaten Shelly.

"What's he saying?" asked Kerristan.

"He's cursing me."

Conversant studied the image, appraisingly, viciously, and then he laughed. "Turn it off," he said. "You don't have to listen."

Shelly grinned abruptly, did it. She brought up the graphics then, planning to calculate a hide-out, a route among the varied probabilities. But once the future chart was on the screen, she sat numb and still. The node that had been yellow was scarlet now, and as she watched, the lines shifted, flared and reformed. She fell back against the seat, gaping as a different pattern emerged. Kerristan lounged beside her, bored and dilatory, watching the rainbow dart of colors across screen.

"What is it?" he asked.

Shelly looked over at him. Derisive and vicious, angry at Kendrick, he was vital with power. She had forgotten he was a major determinant in the paradigm.

They had passed the node.

Shelly laughed suddenly, bitter and exultant. "You know," she said, "maybe I could get to like you, after all."

ABOUT THE AUTHOR

Lela Buis was born in Kentucky and grew up in East Tennessee. She graduated with degrees from The Florida State University and The Florida Institute of Technology, and lived for a long time in Florida, working at jobs including engineering at Kennedy Space Center and teacher of various subjects and levels. She began writing as a child and leans toward genre fiction, having published mainly science fiction and fantasy stories and poetry. She is a member of the Knoxville Writer's Guild, the Science Fiction and Fantasy Writers of America and the Science Fiction Poetry Association.